The Play Is Written

... Life of a Seeker

ıd Rasmussen Faroe

ORIGINAL WRITING

ISBNS
PARENT : 978-1-78237-458-9
EPUB: 978-1-78237-459-6
MOBI: 978-1-78237-460-2
PDF: 978-1-78237-461-9

A CIP catalogue for this book is available from the National Library.
Published by ORIGINAL WRITING LTD., Dublin, 2013.
Printed by CLONDALKIN GROUP, Glasnevin, Dublin 11
Cover: The Seed, by Soham. Photography by Anette Persson.

I wish to thank my copy-editor, Brendan O'Brien
As well as my friends who read the book and gave me valuable support.
Anna Skrine
Francoise Davison
Scott Spanfelner
Kjell Dahlgren
Ewa Gonta
And my wife Ursula

Thanks to all of you for making it possible to publish my novel.

For

My Teacher

With love

The Kingdom of God is as if someone would scatter seed on the ground, and would sleep and rise night and day, and the seed would sprout and grow, he does not know how.

Mark 4:27 (NRSV)

PART ONE:

THE SEED

Chapter One:

PETER

August 1989

I

I met Peter in Copenhagen Airport at the beginning of August 1989, on my way to a conference on New Testament studies in Birmingham, England. The subject was The Gospel of Thomas, one of the texts from Nag Hammadi. These texts had been found in the Egyptian desert at the end of the 1940s, and had interested me ever since I first heard about them.

I was a biblical scholar, but not Christian; at least not in the sense that I went to church or belonged to a congregation or Christian denomination: at that time, my interest in the bible was purely academic. I had studied for many years, written many books – for example, on the origins of the Christian church – and was now teaching at the university in Copenhagen. My secret aspiration was to become a professor, and therefore it was important to be seen and to take part in as many conferences as possible. Things were looking bright: I was regarded as a specialist in the Coptic texts, of which the Gospel of Thomas was one.

Little did I know that this day would radically change my life.

Later, when thinking back on what had happened, it reminded me of the day I had met my wife, some 20 years earlier. I was a dedicated young student at the University of Marburg in Germany, doing very well and enjoying my studies enormously. This particular day, I was having my lunch alone in a corner of the canteen, looking out onto the street and thinking about the thesis I was going to write, when I was suddenly "pulled" out of my introspective state of mind. A young woman entered, looked around, then walked directly across the room and stopped at my table, saying, "Do you mind if I sit down?"

I was surprised, but answered, "By all means – please do."

She smiled at me, looking me straight in the eyes. That day our relationship started, and we married two years later.

Like everyone else, we had had our ups and downs, but we were happy. My wife was a lawyer, our son was 18 and ready to start university, and our daughter was 14. Economically, we were well off; we had a beautiful mansion in one of the best areas of Copenhagen, had good, well-educated friends and I lived and breathed for my work, which, through my biblical studies, gave me a sense of doing something important.

On arriving at the airport, I discovered that my flight was delayed due to ongoing strikes in both Copenhagen and Birmingham. No one knew how soon we would be able to take off; it could be hours, and possibly not until the next day. However, negotiations between unions and the company were progressing, so I was advised to stay and await further information.

I decided to go to one of the pubs in the terminal building. I bought a shrimp, egg and mayonnaise sandwich and a glass of dry white wine, found an empty table near a window, placed my luggage on the chair next to me – I always travelled light on these occasions, and had only a small bag with clothes and toiletries. I started eating, and remember being a little annoyed by the delay, as I was really looking forward to the conference. I was not the main speaker, but I had found some interesting evidence about how to date the Gospel text. The discussions usually turned around two opposing positions: the Gospel of Thomas was older or younger than the known gospels. I wanted to prove that it was older.

I continued eating my sandwich, which was delicious, not really thinking of anything in particular; there was the usual chatter going on in my mind – as if I was talking to myself – but suddenly I "woke up". A man entered the pub and looked around, as if he was due to meet someone. He was dressed in jeans and a dark green T-shirt, carried a green army jacket over his right arm, and had a rucksack on his back. I could not take my eyes off him, which was perhaps what made him aware of me. I do not know why, but after a little while he seemed to make up his mind and, to my surprise, he started walking towards me. He stopped at my table, looked at me inquisitively for a moment and then asked if he could join me. His eyes were peaceful, but very much alive and full of determination, which made it impossible to say anything other than, "Please, sit down."

He pulled out the chair opposite me and hesitated a little.

"My name is Peter," he said, placing his rucksack on the floor and his jacket on top of it."

"My name is Thomas – nice to meet you." We shook hands.

He was going to sit down, but changed his mind and said, "I'll go and fetch something to eat as well." A little later he came back with a slice of pizza and a bottle of water, and sat down.

While we were eating we discussed the delay, and I expressed my irritation. He did not seem to be upset by the delay; he looked at me, almost surprised, and said that he did not mind at all.

"Whenever something like this happens, you always get to meet people that you would not otherwise meet, don't you?" He smiled.

I could not deny that, since I had just met Peter, a person I did not know.

"Are you going to Birmingham also?" I said.

"No, I am going to London, but ..." He stopped and, as if not wanting to give any explanation at that moment, asked instead, "So what are you going to do in Birmingham?"

I told him about the conference, about my job as a scholar in Copenhagen and the theories I had developed concerning the Gospel of Thomas, and was just about to explain my recent discovery when he interrupted me.

"I have also studied theology, so I know about this gospel. I wrote a thesis about it. It is considered to be Gnostic."

It seemed to me that he was waiting for my reaction. I found it incredible that I had met a scholar who had studied the same subject as me. What a coincidence! A thought flashed through my mind and I found myself thinking of how I had met my wife. I had a strange feeling of déjà vu – fate was presenting me with something extraordinary, inevitable, but definitely out of my everyday experience. My mind became alert, and straight away I started discussing my theories with him. Now I could test my ideas on someone who knew about scientific research. He listened, but did not seem to share my fascination with the topic. He finished his slice of pizza and, as if he could read my mind, he said, "I am not a scholar and not interested in the matter from a theoretical point of view. I don't find theories that interesting. When I started at university, I wanted to prove something to the 'world', to show that the church was wrong and that all I had been told throughout my upbringing was false. At the same time, all the knowledge I acquired at university did not make me happy or provide me with the key to living a meaningful life. I left university and embarked on a long journey in search of the truth."

I was taken aback; my enthusiasm melted like a cube of ice in a glass of warm water. Once again, Peter seemed to register what was going on inside me, and continued: "Much later, I met a teacher; not someone from a university, but a real teacher, one who, little by little, taught me almost everything worth knowing. I stayed with him for thirteen years, and when he urged me to finish my university studies and afterwards even suggested that I be ordained, I followed his advice."

Now that my ice cube had melted, all my objections to church and religion surfaced. I was sitting here talking to a priest, who did not find theories useful but had given up his knowledge for ministry. In other words, he was a Christian and not a scholar.

"I have to be honest with you," I said. "For me, the Christian church and its beliefs and dogmas do not lead anywhere. It seems to be against all common sense, and the theologies that the church has developed are not even true from a scientific point of view. They are full of easily demonstrated contradictions. You see, to study the Christian texts from a scholarly point of view means holding nothing to be true, unless it is supported by scientific evidence. And that's what the church has neglected to do from the very beginning. You probably know that there were no Christian theologians in the first years after Jesus, but after, say, the thirties and forties AD there were many, and they all argued, trying to convince each other of their own 'truth'. Science is not like that. You can, of course, interpret a text in many different ways, but you have to discuss it from the content of the text, not from what you subjectively believe, or whether you claim to have had a vision, or that God had spoken to you directly. That is not valid; if you wish to find a consensus between different standpoints, then God has nothing to do with it."

I waited for Peter to say something, but all the time he just sat quietly. He sipped a little water now and then, but definitely had no interest in arguing with me. Then he said, "I know what you are talking about, because I was there myself years ago. But I am sure that no amount of knowledge or scientific discussion could bring me one ounce of understanding on how to live my life. The mystery of life cannot be found in theories, in books or in scholarly studies at university. I know that, and you will probably agree with me when I ask you: Is life a mystery? Or is it something you can read about in books or explain with theories?"

I was a little upset, because I felt that I and my work were being questioned and found to be meaningless.

"Wait a minute," I said. "You are going too fast. Let's stick to Christianity for now and forget about the mystery of life. You see, I was never attracted to ordination and to working for the salvation of believers, but I wanted to study and contribute to our knowledge of history and the contents of religion, from a purely intellectual and sensible point of view. Not through faith or belief or superstition."

Now Peter turned our conversation upside down.

"Everything has a function, including science. I don't want to be right; I want to be happy. I want to know myself, deeply and intimately, and there is only one way of doing that: by observing myself. So what I am talking about is my own experience, and I trust in that. On the other hand, I think you could be interested when I tell you that I know about esoteric Christianity."

When sitting here now, some years later, thinking about that fortuitous meeting, I cannot help laughing. What he had said was like giving an unhappy child a piece of candy, or telling it not to be sad because on Sunday, we were going to the circus together, or we would be going on the merry-go-round. OK? Do you want that? Esoteric Christianity!

That was the heart of my research, and of course I was interested.

"Yes," I said, "I would like that, but I don't know whether you can tell me anything I do not already know."

I regretted that remark almost instantly – my voice sounded ironic, almost arrogant – but Peter showed no sign of reaction at all. I noticed that he was different from other people I had encountered. He was mild mannered; his face had a benevolent expression, showing goodwill, sympathy and tolerance; it was as if he was merely observing himself and me – not absentmindedly, like someone who does not care or is uninterested, but more as a friend, who gives you all the space in the world to share whatever is inside you. My God, *he* was a mystery, and it made me very curious to know more about him, to hear what he had to tell and to get closer to him. Anyway, despite my newly acquired insight, I immediately started to tell him what I knew about esotericism.

"I have always known that from the time the early church became organized, with a hierarchy of bishops, deacons, etc., something was lost. The history of the church, as we know it, is that of an 'exoteric' movement, changing according to the needs of the time and even turning its very message into the opposite of the original; a good example is when the inquisition turned the love of Christ into murder and persecution. But from the beginning, the core of the message of Jesus was preserved in 'esoteric circles' and thus survived the tides of time. My point is that the gospel of Thomas is the foremost proof we have of that."

I stopped. Once again, Peter had poured water into his glass and drunk while he listened attentively to my "speech". Then he said, "I was taught in an esoteric school." He said this as if it was of no importance, but immediately I became very alert.

Over the next hour, he tried to convey to me what this teaching was about. I took it to be something of a secret message from Jesus Christ himself, and became extremely interested. Many questions arose in my mind; I wondered if this teacher had sources of which we, as scholars, were unaware, or if the teachings of Jesus had been transmitted through secret brotherhoods over the past two thousand years? Peter made it clear that what he could tell me about the esoteric teaching would not help me to become a professor at the university. Furthermore, he added, "I am a person who has gone through the esoteric teaching in reality. I gave up everything in my life and through much effort, I succeeded. Do you think that sounds a bit far-fetched?"

Of course it did, and I frankly told him that I had no intention of giving up everything, as he put it; but, intuitively, I felt he was genuine. Here was somebody I probably would never meet again, so I suggested to him that we spend some days together and he readily agreed, which surprised me and made me a little suspicious.

"I will tell you my story," he concluded.

"Yes, please do," I heard myself saying involuntarily, as if someone was speaking through me. I was rather astonished. Then I regained my composure, and asked, "But what is the aim of your teaching?"

He thought a little and answered: "When we are children, we live from moment to moment, knowing that we are divine; but of course, we do not express it in words. We just live it. We are. Then we are given a name and it is like a symbol that sticks to us permanently. If you are in bed, asleep, and someone comes in to wake you up, they say your name and you, without any effort, immediately answer. You are your name. And we cannot forget our name, whereas we easily forget our divine nature. After some years, at around seven or eight years of age, we are more or less conditioned beings, full of convictions and opinions, likes and dislikes, all that circumstances and our upbringing make

7

us believe. From then on, we continue through life with this conditioning and tend to forget the divine nature. I call it the seed that can never be lost, but can easily be forgotten. I would say that we are then only partially ourselves because we have acquired a lot of illusionary values and beliefs which direct all our strivings to being happy, to finding meaning, without really being able to. We think we are conscious and in full control of our lives, but we are not. The aim of the teaching is to re-establish the connection with the divine. But to start searching for this seed on your own is like looking for water in a desert, or digging in a field in the hope of finding a treasure, but without a map. You need a teacher, and his teaching will provide you with a 'map'. Then you will know how to proceed."

I followed him relatively easily. I started to wonder at what point I had forgotten my seed, but was that not a little simplistic?

Once more, Peter sensed my doubts. He said: "I do know I was very lucky to find this path, but I am sure that all of us have the potential to find it. I had help along the way, right from the beginning. I saw an angel who reminded me, and I met a prophet – I usually call him 'the prophet' – who guided me. I went astray for many years with only a tiny hope that there was a seed, a secret to be discovered – not out there, but within – and, in the end, I found it."

I did not believe in angels, and, as far as I knew, I had never met one. I did not, at this point, oppose or contradict Peter, but I was now determined to stay with him as long as was needed to learn about his teaching, through the story of his life.

Only the practicalities remained. We both contacted the information counter in the airport and were told that no plane would leave for either Birmingham or London until the next day, at the earliest. We cancelled our tickets and afterwards I phoned Birmingham and told them about the situation. I mentioned the strike but apart from that I simply said that something unforeseen had come up.

I phoned my wife and told her that I would not be back for several days.

"I know that!" she exclaimed.

"But I am not going to Birmingham. I am staying here in Copenhagen with a friend, a person I met in the airport. We are going to talk about something very interesting. I'll call you from time to time, but at the moment, I have no idea when I will be home."

She asked me nothing more, or what we were talking about. She knew me so well that she assumed it had to do with my research, although it now turned out to be something very different from my university studies.

"It's all right," she said. "I have made my own arrangements now, so please have a good time."

II

We drove to the centre of the city and found two rooms in the SAS Hotel, opposite the main station. The rooms were expensive.

"So what, it's just money," I thought to myself – this had become a habit recently.

We had dinner together, and talked about rather unimportant things, but it was very pleasant being with him. He asked me about Marburg, where the famous professor Bultmann had taught his students about the new paradigm in theology. Unfortunately Bultmann had retired before I became a student, but I had met him on one occasion, at a student gathering to celebrate his birthday.

I said to Peter, "How old are you? I am forty-two."

"So am I," he said.

He did not look that old – maybe around thirty. He was of average height, but strongly built; there was stubble on his face, apparently he had been unable to shave for some days. When he smiled, he showed big white teeth and his eyes were sparkling and alive and seemed to look right through you, examining you and drawing all the right conclusions. It was a little uncomfortable, but I chose to think it was my imagination – he could not possibly know anything about me and what I was thinking.

It turned out that we had started our studies almost simultaneously – he in Copenhagen, I in Germany – which explained why we had never met before. We had no common experiences or memories from the past, but still our conversation was open and friendly, as if we had known each other for a long time.

It was getting dark: we went to my room and sat in two comfortable chairs with a little round table between us, close to the enormous panoramic window, which gave us a view of the night sky over Copenhagen. We watched the many "falling" stars.

"This happens every year at this time," Peter explained, "but they are not stars, just pieces of rock falling through the atmosphere – nothing else. They are not 'dying' suns."

I had always thought they were, but of course it was impossible that suns and solar systems could be "dying" each year when we passed this point in space.

We continued talking over the next days. We went out into the city, visiting museums and bars; we went to the cinema, all the while developing a true friendship. Peter was a very special person; he was always in the "now", in a manner that most people are not.

It turned out that we were like brothers, with much more in common than I had originally thought when I met him at the airport.

Peter told me the story of his life, his search and the nature of his esoteric teaching. He agreed that I could write down his story, but he said that he would tell it in the way he himself had experienced it. He would mention all his uncertainties and doubts, his disappointments and pleasures, the discoveries and insights he had had along the way, until he arrived at the end of the journey. By now, he had reconciled himself to everything that life had presented or could present to him.

I was free to edit his story, as long as I kept the focus on the essential development of the person, Peter. (He sometimes talked about himself in the third person.)

The next morning, after breakfast, I went out to buy a tape recorder. It seemed the best thing to do. If I recorded our talks, I could later present them in a coherent fashion and thus take away any irrelevancies to the main story.

What follows is Peter's story, as reconstructed from the recordings.

Chapter Two:

THE SEED

Childhood

I

We lived a couple of miles outside a little village north of Copenhagen. Our house was old and, according to many people, derelict and in dire need of repair. My father had a small workshop for repairing furniture, but he did not have many customers. He was a restless person, often worried about the future, especially when 11 June approached. That was the final day for paying the mortgage on the house: if you could not pay, the house would be sold at a compulsory auction and you would be homeless. That is why this day was called "the devil's birthday".

My mother, who was a devout Christian, never worried about that particular day. She trusted in the Lord and, as it turned out, the mortgage was paid year after year.

My father wanted a son and, as time passed, he finally prayed to God and promised that if he gave him a son, the boy would become a priest for God. That son turned out to be me. Of course, I didn't know anything about his "promise" until he told me about it later.

He had been born at the beginning of the century, and his childhood had probably been very difficult. This I concluded from what he and my grandfather told me.

He became an upholsterer, but lost his job at the onset of the Great Depression and had to line up each morning at the docks in Copenhagen, hoping to find some work just to earn a few kroner. My grandfather was a foreman in the harbour, but could not help him much. The ones first in line were the first to be hired for the day.

During this time my father became a communist, and a fierce one at that. He went around distributing pamphlets full of party propaganda.

Then he met my mother. She already had a baby girl named Sara, who was born in 1934 and became a part of our family. My parents married just before the war. Denmark was occupied by the Germans, who silenced the government and took over the running of the country. It was during these oppressive times that my "real" sister, Rudy, was born in Copenhagen on a cold December day in 1941.

Eventually the war ended, as all things do sooner or later, such being the nature of time. The recovery was slow and difficult, not least for the economy, but around 1950 my father purchased an old house in the countryside, in an area with small-scale farmers and wonderful nature on the outskirts of the village, or small town.

I was born on the 29th of December 1946 during a stormy night; the midwife couldn't come because the telephone line was dead. A year and a half later my little brother was born, and it was part of my good fortune that he arrived.

II

Childhood for most children is like paradise. There is a feeling of innocence, a joy of being thoroughly true and in contact with the real essence of life, where every little thing has the potential to be wonderful.

I remember many small details about our house. At the time, I did not know that I lived in Denmark but I remember the summers; I felt the warmth of the sun and loved the green vegetation all around.

My younger brother, Jim, probably remembers very little of this time, but he became my best friend and the only one I really loved for many years; he is still a person I love very deeply. Although I beat him and dominated him, and pestered him with stupid practical jokes, he was and always will be someone who is very close to me.

Much of what happened in the early years has disappeared into oblivion, leaving a few vague pictures in my mind. I have often wondered why that is so. Why do we not remember the first years of life? I have no answer, but it is true for most people. The pictures from these years are like paintings, with colours and shapes, without words or interpretation. But a few incidents stand out clearly in my mind. I remember when my stepsister, Sara, moved away from home. She found a job somewhere and only visited us occasionally. She usually brought things for Jim and me, which we looked forward to. My other sister, Rudy, though living at home, did not involve herself with us boys due to the age difference; when she became a teenager there was even less involvement.

Jim and I always played together, winter and summer. We had no responsibilities. From getting up in the morning until going to bed our time belonged to us, with a few minor exceptions. Sometimes my mother would ask me to go to the neighbour to borrow something, for example salt, sugar or flour, and then Jim would come along and we would walk hand in hand over to the old couple Jensen who lived nearby. We would always be given what we asked for, and then we were offered lemonade and biscuits. After a while I would say, "Jim, it's time to go home." Then I would take his hand and off we would go. I think he was happy to have an elder brother, after all.

We slept in the same bed, and had a lot of fun together. When it was cold, we would lift our legs in the air under the blanket, and make cycling movements until we were exhausted and felt the heat in our bodies. That was the "stove exercise". And when my little brother or I felt afraid in the dark, we would cuddle up in each other's arms and sleep safe and sound after saying a prayer.

In the summer, Jim and I liked to go down to the pond near our house. It was not big, but there were all kinds of living creatures in and around the water – frogs that had been born during the spring, insects, and sometimes we even saw a mouse or a rat. In the middle of the pond was a little island with a tree. Once we saw a coot swimming with her small "ducklings" lined up in a row behind her, as if they were on a piece of string; we assumed the nest was on the island. Even when the pond dried up in the summer one could not get out there, because it was still very muddy.

We pulled plants out of the water, which gave off a peculiar smell – not of rotting vegetation but rather of fermentation. The pond was full of life. When we forgot the time, my mother would come and fetch us. She was not nervous or worried for our safety; she trusted in the Good Lord's protection and that was enough for her. She just wanted us to come home because it was dinnertime.

When my grandmother died, grandfather came to live with us. He brought a few things with him from his flat in Copenhagen, including a clock that was hung on the wall over the telephone. It sounded every half hour. Grandpa slept on the couch in the living room and all day long, he sat in his chair doing absolutely nothing. It was interesting, however, to get to know an old man; his perspective on life was so strange to us that we wondered which part of the world he had come from. He told us stories and fairy tales, and it was good to listen to him. But he, like my father, had a temper that could express itself in many odd ways. When he did not have salt for his egg in the morning, he would shout and command my mother to fetch it. He used to say, "Don't you know that an egg without salt is like a woman without a mirror?"

I noticed one thing about old people: they often repeated themselves over and over again. Although we did not object in the slightest, Grandpa told his stories repeatedly. It was comforting to hear a story for the tenth time knowing what would happen, and still being surprised at the end.

Grandfather also had a watch, which he treasured. It was round, mounted in silver, with a chain attached to it. The chain was always visible, fastened to a buttonhole; the watch was hidden in his waistcoat pocket. When he took it out, he did so with an air of importance. He often opened it to check the time, and then, if you asked him what time it was, he would take it out again, as if he hadn't looked at it. It was just a pleasant habit that he did unconsciously.

In the house, there was a photograph of my grandfather from the time he was foreman at the harbour. There were a lot of men standing, sitting and kneeling, all of them dressed in shabby, dirty clothes. Grandpa was standing to one side, dressed in a suit and tie with his arms crossed. You could see the chain of his watch. He was a proud man. He used to say: "I was only a labourer, my son has become a craftsman, but my grandson will be an academic."

He was referring to me as the academic. Father had told me about his promise to God, so of course one day I would go to university and become a priest. At the time, it was not clear to me what a priest was, apart from someone who preaches in church on Sundays. I had been to church with my mother a few times and had seen the priest, but mostly we did not go to church, but only to Sunday school. When people asked me, "What are you going to be when you grow up?" I would always say, "I am going to be a priest."

III

Religion was an essential part of our upbringing. We used to have morning prayers in the living room, readings from the bible, prayers and hymn singing. Our parents were very religious. My mother came from a Baptist background and my father was "converted", as she said, when he met her. His wild life and communist background were exchanged for pious religious practices, which were just as censored as they would have been by any communist country's police. He told us that when the Nazis arrived in Denmark in 1940, he had burnt any evidence of his previous communist beliefs, because it would have been very dangerous.

Now he was a Christian. He introduced many rigid rules of behaviour, depending on his beliefs, which limited our paradise to a certain extent. We all had to live godly lives, which meant that there were many things one could not do; for example, play cards, swear, dance, and go to the cinema or theatre. Naturally that did not apply to us yet, but would become a burden in the future. Furthermore, one should not work or play on Sundays, or drink alcohol, and the boys should definitely have no interest in girls; otherwise God would punish us, as he sees everything. One could not hide from God – even Adam and Eve could not in the Garden of Eden. "Where are you, Adam?" God said, and Adam had to come out of his hiding place and receive his punishment. This was what they told us in Sunday school.

My father was a strange man. He was stern, dominant, but also very highly strung. Sometimes you could almost feel or "see" the struggle inside, as if he was trying to control his emotions and anger, without really being able to. At that point, you knew that some form of punishment was around the corner. The punishments were various, such as a box on the ear, a flogging or being sent to bed without food. Often we did not even understand what we had done, but, as I said, God saw everything and it was not possible to hide from him. My father believed in this fierce God. At the time, I did not understand that he was punishing himself. This understanding came later, when I grew up. Unfortunately, one had to learn to deal with the situation one way or another.

The atmosphere in the house was tense at times. I did not know why my parents had so many arguments, some of which involved shouting and screaming on my father's side – my mother would silently cry. This would be followed by the slamming of doors and then, some time later, there would be reconciliation and everything would be forgotten until the next time all hell broke loose. Jim and I never understood what the quarrels were about, so we would leave so as to not be part of the problem, and disappear into our own world.

But our paradise had a serpent. We ate of the tree and acquired the knowledge of good and evil. The bible tells the story of how

Adam and Eve one day took the forbidden fruit. For us, it was something that happened over a much longer period of time. The bible says: "When you eat of that tree, you will surely die." The idea of death did not bother us much, but we learned to hide things from our parents. Childhood still had a flavour of paradise, but we started lying in order to avoid punishment. If something was wrong, you would say that you knew nothing about it, pretending to be as innocent as possible, even though you knew the truth about what had happened. Without my dear little brother, paradise would have changed into hell much sooner than it did. That's why I loved him so much.

IV

I was about six years old when I had a vision of an angel. I was in bed with Jim in the cold and damp bedroom in my parents' house. That particular night, Jim was asleep, and did not hear or see anything. He told me this many years later. I myself was not sure whether I was awake or asleep when it happened, but it felt as if I was very much awake. I saw standing at the end of the bed an angel – a woman, dressed in bright shining clothes, which appeared to be made of white light. She had no wings, but her arms were stretched out on either side as if she wanted to show me something or embrace me. I wanted to say something but the power of the angel was so strong that I lost the ability to speak. I just looked on in amazement.

I cannot say how long this "dream" lasted. Although the angel did not speak, she "communicated" without words. Then she disappeared. At that moment I was definitely awake, and I felt deep within me that it had been real. An angel had communicated with me.

I remembered the dream vividly and told my mother about in the morning. She smiled and said, "Be thankful, you are blessed."

Later, as I was growing up, I could not explain what had happened. The message was there and I probably added words to the "dream" much later, such as: "Never give up looking for the truth." I was very much aware of the absurdity of the fact that, although I did not hear any words, I "heard" a clear message.

After all, the seed within me manifested itself during childhood as a strong interest in God: not only was I going to be a priest, but also I felt a deep connection with the world beyond. I knew it was there, and I could not forget the angel of my vision.

In Sunday school, we learned about the bible and Jesus and God, and we sang lots of hymns. I think I attended about 400 classes in all; we hardly missed a single Sunday, up to the day I was confirmed. Confirmation ended Sunday school, because at that point one was initiated into the world of the grown-ups and was supposed to go to church instead.

The interpretation of the bible was very one-sided. Its focus was on salvation through Jesus Christ and damnation of unbelievers; however, I loved Sunday school and did not think about the possibility of going to hell. I felt I was a good boy and that Jesus definitely loved me very much. My mother used to say that to me. So why should Jesus reject me and send me to eternal fire? My earthly father might reject me and deny me love, which I believe he did in some way. To him, love was something that had to be earned; it was not given unconditionally. It was deserved through education in the fires of punishment, similar to the making of a precious pearl inside an oyster.

One good thing about Sunday school was being able to meet other children; my awakening interest in girls also revealed itself. During Sunday school, there would be a break when we could run around outside and tease the girls. There was one girl that I liked a lot. Her name was Ulla; it seemed to me that she liked to be teased by me, which felt very good.

V

When I was almost ten, I had another vision. Once again I saw an angel. This time, she was holding a book in her hand.

I thought it was the same angel as before. She opened the book and said, "You shall be able to break the seals of the scroll. You shall read what is there and make it your aim to open it. Open the book of Isaiah and read the 29th chapter. Then you will understand."

When I woke up – and this time I was sure it was a dream – I went and opened the bible at Isaiah chapter 29.

Stupefy yourselves and be in a stupor, blind yourselves and be blind! Be drunk, but not from wine; stagger, but not from strong drink! [1]

For the LORD *has poured out upon you a spirit of deep sleep; he has closed your eyes, you prophets, and covered your heads, you seers. The vision of all this has become for you like the words of a sealed document. If it is given to those who can read, with the command, 'Read this', they say, 'We cannot, for it is sealed.'* [12]*And if it is given to those who cannot read, saying, 'Read this', they say, 'We cannot read.'*

At first, I did not really understand. Chapter 29 contained a lot of different subjects. And of course what I tell you now is an anachronism in the sense that, as a little boy, I did not understand the depth and meaning of the writing. For some strange reason, it gave me a feeling that here was something very important in my life that I should someday investigate.

And later on, the lines about being asleep, being in a state of not seeing, became absolutely fundamental to my search. For me, even at that time, the words conveyed some understanding. They fitted in very well with what I had learned previously. My mother would invariably talk about human beings as being turned away from God and living in sin. She said that they did not want to listen.

So from the moment I read about the sealed scroll, even though I was only a child, I somehow had the feeling that this was a call to me to make it my task to open this scroll, which could only mean opening my life to God or maybe to get away from sin or to be saved, as mother would call it.

The angel had spoken. And in my childish fantasies, I saw the scroll in front of me and I knew that it could not be opened by force, but only with a kind of shrewdness or cleverness, or in some other way, possibly with the help of an Isaiah, a prophet. Of course I did not know whether there would be such a prophet. They were found in the Old Testament, but their messages were very odd. On the other hand, if the Bible was a tool for God to reach us, then why should there not be someone sent by God to teach me?

You might think it strange that a boy of ten had these thoughts, but my childhood had had so many difficult things to deal with that often, when I searched for seclusion, sitting alone in a tree or behind the hedges, I imagined another life – another world with goodness and love, with no floggings, no slamming of doors, spending my life playing day in and day out, coming home tired and creeping up into my mother's bosom and just feeling happy and safe.

VI

I loved Christmas very much. It was the best time of the year. On Christmas Eve, we went to church where we sang all the beautiful carols, which I loved, and there was the feeling of being part of the drama in the stable in Bethlehem, with the holy couple. Christ was born once more. Hallelujah!

I remember the Christmas when grandfather left us. It was quite dramatic. My brother was given a mechanical car with a spring you could wind up and then the car would roll along the floor until something got in its way. This particular car must have been badly made, because the spring unwound and went right through his finger. My father got upset and started to blame him as well as the manufacturer of the toy, but my mother called the doctor and she took Jim down to the village, to have the spring cut loose and put some stuff and plaster on the poor finger. My dear little brother could no longer play with his car and was in a sad mood for the rest of the evening, even though we had Jaffa oranges, dates from overseas, and my mother's homemade goodies made with cornflakes and chocolate.

On St Stephen's day, Grandpa became very sick. The ambulance came and took him to the hospital, and he died three days later, on my birthday. The big surprise was that I inherited his watch. He had said to my mother that it should go to me. I looked at it, opened it. I felt very proud of having inherited it, as if a great honour was bestowed on me.

I was now eleven years old and started to be concerned about my own image, meaning how people looked at me and what they were thinking. To be religious was not popular in school, and going to Sunday school or church was considered stupid. Only weak people did that. But playing football and looking at girls was in. Writing letters to girls and to secretly "be in love" and flirt was what one was supposed to do as one grew older.

My father was very proud of me because I was at the top of my class. He encouraged me to go all the way through college and university to become a priest. I still accepted this idea, but no longer spoke openly about it. I thought that maybe I should take a degree in architecture, or the construction business, or even become a politician and prime minister of Denmark. Then my father would be proud of me. Little did I know or realize that I wanted love, to be seen for what I was, but instead I developed vanity. I wanted to be the centre, always the best. I wanted appreciation, and the more I received, the more I wanted. It was like a drug.

It became more and more obvious that my brother was moving in a different direction. He was happy and was not concerned about being a success. He told me later that he was relieved that nothing was expected of him, in the way it was of me. I was living in a dream world and did not, at the time, understand what was happening.

Paradise was disappearing. Now, we were thrown out into the world of struggle and toil. It was as if the beauty of the landscape of innocence was covered in fog, making it more and more difficult to see the contours of the trees and the lake. We were no longer innocent. Now we were the sinners that the church talked about. We had lost something and did not even remember what it was. We had been "abused" and were wounded children, and thus accused our parents of betraying us. But although the state of paradise faded, the seed was still there.

It was dormant, waiting in waterless, cold soil: but the seed cannot be lost, it can only be forgotten.

Much later I learned how to heal the wounds.

I told Peter a little about my family, mainly because I found it to be very different from his.

"I had a little sister and a brother. My sister learned to play the piano with mother. My brother was into football and became a very good player. When he married he became a professional in France. I travelled to see them when their first son was born.

"My sister married a physicist in Edinburgh and I myself became a scholar in Copenhagen. So we all got well into life. My parents are still living; of course dad has retired now, but he still asks me about my projects. I wrote my PhD thesis, but so far have never had a breakthrough in my career. I travel to conferences, and maybe someday I will be first in the line for a professorship in Copenhagen. When you use the word 'abuse' about your upbringing and being wounded, I cannot relate to you."

Peter said that what he told me was all relative. It is all a matter of degree.

"But maybe," he said, "your father abused you in a way that does not look like abuse. You have like everybody else been formed by norms and rules and beliefs, no matter how 'good' or 'right' they are. Why do you have such a strong hunger for recognition that you travel round the world to all these conferences?"

That shocked me a little, but I returned the question to Peter by asking, "When you were abused, as you put it, how could you then believe in a good God? Would God not rescue his child from abuse? A child who is devoted and innocent?"

Peter said that both his brother and his sister did reject God, but he himself could not do it. He was convinced that God could not be responsible for his father, so how could he blame God?

When he made me aware of my hunger for "academic" recognition, I reacted and I can see now that I tried to hide it. This was the reason I felt I had to "retaliate" with a slight "attack". I asked him, "Could it not be that your vision and your dream were a result of your upbringing, meaning that you would not have had a vision if no one had told you about angels?"

He did not become upset or try to defend anything; he just said that I could be right. On the other hand he knew what he had experienced, and he believed that we all come into this world with something, not like empty-handed children. He had a strong feeling of having been here before.

I felt deep respect for him, and did not venture further into a discussion of the probabilities of reincarnation or angels.

After he had gone to bed, I sat for a long time pondering what he had said about his seed. "It cannot be lost, only forgotten."

What about my seed? Was it forgotten? As far as I could see, I did not have any memory of coming from some sort of paradise. But the way Peter spoke about it, I felt sure that he had some memory of his past that we do not usually have any access to.

But if he was right, if we have all forgotten something precious, then the whole history of mankind was tragic. The bible says that the sins of the parents are inherited by generation after generation. Does that mean that we have simply projected the same mistakes onto our children that occurred to us, and we now live in a state of forgetfulness?

Is that why humanity has not yet found a solution to the existential problems: Where do we come from, why are we here, and where do we go from here? All these questions pressed down on me, in a way they never had before.

Chapter Three:
THE PROPHET

1958

I

A few weeks later, grandfather's old clock on the wall stopped. My father took me with him to the watchmaker in the village to have it repaired.

The watchmaker was a strange man. He was called "the prophet", but nobody could remember why. Someone told me it was because he had once foretold the birth of twins to a woman in the village, though it could also have been because he was religious. Not in the same way as people who went to church each Sunday, and not like my parents, who belonged to their congregational religious group. The prophet did not take part in that. He had his own way, but was considered very pious. He invited people to meet at his house, where they would meditate. That was a foreign custom, maybe Buddhist-inspired, and those who went there hardly ever told outsiders what they were doing.

The prophet had his shop at the end of the main street, on the edge of the countryside. It was part of a villa with a garden in front of it, so that from the street you barely saw the shop; a window facing the street and a large clock told people that this was a watchmaker's shop. The clock always showed the same time: twenty minutes past one. It seemed strange to everyone that a man who was working with clocks did not repair his own, but somehow it was as if time stood still in the prophet's home.

This was the first time I met him in person. I had heard many rumours about him. People talked a lot, and because no one understood him, he was accused of whatever criminal activity there was around. Some said he was abusing children, others that he had secret ceremonies invoking the devil, and so on. Of course nothing of the sort was true. It was just ordinary human suspiciousness about things they did not understand or know about. The worst thing for people is not knowing what is really going on, because in the absence of knowledge, they use their imaginations.

The prophet's name was Carl Hansen. When I first heard about him, long before meeting him, I imagined him to be something like an Isaiah or a Jeremiah, not an ordinary human being with one of the most common Danish names – not in the least exotic.

When we entered his shop, he came out and seemed delighted to see us. "That's a very nice old clock you have there. Where does it come from?"

Before my father could answer I interrupted, saying, "It's from my grandfather."

After examining the clock meticulously, he looked up and said, "Well. It is quite old, but I'll repair it for you." Then he asked, "Now, would you like to come inside and have some refreshments? A cup of coffee, lemonade and some cake, perhaps?"

My father accepted and we went into the living room. The prophet's daughter Maria was at home. She greeted us, and the prophet asked her if she could make some refreshments for the guests. He introduced us, and we exchanged the usual polite phrases. She went out and a little later came back with coffee, lemonade and cakes and sat down with us.

The prophet looked at my father and asked him how he was getting on. My father looked embarrassed, and said that it was very difficult to raise the money we needed. Carl said he could very well understand, but he continued encouragingly, "The only thing to do is to carry on. Do not give up."

These words seemed to give my father strength. He straightened up a bit, and looked almost like an ordinary, happy person.

"And how are you?" the prophet said, turning to me.

"I am good," I answered.

"How is school?"

I pulled myself together, because suddenly I felt that I was being given the space and a place to talk, so I launched into a speech about school.

"School is wonderful; I love it. I am the best in my class and the teachers even let me teach boys and girls who cannot read. I feel so ..."

Here my father interrupted me. "Peter is doing well in school," he simply concluded.

The prophet did not comment on what my father had said. He smiled at me, and I felt that here was a person who understood me.

"And how is Sunday school?" he asked.

I said that I liked it very much, but my father's presence had a restraining influence on me, so I did not develop my thoughts further.

Maria looked at me, but did not say anything. I noticed she was beautiful. I did not know how old she was, but she was definitely not like the girls in school, whom we constantly teased.

Some days later, I was sent down to fetch the clock. The prophet was in the shop, and told me it was ready. I asked how much it would cost; he looked puzzled and then thoughtfully replied: "Nothing, it was a mere trifle."

He told me that all he had had to do was to wind it up. I did not believe him, because my father, being a practical man, would surely not have missed such a simple thing.

Without turning a hair, the prophet said, "I have a little gift for you."

Then he gave me five kroner, for which I was very thankful. He almost laughed at my polite gratitude, and said, "Do come anytime you'd like to talk."

I took this invitation seriously, and walked home much happier than I had been for many days.

II

When I went to see the prophet he always welcomed me, and Maria, when she was there, was kind and talked to me a lot, especially asking questions about life, school, friends, and so on, to which, most of the time, I did not know what to answer.

I remember once I told him about Sunday school. We had the parable about the sower, who went out into his field and sowed seeds by hand. Some fell on the path where birds ate them, others fell on rocky ground and could not take root; still others fell among thorns and were choked. But there were also seeds that fell on good soil and grew and brought forth grain – some a hundredfold, some sixty and some thirty. Let anyone with ears listen.

Whether this last exhortation was meant as an invitation to go deeper into the meaning of the parable, or simply a request to open the eyes, or rather ears, our Sunday school teacher did not say or explain. For him, the meaning was clear. It was about people who had no faith and therefore did not bring forth fruit. The good people brought forth manifold fruit.

This meant that some people were doomed; they would perish and go to hell. Was I one of those fortunate few to be saved or was I among the lost? What did it mean to bring forth this "fruit"?

I had a feeling that it meant something like living your life with God, as my mother would say, but sometimes I had the feeling that my life was only dedicated to football, being clever in school, looking for friends, having fun and, in between, being interested in girls.

I could not help thinking about the last Christmas celebration. Each year, we had a celebration in Sunday school on the 28th of December. In the vast hall, there was a Christmas tree several metres high. We would receive goodies and dance around the tree, and then we would play all the Christmas games, running around and sometimes even holding hands. And I happened to hold hands with Ulla, the girl from my class. The whole evening was blissful, and I couldn't sleep that night for sheer happiness.

At the same time, no one was supposed to know that I liked her, and when we met in school after the holidays, we hardly ever spoke a word to each other. This made me sad, but in my heart I understood that I was skating on thin ice. I was not thinking about God or salvation but constantly about worldly things.

I told the prophet about it. The parable about the sower made it clear that there should be another way to live, in order to reach paradise – where, by the way, you could not play football. The teacher had said that. He said we would be like angels, singing and playing the praises of God the whole time. I felt that was stupid and it was not what I longed for. But the teacher did not understand. He was looking forward to that. As a matter of fact, his father, who was a very old man, would talk about Jesus all the time, and when he visited us, my father thought that he was a bit crazy.

"You cannot talk about Jesus, and Jesus and nothing else. You have to live as well," he shouted almost angrily.

My mother tried to modify this statement by saying that this world was a place of sorrow and the heavenly world would be one of joy, so there was nothing wrong in longing for that.

The prophet laughed at all this. "Don't think about it like that," he advised. "This is not what Jesus is telling us. I shall tell you what the parable means: You are the field where the message is sown as a seed, and you are full of all kinds of thoughts, feelings and impulses; sometimes you follow one of them, and another time, another one. At times you even discuss within yourself which one of them to follow.

"The parable is not about good and bad people but about our own inner landscape where thorns and lilies grow side by side, where hard and unforgiving feelings exist, where indifferent and passive tendencies govern, where nothing matters and carelessness leads us into a feeling of emptiness. In that landscape, there are also green pastures and brooks with water glistening in the sunshine, and there you experience joy; here is the good soil where the seed grows, bringing forth grain for a plentiful harvest. There is even a football ground where you feel the pleasure of using your body fighting for the ball. Jesus wants that also, that we enjoy our lives and go home from the football match, tired and dirty and, after washing, go to bed, say our evening prayers and sleep soundly in the company of all God's angels." He said this while looking teasingly at me.

"And remember," he said, "God does not forgive, because he never condemned you.

Believe that." Then he patted me on my shoulder.

"You are a good boy. Do not forget that. Do as well as you can, but don't forget to be happy and enjoy your life. God loves you as he loves every human being he created."

This gave me a beautiful feeling of peace: if this were really true, I had nothing to fear. I wished to tell my Sunday school teacher about it, but I thought that he would probably not understand. So it became my own secret, shared with the prophet.

III

One day Jim and I built a little "cottage" in the garden. It was made out of thin branches and we used straw to cover the walls. The straw was twined between the branches like a plaited basket. It was beautiful. You could not stand upright in it, but we loved sitting there, with a table for biscuits and lemonade from the house.

Then our neighbour's two sons came along. We did not play with them often, but on this day they came with some other boys. We split into two groups to play hide and seek or cops and robbers. The game started, and while one group was hiding, the neighbour's oldest boy drew our attention to the part of the field we should search, while he went straight to our cottage and demolished it. I saw what he had done from a long way away and ran towards him. He was fleeing; I chased him across the field which, at that time of the year, was ploughed, and just before catching up with him, I fell. It was strange because in our playing, I had done this catching many times – throwing myself forward and catching the legs of my opponent – but this time I missed. He ran home, laughing hilariously, while I was left on the ground. I wanted to beat him to death, but I did not get the chance. I was devastated and hated the boy for what he had done, although I was aware that it was a sin to hate anyone.

I told the prophet about this. I said that I had wanted to kill the neighbour's boy, but somehow I knew it was not a good idea.

The prophet said to me, "Do you remember the parable of the sower?" I did.

"There is another parable following that in the bible." He told me the parable.

"A man sowed good seed in his field; but while everybody was asleep, an enemy came and sowed weeds among the wheat, and then went away. The workers told the householder that weeds were growing among the wheat, and they suggested pulling them up. The householder said no, leave them. If you pull up the weeds, you might uproot the wheat as well. Let both grow together until the harvest; then you can collect the weeds and burn them.

"You see," he explained, "you cannot take away what you do not like in yourself. It is all about not feeling guilt or shame and condemning yourself, because when you focus on your sinful nature, you strengthen it, and even neglect what is good in you. You can work on making the weeds passive, by leaving them alone and trying to learn to love yourself as your neighbour."

He said all this in a way that made sense to me. I knew what he was talking about.

"And at the time of the harvest," he went on, "God will take the last step. But, you know, when the harvest will come is another question. And about that, I can talk much more later on. It is good you did not kill him. Well, I am sure you wouldn't have done it. But try to understand that there are two beings in us: one being who wants to hurt and the other who wants to do well. Which of them will win?"

"I don't know," I said.

"Of course the one you feed. It is quite normal to feel unjustly treated. But try to see the whole thing in a different way. Unjust treatment will not be eliminated by vengeance. That will only create more injustice and even more struggle. Leave it and be glad that you did not hurt him. He is carrying his own punishment. Some day he will know; you do not have to inflict the punishment on him. He will do that himself, so help him God."

Some days later he showed me his guitar. He played for me and asked me to sing with him. He was a really good guitar player and had an excellent voice. I liked listening to him, but he always wanted me to sing along.

"It is healthy to sing," he repeated many times. I had some difficulty with that.

Anyhow, it was always good to listen to the prophet, and I savoured all the words he spoke to me and I kept them in my heart.

We moved into a new decade, the sixties, and from then on, the economic situation changed radically. It now became possible to buy all the things we could only dream of before, including a television in 1960. The good new era was marching on.

The next day, Peter continued his story.

1961

I

Some months before I was confirmed, grandfather's old clock on the wall stopped again. This time I went to see the prophet on my own, with the clock under my arm.

I had not seen him for some time, and I missed him. But the days went hurrying by, filled with school, football and girls in class. I was fourteen and feeling almost grown-up. Confirmation was the entrance into adult society.

The prophet was not at home that day. Maria came into the shop. And then something quite unexpected happened. I fell in love with her, and for a moment I was in a very different world.

It was as if lightning had struck! She was wearing a red dress, tight on top with a wide skirt. I noticed the shape of her breasts, her black hair hanging over the shoulders and her smile, like an invitation from a goddess.

I was speechless, and just put the clock on the counter.

"How are you today?" she asked. She came closer and smelled heavenly. I could not find any other words than "I am fine."

At that moment, I was definitely fine; bewildered, yes, but fine. I looked at her with no thought of the clock, the time of the day or any other important ideas. She must have noticed, because she laughed a light, almost flirtatious laugh. (At the time she was about twenty-two – a grown woman.)

"So," she said, as if she was going to do something very decisive or important. "So, the clock has stopped working again."

"Yes, that's right," I affirmed, looking at her beautiful dress and her breasts. I now felt a warm, unpleasant sensation in my cheeks. I was blushing. "It is not working," I repeated and looked her straight in her eyes, as if confessing my attraction.

She smiled knowingly, and told me that the prophet, or Carl, as she called him, was at a meeting and would not be home until the next day.

"What meeting?" I stammered, not really interested but simply because I had to say something.

"Well," she said, "he belongs to a group, which meets regularly. They have a house in Gilleleje on the north coast. Of course he cannot go that often ... but ..."

"What kind of group is it?" I interrupted.

"It is a spiritual group gathered around a teacher. But please, I am only telling you this because you are a friend of his. Do not babble about it all around in the village. They do not understand or like these things."

For a moment I forgot about Maria and her beautiful dress. A spiritual group, I repeated in my head. Strange that he had never told me about it.

"And when will he be back?"

"Tomorrow, I told you."

"Yes," I said, "of course you said that."

This little extra remark, "I told you", made me feel stupid.

"OK, then. I'll leave the clock and come back ... in a couple of days."

I walked towards the door and she followed me, to say goodbye. I walked home in a trance, all the time trying to tell myself that I was stupid. She was so much older than me, and ... yes, but why? Why had I never been in love like this with the girls in the school? I did not know, and I decided to forget all about her as soon as possible.

As a matter of fact, I managed to do that, so when my father asked me to fetch the clock I excused myself, explaining that I had much homework to do. Then he fetched it himself.

From then on, I tried not to go to see the prophet. I felt that what I had experienced was dangerous and I would never be able to handle it.

II

When I was confirmed, I stopped praying to God. My childhood religion was abandoned. I wanted now to be my own person. I had to leave everything that my parents represented. I had to revolt in a way that bordered on a type of revenge. When my anger was strong, I promised myself that I would go the whole way, through high school and university where I would study theology, not to be a priest but to prove to them that all they believed in was false – the image of an angry and revengeful God, the bible, sin, praying, and all the naive stories they had made me believe during the years in Sunday school.

From then on, my relationship with my dear and beloved brother changed further. We did not have much in common anymore. He did not want to go to some stupid dusty high school to read books about all the things you did not need in this world. Later he began an education, became a teacher and entered into an accepted way of life.

I did not follow suit. I started reading books and listening to classical music, as I had managed to buy a record player with money I earned working during the holidays.

I often felt lonely and sad, a feeling of something missing. I thought a lot about Maria, and wanted to visit her, but since I had not been there for a while, I thought I needed an excuse to go. I was shy and very self-conscious, a common trait of teenage boys. I did not feel able to go round to the watchmaker's shop and say, "Hi, I would like to talk to Maria."

But then I hit on an idea. I had grandfather's old watch. I could take it to the shop and maybe then be able to talk to Maria; but what if the prophet came into the shop when I arrived – could I just say to him that I badly wanted to see and talk to Maria? That seemed both stupid and embarrassing.

I could go with the excuse that my grandfather's watch needed repairing, and at least get a glimpse of Maria that way. There was, however, one problem with this: the watch was working perfectly. My bright idea was to damage it a little. I took it out and banged it on a stone a few times, so that the glass was smashed.

I went to the prophet's shop to have my grandfather's watch repaired. "So what can I do for you, young man?" the prophet asked. Then he continued without waiting for my answer, looking closely at me.

"It is a long time since we discussed the world situation or the state of theology, isn't it? How is your singing? Have you sung anything lately?"

I was really glad to see him again, and it seemed as if I had been there only yesterday.

"Well," I said, "I haven't been singing but I have seen a lot and learned a lot, which has been put to the test, because I have been confirmed."

"All right, so what do you think about it now?"

"I don't know. I am familiar with the bible and the church and the theology of the church. You see, sometimes I wonder what it's good for. I loved the celebration and everything was great, but I do not feel any different regarding faith. I did not really catch the mystery of it all."

"I see," he nodded, "I see." He continued: "But do you know what? Maybe it is not so important to think about the form, because as a matter of fact, it is just a form, and there is nothing inside the form unless you put something into it. Do you understand? So if you attach no meaning to it, then it is empty."

"Yes. I mean no, or maybe." I had not thought about it in that way, but then I said: "It is a form, solid matter, the party, the service, the presents ... well, it was all right, I even had a new bicycle, but otherwise I don't know. We had Holy Communion, but is that a miracle?"

"No," he said, "it is not. But don't worry. You will find your own meaning in theology one day. Trust me."

I was about to ask about the spiritual group that Maria had mentioned, but before I could, he changed the subject.

"Now, what is the purpose of your majesty's visit?" he said jestingly. I remembered my ostensible purpose.

"Yes, you see the glass is broken on my grandfather's watch."
He looked at it. "Oh, I see. It has had a real thrashing. The silver case is damaged as well. OK. What shall we do about it?"

And he gave me a knowing look, a scrutinizing glance which said that there was something more to the damage of the watch.

"Do you want to talk to Maria?" he said.

"Yes!," I burst out, straight away. I repeated: "Yes, I would like to." Although I was blushing, I was proud of myself for being honest and brave.

"I would like to talk to her," I repeated once again.

He smiled, and showed me into the living room. "Maria," he called out, "you have a visitor." Then to me he said, "Stay here, she will be with you in a moment," and he walked back into the shop.

Maria came down the stairs. "Peter!" she exclaimed, "Nice to see you! Where have you been for so long?"

This is the kind of question you cannot answer. Where have I been? Hiding from you, I could have said, but no, not now that I was here.

"It is nice to see you too," I said.

"Come on in and sit down."

And then she started talking. I did not have to explain or excuse. Probably she did not even know that I had been, or was still, in love with her. She asked me about everything between heaven and earth, which is quite a lot, and our conversation flowed very naturally and truthfully, due to her natural friendliness. From that day on I had a friend, a real friend to whom I could talk about what was in my heart. The prophet had also been that, but this was different, because she was young, and a woman, and I liked her very much indeed.

Now I started to visit the watchmaker's shop frequently. The prophet made no comment, but it was obvious that it was Maria that "pulled" me. He smiled and laughed whenever I came, and asked the same questions as before.

Maria taught me to play chess. She showed me the moves and I learned quickly. After some time, I could beat her and I don't think she lost on purpose.

Our relationship changed, and even when I could not help admiring her beauty, looking into her dark eyes and melting for a moment, we were still relaxed around each other. I loved it.

One day she said, "My father told me you are a good singer."

"I don't know about that," I began, a little unsure of how to react.

"That's what he told me, but he didn't say maybe." She laughed. "Would you like me to teach you the guitar? You know my father is a good guitar player; he taught me and he thought that you could be an excellent guitar player too."

I had never given it much thought, but because Maria offered it I had to accept. It was wonderful that she was going to teach me the guitar; she had already shown me how to play chess and she was welcome to teach me anything in the whole wide world. She was the best – a beautiful angel.

So we started lessons; I came every week and soon I had learned the most common chords and was able to sing and accompany myself. I was very shy at the beginning, but after a while my confidence grew.

Maria said to me, "You have to express yourself more, let go of your inhibitions – just let yourself go, sing loudly and don't be embarrassed."

I followed her advice, and really it felt very good.

My watch was repaired, and I never damaged it again. I keep it as a memory of my dear grandfather and I still have it here ... in a way. But it has changed its value.

That's another story, which I'll tell you later.

I told Peter: "I also have a thing from my grandfather. It is a book: Tischendorf's *Critical Text of the New Testament* from 1878. It has an introduction in Latin. He wanted me to have it, since I was going to study theology and he himself was a scholar at a university in Germany. I am very proud to have it, but I was a little older when my grandfather died. I had just started at university. I couldn't use it for meeting a beautiful woman by damaging it."

Peter couldn't help laughing at the idea.

III

My time at the village school was coming to an end. I was sixteen. The principal had suggested I should go to high school which, over three years, would prepare me for university. I passed the entrance test and, although I would still be living at home, each day I would travel into the city by bus to enter a new and foreign world. I was proud of getting top marks in my class, straight A's for every subject.

I went to tell Maria.

When the door opened, a young man stood there in front of me. He said, in a harsh and very impolite way, "Who are you?"

I caught a glimpse of his eyes. They were a yellowish green and staring at me. I looked down.

"Oh, I am sorry!" I exclaimed. "I have come to see Maria. She is teaching me to play the guitar."

"Is that so?" he said in a condescending way. "Come on in then."

I walked into the room and when Maria came down the stairs, I stood there full of questions. The appearance of the young man had given me such a surprise that I knew I most certainly looked confused.

"There was a man at the door ...," I started.

"Don't worry. He is my brother; or, that is not true, he is my half-brother." She stopped.

"As a matter of fact he is neither my brother nor half-brother, but he is a young man that my father adopted many years ago; he is eight years older than I am." She paused a little again.

"Of course," she said, "you have never met him. He left home long before you came here the first time; I think it was when you and your father came with the big clock. Is that right?"

"Yes," I said, "it is."

"Good. His name is Jude – my father calls him Hans – and he finished a degree in economics four years ago, actually at Oxford, and has been offered a job in a big firm somewhere in England. He was English from the beginning, you see. He has been working in Copenhagen until now, but he is moving ..."

She obviously felt a bit uneasy and I couldn't understand why. She was usually so relaxed and composed. What was going on?

She continued: "He is here for a couple of days to collect some things, because as I said, he is moving."

I tried to change the subject. "Where is your father?" I asked.

"He has just gone out on an errand. Unfortunately, the thing is that Carl and Hans do not get on very well. My father introduced him to the teacher of the group – I'm not sure it was a wise decision – but let's forget about that for now."

As a matter of fact, I had tried to forget about it, but the latest information made me think. I was sure that Carl, as she called him, or the prophet, could not have any difficulty getting on with anybody. From what I knew, he was a master of empathy and the most pleasant and understanding person, who could deal with anything and solve any problems, which he had done for me so many times.

Maria said, "Hans is a difficult person, you know. He did not have a good life before he arrived here. That was before I was born, but we grew up together. I think there were some problems with him in the group. But I really don't know."

After the guitar lesson, which had a gloomy feeling about it, I left earlier than usual. I did not feel well. Maria noticed, and we ended the session for the day.

On my way out, Hans came to the door. "So you are leaving?" he asked.

"Yes."

"Good. You spend a lot of time with Maria, I understand, but take it easy. She is my woman and we are getting married."

I just left – didn't even say goodbye. All right, Maria was getting married. So what?

But on the way home on my bike, I was sad. Maria was getting married. Why hadn't she told me herself?

IV

After the summer holidays, high school started. Had I known what a nightmare it would introduce into my life, I would probably never have gone. I came from a small country school, where I was number one, to a large school in the city, where I totally disappeared. I did not make any friends that first year. I was very lonely and wanted to leave, which my father would not allow, since I was on the way to fulfilling his dreams concerning me.

My luck changed in the second year, when I found a friend. His name was John.

In the beginning, we were like boys of that age. We talked about girls, but the difference was that we could talk honestly and openly about everything, even allowing ourselves to expose our weaknesses. At the same time, we gave each other what we badly needed: approval and honesty. Our friendship lasted the whole way through high school and beyond.

We both seemed to be interested in religion from an alternative point of view. We discussed the faith that we had been brought up with, although his background was more liberal. His parents were teachers and not engaged in any congregational group.

When the teacher in the religion lesson drew our attention to a passage from St Mark's gospel, we were stunned. It said:

To you has been given the secret of the kingdom of God, but for those outside, everything comes in parables; in order that they may look, but not perceive and may indeed listen but not understand; so that they may not turn again and be forgiven.

This was very puzzling. Nobody had ever pointed out this passage to me before, or to John, maybe because it did not fit into the dogmatic pattern. Was it saying that Jesus decided to whom the message and the salvation would be given, and the rest would have to find their way through some parables so that they should not be forgiven?

Of course I wanted to ask the prophet about it. But I had been hesitant about visiting him recently, partly because I would have some difficulty with meeting Maria after what happened. Then I suddenly remembered that Maria had said Hans was to leave for a job in England. If he was leaving, what would become of the marriage? I pulled myself together, and one afternoon I went to see the prophet and Maria.

She was not at home. The prophet welcomed me as usual and we sat down at the kitchen table. I brought up the subject of the religious lessons – I did not mention the marriage.

The prophet asked me whether I still remembered the angel and the book of Isaiah – I had told him about my angel many times, and also chapter 29 in the book.

"Yes, of course, I'll never forget about it. Besides, number 29 is the date of my birth."

He fetched a bible and quoted the following lines:

[10] *For the* LORD *has poured out upon you a spirit of deep sleep; he has closed your eyes, you prophets, and covered your heads, you seers.*

The vision of all this has become for you like the words of a sealed document. If it is given to those who can read, with the command, 'Read this', they say, 'We cannot, for it is sealed.' [12]*And if it is given to those who cannot read, saying, 'Read this', they say, 'We cannot read.'*

He closed the book and looked at me. "I will try to explain these passages to you. Let us go and sit comfortably in the dining room." Then he started:

"Someone once said that we have come from the stars. It is a long journey through eternity, into the time and space when we entered our solar system, where the sun sustains us and where the planets form our innate abilities, and create a being with its own potentials. Finally we end up on earth where Mother Nature created our bodies.

"I suppose this is a myth or possibly a parable that gives us a sensation of the great mystery of life, because whenever I see a newborn baby, I have a strong feeling that it existed before its birth; in other words, we do not come empty-handed; we carry something with us, and this is the seed of life that, when planted in fertile soil, will grow and perhaps develop into a tree where the birds of heaven can build their nests.

"But we are all faced with one problem: The seed of life is very quiet. It does not shout and scream; it does not even use words; it is silent, and like a faint vibration in the heart, which we tend to disregard when we are in the midst of the many activities of life. When the tiny voice from the seed reaches us, we are like the people in the text: we excuse ourselves, saying it is not possible. I cannot open the sealed document or I cannot read wordless messages."

He looked at me, full of compassion. "I think that was the message from your angel!"

I sighed deeply, recalling my dream when I met my angel. Suddenly, I felt I understood the whole meaning of life, and I was filled with joy.

"So what about the Gospel text?" I asked.

"You see," Carl continued, "most people are not looking for God or ways to wake up, so it would be useless for Jesus to try to convince them. They would either not listen, or they would argue and go on living their lives, judging and criticising and thus neither being forgiven nor coming closer to a new understanding. Therefore, the only way forward for Jesus was to speak in parables, because the parable speaks to the emotions. It may then be possible for a person to feel something within himself by listening to the parables, which could enable him to begin accumulating pieces of the truth. When reaching a little understanding through listening to the parable, a man might one day start to search actively and, later, be ready to be *given the secrets of the Kingdom*, as the text says. It must be voluntarily, so you can say that the Lord put us to sleep by placing us where we are, but at the same time, we are given possibilities by the same Lord, to help us wake up."

Now I wanted to ask him about the school that Maria had mentioned. I said, "All this is something you have learned in the school, isn't it?"

He shook his head with a benevolent expression on his face. Then he laughed, and I did not press him anymore.

And he did not tell me about his group until a couple of years later.

Chapter Five:

UNEXPECTED EVENTS

1966

I

My friendship with John deepened during our last year at high school. We were nineteen and we could now decide things for ourselves – something we had longed for since our confirmation. Free at last, but there again, what was this freedom to be used for? What would I do with it?

One day, John was not in school. I caught the bus out to see him as I thought he might be ill, but he was at home because his father had died.

I did not go to the funeral, but some days later John asked me to help him sort out his father's books and take them to a second-hand bookshop to sell.

We spent most of Saturday looking through the books – his father, whose name was George, had a lot of books. We worked hard, and then we came across a box with letters and other papers inside; the bundle was carefully tied together with string. John said that we should close the box; his father had told him that he, as the oldest son, should burn these letters and leaflets the day he was not around anymore.

"Why is that?" I asked.

"Because my father belonged to a secret spiritual group. I do not know which one, but I presume it was the Freemasons."

John did not know what the Freemasons were about, but having discussed the matter at length, we decided to follow George's wishes and not read the papers in the box. However, our curiosity made us look at the open letter that was at the top of the bundle. It was impossible to avoid reading it. It read as follows:

Dear Carl.

I want to warn you about Hans, the Englishman. He is not reliable.
Since you are his father, I thought that maybe you should talk to him first.

Love and peace

George

We looked at each other and knew we had come across a secret that was not meant for us. But there it was, right in front of us.

"What shall we do?" John asked.

"I know these people," I said.

John did not hear me and he went on about getting rid of the papers.

"There is a secret recess at the bottom of the shelves, right in the corner, where we could hide the letters until we can make a fire to burn them."

"But I know who your father is talking about in that letter."

"What? Why didn't you say?"

"I just did!"

And then I told him about the prophet and Maria – even my love for her – and about meeting Hans.

"Do you know," I continued, "that since the letter from your father is here, it means that he never sent it?"

John also realized that now.

"But suppose it is an important message?"

We took out the letter, and looked at the date. It was only a couple of weeks old.

"I could take it to the prophet and then it would be up to him to make up his mind what to do."

John agreed. "There is a reason we have seen the letter, so I think you should go and show it to him."

Then we hid the rest of the bundle in the secret recess.

I took the letter with me and on the following day, after school, I went to the watchmaker's shop to show him the letter.

I must admit I was a bit tense, as the last time I had been there the difficult subject had been avoided, namely Maria's putative marriage. I recalled my relationship with Maria, and Hans's strange attitude towards me.

The shop was closed. There was a sign on the door. I rang the bell and after a while Maria appeared. She was wearing a dressing gown, and it was obvious that she had just had a shower.

"Hello, my dear friend Peter!" she exclaimed.

She was glad to see me, there was no mistaking the sincerity in her voice and I was pleased to see her too, as you may imagine. I could not believe what I saw: she was so beautiful and I wanted to throw myself in her arms and kiss her. I had kissed a couple of girls, for instance when the whole class had travelled to Germany with a school teacher. It had been in the evening, just before we were supposed to be in bed, and we had sneaked in unnoticed after the lights were out. Nobody knew except the two of us, and the kissing did not lead any further. I was now nineteen, so of course there was no reason for me not to kiss Maria, even though she was some eight or nine years older than me. All these thoughts rushed through my head; I forgot all about my letter and did not ask for her father.

"Come on in," she said. I needed no second invitation, and was in the hall and on my way to the living room in a flash. I felt immediately at home.

I knew I had to ask the question uppermost in my mind since I had met Hans.

"Are you married now?" I cautiously asked.

"Where did you get that idea from?"

"Hans told me when I visited you one day, and I did not want to intrude. Last time I was here I said nothing, only talked to your father about theology."

She shook her head vigorously.

"No, I am not marrying. You know I told you Hans is different. He was always in love with me, he even tried to force himself on me. He seems to be possessed at times, but don't think about him; he is now living in England."

Maria looked at me and smiled in a way that told me she wanted me. Her lips said that. They spoke silent words, understood only by the heart; and her hair, which was still wet, hung down her shoulders, and there was a joy in her eyes, almost like tears, when she said:

"Why have you been away so long? Were you afraid of me again?"

There was no time or space for talk, no time for words or explanations. There was only this very holy "now" of meeting a beloved friend after what seemed to be ages.

Then all of a sudden she let her dressing gown fall to the floor and she was naked. It was the first time I had ever seen a naked woman, and I was speechless. She looked marvellous, fantastic, inviting and, like a goddess, she stretched out her hands towards me.

"I would like you to take off your clothes," she said with a smile.

I started to undress, feeling a bit embarrassed.

"Come," she said.

She pulled the cushions from the sofa down onto the floor and made me lie down on my back. Then she caressed my naked body for a long time, and after a while she sat herself on top of me.

This was the first time I made love to a woman.

We woke up in the middle of the night. It was dark. "You had better go home now," she said.

I was half awake, my mind flooded with the memories of the evening before, and somehow I could not understand what had happened, but I knew it was true.

"I have to go," she said, "early in the morning."

I did not argue or insist on staying. I was too sleepy to think about where she would be going so early in the morning. We kissed, and then I wanted to say something about seeing her again, but she laid her finger over my lips and kissed me one last time. Then I left, walking home on a cloud of supreme happiness and wonder.

Nobody was awake in our house when I arrived. I tiptoed in and lay down on my bed wanting to sleep, but for a long time I dreamt of the beautiful Maria. I wished to be with her for the rest of my life – for ever if possible. She was so full of surprises and joy, a miracle created by the good Lord, which at this moment appeared to be real. Goodnight world, and thank you for Maria and for being alive.

II

When I called on the prophet two days later, I was relieved to find him at home, since it was important to tell him about the letter we had found at John's place. As soon as I came into the living room behind the shop, I bluntly asked whether Maria was at home.

"No, and she will not be for some time, I think," he replied.

"Why?" I asked, becoming a bit agitated.

"She has gone to live with our group and the teacher."

"But she did not say anything about that the day before yesterday."

"I know. She told me, but do not get upset. Everything is fine, and please appreciate that what she did was to give you a precious gift. Be thankful for it. She knew she was leaving and naturally she could not tell you."

"But why not?"

"Because in your immaturity you would not understand and would just make things difficult. That is why."

I suppose I was absent for a while until I recovered my senses.

"What is it with this group? Now you must tell me," I demanded in anger and disappointment.

"Sit down," the prophet said, "and I'll explain."

"This group, as you call it, is not some secret brotherhood. We are all ordinary normal people, but we are working with a system, working on ourselves. This work is about waking up from the natural 'sleep' that people, you and I, exist in. That is all it is; nothing more.

But we do not talk much about it to the outside world, because people do not understand."

He looked at me as if he was waiting for me to take in the information, and continued:

"The teacher we have shows absolute unconditional love, and that is what people are afraid of. Maybe you would say that one cannot be afraid of love, but it is so. Do you know that unconditional love is to leave your whole life in the hands of something greater – God, if you like – and to give up all decision-making, plans or agendas, and just follow this higher power, and there is nothing in the whole world that makes us more afraid or stirs people up more than this idea? To follow wholeheartedly – that is what the first disciples did, according to the gospel, although it is stated in a way that does not allow for their doubts and struggles, but in the end, they had to follow unconditionally. And when people see this, or hear about it, they think we are crazy. They believe us to be small obedient lambs, and then their next thought is: they are being manipulated. Someone is taking advantage of them. This is criminal, so we must help them; and then they start to act violently. Have you ever thought about why Jesus was killed, or Gandhi, or others in a similar position? It is dangerous for people to know the truth, when they are not ready for it." He paused.

"But I am ready; I want to go," I replied. "I want to go to Maria and the teacher."

Carl kept quiet at this point, in order to allow me to let out all my emotions. I knew he fully understood. Then he said very calmly:

"You will be ready one day. What one calls destiny is very difficult to explain, but it is not like predestination; it is like a magnet. We carry a magnet around inside us and because of this we are drawn to different places and circumstances. What draws us is what is in our minds. If you are thinking about misfortune the whole time, you attract misfortune. You can even attract illness, if you worry about it, or are afraid of being sick, and contrary to that, you can attract happiness, good friends, maybe even a good job and become wealthy. But we are not aware of what is in us. Much of the time, the mind spins around and creates thousands of wishes; some of them group themselves around certain strong desires, and that is what we attract."

He got up from his chair and walked towards the window. He was deep in thought for some time. Then he turned around and, standing there, he continued talking.

"What I am telling you explains why the teacher does not advertise for students: because it is possible they would come simply out of curiosity. Many people look for miracles and wonderful things. When they hear about a teacher who performs miracles, they want proof, and the more proof they get, the more they will want. When it is denied them, they become negative, and turn their backs on the teacher and start squabbling. They gossip and make everything negative, cruel and unjust, and then all is destroyed. In the gospels, Jesus often told people after he had performed a miracle not to talk about it, and I have just explained why."

The way he spoke to me made me relax and feel confident in whatever would come.

"You will always attract what you desire, positive or negative. For, you know, where your treasure is, there your heart also will be. Or in other words: your being attracts your life. And do you know that I have talked to the teacher about you, and one day you will come, when you are ready. But at the moment, do not ask any more questions; just wait. Purify yourself and your wishes. You will be ready. Maybe you will have to live through many difficulties, maybe you will travel around the whole world, the East, India and maybe even further, but one day, I promise you, you will be ready. Maybe you will find yourself in total despair and just want to leave this world, but don't. Stay and have patience."

He came back and sat down.

"By the way: India is a good place. I once spent some time there visiting a friend. We worked together, which is how I met him; he is a good man, who taught me many things and he also visited me here once."

The prophet sat in silence for some time. What he had said sent me a strong message, which I promised to keep in my heart and not mention to anyone.

Then I remembered my letter.

"Oh," I said, "the reason for coming to see you is this: I have a letter you should see."

I told him the whole story about John's father and the letters we had found. He read the letter and then he exclaimed, "I knew it all along!"

"Please tell me, what did you know?"

After a little while he told me the story of his life. It was a short version pertinent to the immediate problem.

"First of all, I knew that Hans would create problems. When I introduced him to the teacher, I thought he was ready but then I thought I was mistaken. But the teacher said that he should stay. He seemed to see a purpose for having him there.

"When I was young, as a newly qualified archaeologist, I had the opportunity to go to Israel to work."

"You are an archaeologist?" I said with great surprise.

He paused. "Yes, we worked in Israel, but at that time, there was no state called Israel. The excavation took place near the Sea of Galilee, or as it is called, Gennesaret. There, I found a little fragment with a Hebrew inscription. The Hebrew alphabet consists of consonants and the vowels you add yourself. The letters on this fragment were: MGDL. Knowing the Hebrew language, you would automatically add the first vowel as the letter I, so it would read: Migdal. And then we realized that it was the name of the town, Magdala, a town whose whereabouts are unknown and have never been found, but it is mentioned in the gospels that Mary came from Magdala. We found many interesting items there. It was a village inhabited by fishermen, and the later Greek name translated to mean the village of salted fish."

It was clear to me that memories were coming back to him.

"Now, by telling you all this, I want you to understand my background. I found Magdala and many other clues about the time of Jesus. My Indian friend was with me there, and we both felt a strong desire to go deeper into the gospels and the message of Jesus. We were at that moment in the place where Jesus grew up, and we almost felt his presence. It was the first time I became interested in what you could call religious matters."

"But during our work, I fell in love with a Jewish woman. She was the most beautiful and wonderful person in the world. We married in 1930 and when things in Europe became difficult, we moved to Denmark, and no one imagined that our country would be occupied and violated. After having been married for some years and having no children, we decided to adopt a child. A friend of ours from our work in Palestine had some relatives in England, and we managed to adopt a boy from there in 1938; his name was Jude. He had had a very traumatic childhood, but he seemed to be a good boy and we gave him the name Hans, since that made more sense in Denmark. Then Maria suddenly and unexpectedly came along a year later. She was born on the 22nd of July, the day of Mary Magdalene; that's why we called her Maria. Hans, who was then eight years old, liked the little girl very much."

"Then the war came to Denmark, and the persecution of the Jews began. I was married to a Jewish woman and had a Jewish child, which was a very difficult situation to deal with. In the early part of 1943, some Danish people starting blaming the Jews for everything, and one day they stood outside my shop, shouting at me to send out my Jewish bastards. They threw stones at the house and they smashed the glass on the clock outside. Later that year, I decided to send both my wife and Maria out of the country to Sweden. I arranged for their passage with a skipper and they went to Gilleleje to wait for the boat that evening. For some inexplicable reason, the boat never came. The refugees – and there were quite a few of them waiting for the boat – hid in the church overnight, but some law-abiding person told the Gestapo and they stormed the church and took everyone and sent them to a concentration camp. At the time, I did not know what had happened. Little Maria, who was only four and a half years old, managed to hide under one of the benches, holding herself up on the heating pipes.

"Later that day the skipper came, and there was only Maria and one man, who had managed to hide in the organ. They went to Sweden.

"All this I was told later when suddenly, one day in 1946, Maria came back to me. She was a very clever girl and remembered me, and with the help of good people, she came back. She did not know the name of our village and could not remember my first or second name, but she remembered the clock. And the reason why I never repaired the clock in the window is that it was damaged the day I lost my wife."

Now he was silent. This was the first time I had heard the prophet's sad story, which he was now sharing with me. Then he spoke again.

"Hans is a very difficult man. He is grown-up now and has many strange ideas. He hates foreigners; he is a communist, and despises our capitalistic society. He has been attracted to Maria from the time she was thirteen. He has tried to force himself on her and had it not been for me, he would have succeeded. But I forgave him. It is very strange that he came into my life, but I believe that God has a plan for all of us, and sometimes only much later can we understand it. I still do not think that I have understood why Hans came to us, but one day I hope I will.

"Hans is now in England pursuing a good career, which, by the way, is in a capitalistic company, as he would put it, being a socialist; but I think he is doing it just to get some money and position and will later find a use for it. Often I wonder what goes on in his mind. As he became older, he never confided in me and we have hardly ever had an open, honest conversation."

The prophet rose and put his hand on my shoulder.

"Please, do not talk about this to other people. Just keep it to yourself. It is to you I have told the story, and it is just between us. I will talk to JC about the letter, but somehow I am sure he already knows."

"Is JC the teacher?" I asked.

"Yes," he said, "his name is JC."

Chapter Six:

THEOLOGY

1966–1968

I

The old university, built in 1479, was situated in the centre of Copenhagen. The buildings were anything but modern, being mainly built in the Renaissance style. Most noticeable were the auditoria, which were our lecture halls. They were furnished with old wooden benches and the rostrum was placed at a much higher level than the rest of the auditorium. This gave us a feeling of inferiority, as we had to look up at the lecturer in the "pulpit", from where he would feed us the knowledge we needed to pass the exams and acquire a degree.

Brand new premises had been built in the suburbs of the city for the so-called exact sciences, whereas the students in theology and the other arts subjects were accommodated in the old buildings around the cathedral. Sometimes even the auditorium in the zoological museum was used. I attended classes in Latin in a room surrounded by stuffed animals and a smell of various disinfectants and preserving substances.

I sometimes asked myself, "Why did you choose to study theology? You are not a Christian in the usual sense of the word."

In a way this was true, but I still wanted to find answers to my question about the teachings of Jesus. The prophet had set me off on my search by interpreting the parables in a new and unexpected way, and I had to continue in the same direction.

What I learned after the first term confirmed my assumptions about Christianity. It was not the teaching *of* Jesus, but rather a teaching *about* Jesus. It became clear to me that if I wanted to find the teachings of Jesus, I had to read between the lines. Undoubtedly the texts quoted Jesus, but these pearls of wisdom were mixed in with the beliefs of the early church and the task, therefore, consisted in finding a method of determining what the essence of his teachings were. There seemed to be an exoteric gospel, accessible to everyone, and an esoteric gospel for those "who had ears", which were fused together in one.

I became obsessed with finding the "real", true teaching of Jesus.

Of course, I knew that other scholars had tried before, without success, so why on earth did I think that I would be able to find it? I reminded myself that Aristarchos of Samos had put forward the theory that the earth moved around the sun in 250 BC. He had even calculated the size of the moon almost exactly, but his theories had been forgotten and not formulated anew until around 1500 AD by Copernicus. Similarly, the teachings of Jesus would surely have been known in the beginning of our era, but apparently they had also been forgotten – as I understood it – and would then have to be rediscovered.

When I visited my parents, I couldn't help noticing that my father was delighted that I was studying theology now. He saw his wish being fulfilled, but he did not know that, for the time being, I had absolutely no intention of going into the priesthood. He had no idea what was going on inside my head, and I did not tell him. I even kept my address secret. When asked why, I said that my room was nothing more than a cupboard, and since I came home quite often, they did not have to write to me.

The truth was that I did not want them to arrive unannounced, when I was unprepared – not that I was doing anything illegal, but I wanted to keep them out of my life, my whereabouts unknown.

The first room I had was opposite the central station, with access to a kitchen and a toilet, but no bathroom. The room was only nine square metres, but I enjoyed having my own space where I could study undisturbed.

In the beginning I made no friends, but then I met Nadia. She was studying history and had a room, not much bigger than mine, in another part of the city. After a couple of months we started sleeping together; sometimes in her room, other times in mine. To be with her felt good, and often we had great fun – naturally our interest in history gave us opportunities for discussing our studies – but at other times we argued a lot. She wanted me to be a doctor, not a theologian; to change me into her idea of "the ideal husband". She wanted us to be the perfect couple, she to be supported by an important husband, to live a life of luxury, belong to the right "set" and then to have children who, in their turn, would be successful citizens. I also tried to mould and model her. I corrected her speech, criticized the way she dressed and, without being aware of it, she became part of my image, like a trophy of which one could be proud. Nevertheless we stayed together, probably because both of us needed a companion to fill the loneliness in our lives.

John told me that he also had a girlfriend now. They got on very well together and were even talking about marriage. He was not studying at university but had found different jobs, mainly in factories.

II

Then something happened. When I was looking for a book in the theological library, I saw another book on the shelf: *The Gospel of Thomas*. It was translated into Danish. I took it out and read the opening passage:

> *These are the secret sayings which the living Jesus spoke and which Didymos Judas Thomas wrote down. Whoever finds the interpretation of these sayings will not experience death.*

When I read this sentence, I immediately understood that this was the first and probably only esoteric text containing the teachings of Jesus. From now on, I sensed what the content of an esoteric teaching was like. The gospel contained a 'secret teaching' which was considered heretical by the established church and was therefore hidden.

I wondered if the prophet had been taught this teaching. Had he actually come across something similar in the days when he worked in Magdala?

Before I go on, I wish to pass on a little information about the Gospel of Thomas. Of course both Peter and I knew about the teaching, but for you, my reader, I will add a short introduction.

In 1945–46 some peasants in the Egyptian desert, near the classical town of Chenoboskion, the modern Nag Hammadi, found a jar containing some old manuscripts – around 13 books. Probably disappointed at not finding gold or other valuable material, one of the men took the contents of the jar home, where his mother used at least one of the manuscripts for lighting the fire in her house. However, a local priest heard about the find and realized that the books were written in the old Coptic language and thus were very valuable.

After the English had to leave Egypt during what was called the "Suez Crisis" in 1956, a Danish scholar, Soren Giversen, later a professor at the university in Aarhus, succeeded in gaining access to the manuscripts. He managed to translate and publish the Gospel of Thomas as early as 1958. Otherwise, these texts were not publicly available until 1961.

Peter continued:

I had heard about these manuscripts, since the professor was a distant relative of the family and because my father took a keen interest in the gospel, in order to discern whether or not it was at variance with the canonical gospels in the New Testament. I saw my father's relief when Giversen claimed that the gospel was very close to the known gospels, although there were differences. At the time, I did not find the idea very appealing and it was not until now, in 1967, that I came across Professor Giversen's translation by chance in the library at the theological college.

III

Over the next few days, I felt an urge to visit the prophet, so I promised myself that I would see him the next time I went home to see my parents – which I did a couple of times a month. It turned out that he had visited my parents recently and asked for my address, but since they did not have it, there was nothing they could do. Carl had stayed a while, had coffee and said that he would talk to me some other time.

He had left a short note for me.

Dear Peter

I hope you will dedicate yourself to your studies, but remember that life will teach you something much more important than any book is capable of doing.

We will meet again.

Love
Carl

I did not understand the purpose of his letter because it sounded so strange, almost like a farewell letter. I walked straight down to see him. I wanted to tell him about Nadia, about Copenhagen and the students there, my theology and the Gospel of Thomas.

When I walked towards the house, I saw a lot of people and many cars parked outside, even on the street, which was strange. Was he having a party?

When I came to the door it was open, and on entering I heard people talking inside. It came to me suddenly and painfully that Carl was not there. I had missed the 'For Sale' sign outside in my eagerness to see him, but instead of Carl, I saw a real estate agent showing a group of people around the house.

I walked into the living room, where Maria had made love to me, and I went into Carl's study; the guitar was still there, and all the familiar furniture seemed to be in its usual place; I supposed the furniture would be removed later.

I asked the agent about Carl Hansen, but she said all negotiations were to be made through her and she could not give out an address. A very sad and almost frightened feeling came over me: Would I ever see the prophet again? I did not know where he was, and any attempt to find him would probably be doomed to failure. Maria was long gone, and I now felt such an overwhelming feeling of loss that I tried to find a counterweight, something positive to balance my heaviness of heart: John was my friend and I had Nadia, my parents and my little brother Jim, although we did not meet as often anymore, but all in all, things would be all right and there was nothing else to do but to struggle on. I wanted to find out the truth about Jesus through my studies, and as Hamlet said in the play as his last words at Elsinore: "The rest is silence." There were no more words to be said, and in a way I was empty.

IV

In the summer of 1968, the student revolt spread throughout Europe, even to Copenhagen, and it was the main topic of conversation. The Soviet Union invaded Prague in August because the Czechoslovaks had started a reform programme to try to establish what the newspapers called "socialism with a human face", instead of the old Stalinist model. Many students demonstrated against the Soviet Union, and also against the Vietnam War, but I could find no real reason to take part in the socialist movement, as I did not believe that anything could be accomplished. Would the Soviet Union listen to us? It turned out that they didn't, so not much changed. The Czechoslovak leaders were silenced, and the world went on as before.

At the same time, the Flower-Power movement reached us from the US, and it seemed to be welcomed by many young people, in and outside university. It brought so many new ideas, new music, long hair, smoking hash and an alternative vision of the world, where suddenly a new religion and a general anti-authoritarian attitude developed. It was a new age for all of us. Many young people – hippies, as older people called them – started living in communes. Living together and sharing everything was the mantra of the day. The maxim "Make love not war" became very popular; it was almost the description of the "New-Age programme".

I told John about the Gospel of Thomas – although he had not studied theology at university, he was very good at imagining possibilities and asking useful questions.

"But," he said, "if there is a teaching of Christ which has been hidden, then one could as well imagine that the same teaching has been kept alive within esoteric circles through the centuries."

I agreed.

"And maybe this gospel *is* the teaching of Christ: maybe not the only one, but it does not matter if it is not; perhaps there have been different versions, which we know nothing about, but still the one we know about proves that there was an esoteric, secret teaching. And the fact that it was secret explains why we, or almost no one, have any knowledge of it, apart from ..."

I interrupted him. "Wait a minute! You know when we found the letters amongst your father's books?"

"Yes, and what ..."

"When I took the letter to the prophet, the one we took out of the box, remember?"

"Yes, and ..."

"He told me about a group and a teacher called JC ... This means ..." I paused, holding him in suspense.

"It means," I repeated, "that your father was a member of that group and not of a Freemason order or some such. He was a member of the group that Carl talked about."

"Of course, now it is obvious."

"... and the prophet said that it was secret, in the sense that they did not speak openly about it, since people would not understand."

John's face lit up, like someone having a brilliant idea.

"I think ... that ... maybe ... although we cannot be sure, but whether or not ..." He said this slowly, as if he was putting together all evidence while he was speaking, wondering about the fact that his father could have been an esoteric Christian. He found this strange, slightly amusing and bordering on the unbelievable. Then he said, "We must further examine his papers now, so that we can find out for ourselves what kind of group my father belonged to, and if it is the same group that the prophet is a member of."

There was no doubt about what we needed to do, so we decided to look through his father's letters on a day when his mother was teaching, and nobody else would be at home, to give us time to go through everything properly. We almost felt as if we had found the "jar" in the desert.

V

We managed to find a suitable day. It was a Wednesday at the beginning of September. John's mother and his younger sisters would not be home until about 4 p.m. John had inherited his father's old car, and fetched me from the station. It was raining heavily and we arrived around 1.30 p.m., parked on the driveway, ran up to the house, and then we suddenly stopped outside in the pouring rain. The front door was open. It looked as if someone had tampered with the lock. There were clear signs of forced entry on the frame and the door.

John was about to shout out, but restrained himself and put his hands up in front of his mouth. Then in a whisper he said, "What is going on here?"

We carefully pushed the door fully open and went inside. Water was dripping onto the floor from our wet clothes, and we clearly saw footprints all the way to the kitchen.

"There is someone in here," I whispered. "Should we call the police?"

"We can't – the telephone is in my father's study."

From the kitchen, a door led into the dining room. It was wide open. We tiptoed through the kitchen and listened at the dining room door, but could hear nothing. Then we opened the door and went in. The wet footprints were not so obvious now, but we could still see them on the floor leading to the study. We heard a noise, like books falling to the floor. Then silence. John and I looked at each other and, I think, we were both considering whether to find weapons with which to defend ourselves. We looked around, but could find nothing suitable, then John disappeared into the kitchen with cat-like agility and, seconds later, reappeared with an empty wine bottle in his hand.

Once more we listened, and just as we were going to open the door to the study, we heard a window pane being smashed. The sound came from the room behind the study. Now we rushed in and saw books from the shelves lying spread out over the floor. I ran to the next room, where the curtain was fluttering in the breeze coming through the open window, and I saw someone running across the lawn, heading for the gate and disappearing behind the hedge.

John came into the room.

"He has gone," I said.

"Did you see him?"

"Yes. I saw him. It was a man."

It became clear that the intruder had had to break the glass of the locked window, as he could not find the key, in order to get away.

"He must have heard us," John said.

Then, remembering about the papers we were going to examine, we hurried back to the study and found the little recess open and empty.

We called the police. By the time they arrived, three hours later, John's mother was home, and had gone through the rooms and drawers to check if anything was missing. As she had known nothing about the secret letters, she told the police that nothing was missing. The police left, shaking their heads, but probably relieved that they would only have to write a short report – name, address, burglary, nothing missing. Case closed.

John drove me back to the station. "What are we going to do now?" he asked.

"I don't know. I suppose we will never see the papers again." Then I started thinking, attempting to make sense of what had happened.

"What puzzles me," I said, "is who could have known about the letters, and why was it so important to come and steal them? I just don't get it."

"Well," John said, "I'm sure it must have been one of my father's acquaintances, someone who knew about his affiliation to the group – maybe even someone who was or is a member."

I sighed. "If only I knew how to get in touch with Carl, I think we could resolve and settle the whole business, but I can't."

John parked outside the station. We went into a pub on the corner and ordered two beers. It was almost seven o'clock and getting dark outside, but the bar was always gloomy even in summer, because the curtains were always half drawn, as if the owner wanted to protect his customers from the light. We sat by the window and talked. I took up the subject of the Gospel of Thomas again: how it differed from the other gospels, not being set in a place or a time, and not related to the events in the life of Jesus.

"In fact there is nothing about the crucifixion or the resurrection, but only quotations from Jesus."

"But still, although we have discussed this back and forth, I do feel it is strange that no one knew anything until about 20 years ago?"

"Yes it is. I agree. On the other hand, the church did a clean sweep when they burnt all books they deemed to be heretical."

I then said to him: "An interesting thing about the gospel is that it resembles the non-dualistic teaching in the Hindu teaching of Advaita Vedanta or even some forms of Buddhism. Do you know that Thomas is said to have travelled to India, where he founded his church, and maybe founded an esoteric group?"

"Really? I didn't know that. So let's go to India," he laughed.

Then I remembered something that the prophet had once said to me: "maybe you will travel around the whole world, the East, India and maybe even further, but one day, I promise you, you will be ready."

"I think I will go to India!" I exclaimed. "I really think I will go."

I pronounced this as if it had been a long and difficult decision – something I had pondered for a considerable period of time – but in fact it was a complete impulse. John looked at me in surprise, and simply stated:

"You are a dreamer."

VI

I took the train to Copenhagen, alighted at the central station and started walking towards my room, thinking about India and esoteric groups. The prophet was gone; the papers in John's father's study were gone. I had lost every possible connection to JC's group. I was in an unusual mood, and my mind was flooded with thoughts about life: not only my own; not only my problems with my family, Nadia, students at the university; but life in general, God, the world, humanity, and the many questions the answers to which I did not have. I felt that I was getting closer to making up my mind – not as to whether the truth about Jesus was to be found in books, or whether I would one day conquer what I sometimes called superstitions, but about clearing myself of the conditioning and thousands of impressions that had made up my life to this date.

Hesitantly, I started to pray. I did not know to whom I prayed; maybe I was simply talking to myself. "Where are you, God?" I asked. No answer. I fell asleep.

In my dream, I met an old man by a river somewhere. I said to him, "I am looking for God, but cannot find him."

"Where have you been looking?" he asked.

"Almost everywhere."

He shook his head.

"God is not 'in' the universe. You cannot find God anywhere; he is not under your bed or in your cupboard, or in the church, not even in a remote galaxy."

I looked at him in surprise. Then he pointed at my chest with a long, bony finger; it felt unpleasant when he pressed against my sternum.

"God is inside you," he said.

During the following few days, a decision formed inside me. I would travel to India, find a teacher and withdraw from the worries of the world; go into seclusion, or to an ashram. First of all, I would finish my university studies as quickly as possible: I was no longer concerned about marks, but simply wanted to get to the end. Then I would go on my quest and, with the help of a teacher, I would find this God inside of me.

Chapter Seven:

NADIA

1972

I

On a cold, cloudy day in October, four years later, I was standing, looking out of the window of my flat. I had moved in recently due to certain circumstances. I saw a couple walking on the opposite side of the street, hand in hand, which made me angry.

At that moment, I remembered what the prophet had said, and not only the part about travelling to India: "Maybe you will find yourself in total despair and just want to leave this world, but don't. Stay and have patience."

Indeed, he was a prophet. Things had turned out in an unexpected and disastrous way; nothing had gone as I had hoped. Let me go back and explain.

My decision to travel to India was not realized. I had promised myself that I would finish my university studies, but resistance to my studies grew, month by month. I started studying the Coptic language, in order to obtain first-hand information about the Gospel of Thomas. The Danish translation was probably quite good, but there were so many phrases that did not make sense to me. I came to think that it was written in a kind of code-language, where the words meant something that the translation could not convey.

The Coptic language was very different from European languages and I spent a whole year familiarising myself with the grammar and the vocabulary. Because of this, I neglected my university studies: the history of the church and many other subjects. I remember one particular exam for which I had to read several thousand pages. It was a major effort trying to remember all the names and theologies: some of them differed in minute detail, but they also constantly challenged each other's teachings. Sometimes I was not even clear what they were arguing about.

As I saw it, the first 500 years of church history was one long battle over nonsense, spent discussing whether Christ was human or divine, and if so, to what degree he was human and how many ounces of divinity there was in him, torturing and killing each other over these points. The church became the church of the state during the fourth century, because the emperor wanted a strong central power to help him hold the empire together: a force with which to unite his scattered provinces, as well as enabling him to thwart all the people trying to usurp his power. It was also to give the emperor strength and authority against the invading peoples from northern Europe. It made for depressing reading; the church of Christ engaging in murders and disputes.

And then I blew the exam. I was asked about a period of which I knew hardly anything. I had wasted a whole term, and could not re-sit the exam until the end of the following term. But there was more to come.

When I arrived back at my room on this unfortunate day, Nadia was sitting outside, waiting for me. She had been crying. We walked inside, and then she told me: "I am pregnant."

It was like having a bucket of cold water thrown in one's face.

Then came all the questions, the feelings of blame, the regret, the sadness, the anger, the self-pity, but nothing would change the fact that "reality" had entered my life and a scenario had arisen that I had to accept and do something about.

I said, "We will have to get married then."

Both sets of parents were in favour of this solution, so without any discussion, Nadia and I agreed to the marriage.

The following week I did not go to university but to my parents' house, where I stayed for a few days. As you can imagine, the atmosphere was not good and I tried to keep out of the "interrogations" as much as possible. One day, I drove to Gilleleje to try to find the house that Maria had mentioned in connection with the group – probably the prophet would be there; maybe even Maria.

If I could find them, it would change the whole perspective. However, no one had heard of a person called Carl Hansen.

Life went on, but it was a long winter. We spent Christmas with Nadia's family. Nobody was really happy, but we sang the usual hymns and exchanged gifts with each other, and that was all.

We managed to find a small flat halfway to Copenhagen, which would make it easier for me to continue at university, at least for the time being. What would happen next I could not predict in any way, except that one day I might have to get a job and then my studies would "suffer".

The wedding was held in January, before people could see that Nadia was pregnant; but they all knew. I had the feeling that I was not the most popular person on the planet.

II

In June our little boy was born, and his arrival brought a lot of joy despite all the difficulties surrounding us. He was baptized Julius.

Needless to say, there was not much progress with my studies or with Nadia's. I should have had my degree by now, but I had resolved to share the "burden" of being a parent, and helped as much as I could. I took care of our dear little boy many days and nights and my love for him grew deeper – so he was not really such a burden. Nadia and I, on the other hand, were not getting on too well. It was difficult finding a balance between studying, free time and all the other responsibilities. It seemed at times that we would not be able to go on for very much longer.

Nadia and I lived in the flat for the first two years. I had a part-time job at the main post office in the city, but it was difficult financially. So when one of the postmen told me about a commune he and some friends were building up, and asked if Nadia and I would like to move in, this seemed a way out of our financial problems.

I spent several days persuading Nadia to come with me, mentioning all the advantages of low living costs and, at the same time, having people around us. Finding a babysitter would be the easiest thing in the world. In the end she gave way, reluctantly.

We found, as time went by, that there were many advantages to collective living. You were never lonely and you always had someone to talk to. The disadvantage was the perpetual challenge of trying to be open and to be ready to leave the comfort zone you had reserved for yourself. In every situation, you had to be ready to cope with others, and the only escape, naturally, was to your own room.

Nadia wanted us to keep the flat as a safety net, in case it did not work out in the commune. Luckily my brother Jim was ready to take it, and he moved in with his girlfriend and thus solved that particular problem.

I decided to do something about my studies. I still had unfinished business with church history, but studying in the commune turned out to be nearly impossible, with so many visitors around and the frequent parties, even during the week. Nadia and I agreed that she should stay in the commune and I went to my parents' house in order to concentrate on my studies. This arrangement started at the beginning of May; the exam was to take place in the first week of June.

When I returned to the commune after the exam in June, I was fetched from the station. Nadia was standing in the doorway of the house with Julius, and he smiled happily when he saw me, as if he was saying, "Welcome home daddy!" I kissed both of them and held him in my arms.

Nadia looked different, and intuitively I knew something had happened. We went into our room in the house and sat down, and I waited: I didn't know for what.

"I passed my exam," I said.

"OK," she just nodded.

She did not seem enthusiastic or congratulate me. A threatening silence filled the room.

"What is the matter?" I asked. "You look worried."

"I am," she replied. "I am."

"Why?"

"I have fallen in love with another man."

Time stood still. A long time passed before I said: "What?"

"I have fallen in love with another man," she repeated.

"So?"

"I do not know."

She looked down, sad, bewildered, confused. She said, "Well. It is difficult. I am so much in love with him, but I am also afraid to leave you. You know yourself that we have never got on very well, but now we have a little boy. It's all so complicated."

She had tears in her eyes. Inside me thoughts started spinning around, telling me that this was real. Once again, life had caught up with me and my plans. I was on the verge of being discarded, thrown out. I was, at this moment, like a piece of refuse. My pride was hurt, and I reacted with a load of self-pity.

"Come on now," I said, "We could try again. I should not have left you for so long. Let us try again. Please."

I noticed a slight shaking of her head. It probably meant: No.

After a month, it became clear that Nadia wanted to live with this new man. She went to see him at his house a number of times, which made me feel even more worthless and miserable.

We started divorce proceedings and since we both agreed to the divorce, it did not take very long. When we left the commune to go our separate ways, I talked to Jim about the flat, and having always been lucky in my relationship with him, he told me he was getting married and that they were going to buy a house, so I was able to move back into the old flat.

The divorce was finalized. In court, it was decided that Nadia would have custody of our son, as was usual, and I would be allowed to see him twice a month, or as often as we could agree.

But, such was the state of affairs, we could not agree on much. As she was regarded as 'the guilty one', leaving her marriage because of another man, I was not obliged to pay alimony. As time went by, I lost all contact with Julius, which I regretted for a long time.

III

As I said: On this cold and cloudy day in October, looking out of the window, I saw a couple walking on the opposite side of the street, hand in hand. It made me angry.

I was surprised that I had reacted so strongly. Inside me was a huge bottomless hole filled with anger, envy and a previously unknown feeling of hopelessness. I forgot about the meaning of my life; it was as if it had disappeared and was never to be found again. I worked at many different jobs to earn money, and left as soon as I was told to come in on time in the mornings. I became upset over nothing and there were days when I felt dead, in a dreamy state, hardly recognizing the reality around me.

The prophet had been right in his predictions. Life had presented me with difficulties hitherto unknown to me.

I decided to give up the flat. I could hardly afford it.

At the end of November I left and found a new place to live, in one of the many communes around at that time. I did not know any of the people there, but I moved in anyway. My drinking and misuse of hash became worse, and even though I tried one last time to concentrate on my studies, it was impossible. In December I gave in. The way I lived my life at that time was driving me into depression, and that winter was like living in hell.

The commune I lived in was situated in the Copenhagen area. I started going out with my fellow members on nightly sprees, and then early in the morning we would go to a bar where they served breakfast, and then go home and sleep.

It was during this period that I met Kumar. He was a gift from above, but I did not recognize this at first. I think it was in the early months of spring 1973 in Charlie Brown's discotheque. Kumar was sitting alone at a table with a drink in front of him. I guessed that he came from India.

I walked over to him and introduced myself. It was a completely impulsive action, as if it was something I had to do, like playing my part in a play. We greeted each other and talked a while. I found out that he was from India and was surprised that he spoke Danish so well. The mere sound of the word "India" recalled my forgotten dreams of travelling the east. After some time I said, "I have had the idea many times of travelling around India and possibly finding a religious teacher. What do you think about that?"

He smiled. "Well, there are many of them. But don't be disappointed if no one turns up for you. Indian gurus are not like those from the west, and their lifestyle is very ascetic and different from the priests here; they might not suit you."

I had read about this, and I sometimes wondered what my limits were. How much austerity could I endure? Judging by the past seven or eight months, I was not hopeful, but I knew that some teachings focused on the mind, not the body. That was my chance, I thought.

"I think I will try anyway," I said in a not-too-convincing voice.

I looked into his eyes. They were sad, no doubt about it; Kumar was not happy. Like most people from India, his eyes were dark and deep. When I had first thought of him as Indian, it was because of his dark brown complexion; his hair was black and his whole being radiated physical but not mental health.

"How come you are here in Denmark?" I asked.

He sat quietly for a little while, as if he was deciding whether to tell his life story to a total stranger, but maybe, due to my openness, he felt able to tell me about himself. I suppose he needed to.

He said that once when he visited his father, who worked in a factory in New Delhi, he had met a girl in the coffee shop in the centre; she was English and he fell in love with her immediately. He stayed for a few days in Delhi, and they met each day. She probably found it exotic and exciting to be attractive to a young Indian boy. One day, she invited him to her hotel room and they had sex. For him that was the final proof; she would be his wife. Indian couples do not engage in sexual relations until their wedding day, and now it had happened, so although he was already promised in marriage to a girl from his village, he had found love on his own.

She needed to go back to England and he followed her. He fled from India and all the expectations that rested on his shoulders, but when he arrived in England, he found out that she was already married. Obviously she did not have the same social mores as he did, so for her there was no problem. Unfortunately, for Kumar it was a disaster. The only solution seemed to be to swallow his pride and go back home, but he found this idea unbearable. So he applied for a work permit, which was granted, but he couldn't find a job. Then, by chance, he met someone who offered him work in Denmark. He went to Copenhagen – helped financially by some Indian people in London – and now he was working in an Indian restaurant, as he was very good at cooking.

"What a story," I said. "It must have been very difficult for you. Don't you ever think about going back home?"

"Sometimes, but I am ashamed of myself."

"You don't have to be. I imagine life here in Europe is different to the life you know, but you couldn't have known that she was married. Things like that happen all the time here."

Then I reminded myself that here I was, talking to him about not taking things too seriously, when I had already gone through so much shame and upset. My God! It was like advising on something you read in a book but had never put into practice yourself; a case of the blind leading the blind.

I ordered a beer for him and we sat silently, while the music from the DJ became louder and louder.

"Let's go outside," I suggested. We went out and together walked up over the bridge past the parliament buildings and into the pedestrianized area. Life felt so uncomplicated walking beside him.

"Do you want to visit my family when you go to India?" he suddenly asked.

"Why, yes, of course. I would like to. Where do they live?" He gave me the address, and that's how I had a family to visit in India in a place called Bilga, which is situated in the northern state of Punjab.

We walked up to the city square and he invited me back to his place, so I went and we talked all night.

IV

I did not see Kumar again for a long time. My situation was still desperate and I seemed to forget all about India. Black clouds kept rising up on my horizon, and daily life was dull and uninteresting. I didn't visit John, Jim, my sisters or my parents, and I even isolated myself from the people in the commune. I started taking stronger drugs than hash. I felt an urge to fill the hole inside me with something other than nothingness.

First I tried amphetamines, but they did not have the effect that I expected, since I became more restless and could stay awake for 48 hours at a time. Then I tried LSD, but that was a difficult drug that almost frightened me. It did not enable me to sleep or soothe the pain; instead I became very awake and alert, and transported into a state of unbearable awareness of life, enabling me to see my twofold personality – the one who had ambition and wanted to strive to succeed, and the one who wanted to run away when things became difficult. I was looking down into an abyss of nothingness and filled with confusion. Then I tried heroin. That gave blissful relief, but I had taken a very dangerous road. I did not work much, only when I needed money, and I even stole things from shops because I had no money, but had no pangs of conscience.

Then the heaviest depression I had ever had took hold of me. I wanted to die, which would be the ultimate escape. I forgot about Kumar and India.

"Why should I go there? I would not find a teacher anyway." I was incredibly tired of myself and of life, drank a lot, smoked hashish and tried to find ways to get more heroin.

In early spring, when nature put on its most beautiful dress, I was so hopelessly down that I knew I needed help; otherwise I would die of an overdose sooner or later.

"Problem solved," I said to myself haughtily, and a slight shudder went down my spine; I knew many people around me had already done it.

Peter stopped talking for a little while. He seemed to be reflecting on something, but then he went on.

I'll tell you about taking drugs. A drug like heroin is like seeing a woman from afar, a beautiful woman that you want to meet, so you take one more dose and get closer to her. It is a state of bliss, pure heavenly bliss. You get closer and closer, but after the tenth or eleventh time, you suddenly realize that she is moving away from you. Then you take more drugs and still you believe you will meet her, and in the end when you do, you see to your surprise that she is not beautiful; she is ugly. She is even laughing at you. You have been lured into believing in her existence, you think it is because you have had too little and that you must have more, but you never find those feelings that you had in the beginning.

It just gets worse; it is like a shadow of what was once within reach, but is now almost impossible to achieve. Now a dose is just a few moments of release before you slip back into depression, but you are still ready to sell your soul to the devil for just another shot. The body becomes addicted and does not function without the drug. You need more and more each time, and heaven is replaced by hell. There is absolutely nothing else to live for, other than to continue with the drugs until the end of the world, or the end of your life.

It was on one of those days, when I really did not care about anything in the world other than trying to think of where to meet a pusher and get another dose, that something happened; maybe it was an answer to one of my weak and uncertain prayers. I had a little money, but not enough for a dose, as the price of heroin was high. I was alone with my ghosts and had no plan for the day, apart for finding a moment's release from pain.

I remember passing the Botanical Garden. The spring flowers outside seemed to smile at me, and to remind me that life still had possibilities, so I went inside the tropical glasshouse, where it was warm and humid and the virgin forest grew up to the glass roof. I looked up and saw a glimpse of the sun in the sky.

There was a movement and I felt a presence beside me. I sat down on a bench, and maybe I dozed for a moment or two, but suddenly I saw my angel standing in front of me – my childhood angel. She was wearing black and looked seriously concerned.

"Have you forgotten?" she asked. "Have you forgotten your seed and your task? What are you doing here? What about your quest? Why don't you stop now and go on your journey? They are waiting for you. Come with me now." She stretched out her arms to me and smiled a smile full of love.

I woke up, and as I came out of that dream world, I realized who I was.

"Yes," I said. "Yes."

I repeated my "Yes" many times, and then I walked to the nearest hospital and asked for help.

PART TWO:

THE FLOWER

Chapter Eight:
INDIA

1973

I

By August, I was free of drugs and even though a tiny thought or wish often crept into my mind, I had no difficulty in resisting them. I had reached an irrevocable turning point, which one could call "repentance". This was not the old way of repentance in which I was brought up, but rather a nurturing of an understanding inside, which told me that from now on I had to think in a new way. I had been through so much, I had found God, in my own way and by studying the eastern religions, and it was now clear to me that this was where my search would continue.

I could not understand why Maria and the prophet had disappeared and were no longer in my life, but I felt that, having gone through hell, I was ready now to meet the teacher. However, I had to wait because, as I had been told, only those who are ready will be called, and since there was no way in which I could accelerate the process, I had to move forward in a way that felt right to me.

I felt sure that my decision to travel to India was the right one, since all signs in heaven and on earth pointed in that direction. I wanted to follow what was called the happy-hippie trail, meaning the route from Istanbul overland to New Delhi. The only question remaining was when I should go, or rather when I could go. Everyone who had undertaken this journey, especially my friend Kumar, advised me to travel from Istanbul in September and arrive in India in October, when the temperature would be more agreeable for me, as I was not used to the semi-tropical heat. It was already August, so I could not make the journey that September; the required vaccinations would take almost two months, and besides there was the crucial problem of money. I needed a job and at least 6000 Danish kroner, which unfortunately would take me months to save.

Help now came from an unexpected source. Someone I knew from the first commune invited me to live in his flat. His name was James and he was from York, England. I did not know him well, but I had only positive memories of him. He was not given to self-importance, so when he spoke, he always had something profound to say.

I had met James many times at parties – he liked parties, enjoyed them in his own way; sometimes he just sat and observed people – but I had never really talked with him in the deepest sense. I knew he was a good guy, reliable and straightforward. He did not do excess – no hard drugs; he smoked the occasional joint, like most people at the time.

He was a world champion hitch-hiker. We once went from Copenhagen to a place way out in the countryside, and as soon as he stretched out his arm, cars would stop, as if compelled to do so.

James had a two-bedroom flat, owned by the joinery where he worked; he offered me one room and so I had a place to stay without having to put up with the bad company of my so-called hippie friends.

He said that the only conditions were that firstly, I paid half the rent and secondly, we never spoke about people who were not present. This last point turned out to be a very useful exercise. He also had another principle, namely that if one did not have anything to say, it was a bad habit to talk just because one was afraid of, or embarrassed by, silence. During the year we lived together, I came to appreciate him as a person, far more than many of the other acquaintances I had. I enjoyed living with him.

The money problem was also solved when I was offered work in the joinery. I accepted gratefully and worked there all through autumn, winter and the following spring. Now life became quiet and peaceful and for the first time ever, I adapted to an ordinary working life. We started at seven and worked until four in the afternoon. Free time was spent reading or listening to music.

There was no television in the flat and no newspapers, so it was a little like living on a desert island, or in a monastery, with only the tasks of daily living to take care of, such as cooking, cleaning, shopping and going to work.

I started to read about travelling in India, had the required vaccinations, and gave away any belongings that I could not sell. In the end, all that was left was a box with some books, which I stored in my brother's place.

I was quite proud of myself. Was I now a disciple? Sell all you have, give it to the poor, and come and follow me – but of course, it was not the same way as the apostles; I did not give away my money to the poor as I badly needed it for my journey. Anyway, I had a longing to go more deeply into the realm of discipleship. My knowledge of spirituality was mainly gleaned from what I had read in books, and I did not really understand what was required.

When I told my friend John about my plans for India, he was entirely happy. I had the feeling that he also wanted to go, but he said that he was not ready for such an adventure at the moment; perhaps that explained the slight envy that I undoubtedly detected under the surface.

"Why don't we try to find the teacher your prophet spoke about?" he asked.

"I don't know where he is," I said.

"But do they not advertise to attract new members?" John asked.

I told him that Carl had said that whoever was meant to come would find the teacher, and I was sure I had repeated this several times, to him and to many others.

Eventually he accepted what I said and encouraged me to go on with my project, but asked me to write to him whenever possible. I told him that I had prepared a farewell party: Kumar would make the food and I wanted to invite everybody, meaning the closest "family".

"Then you can have the party here at our place," John said, and so it was decided.

I managed to get enough money together, partly from my job in the joinery and partly with a loan from my parents. I assured them that this was a journey where I would search for communion with God. They liked that idea, but could not understand why that could not be found in their church or Christian fellowship, and my father was worried about my leaving university.

I bought a rucksack and a sleeping bag, and made a little purse for my American traveller's cheques, to be carried under my shirt, to thwart the thieves. I was ready to set off.

On my last night in Denmark, Kumar came to John's place where we had the farewell party. He served fantastically good food, but I noticed that he was still not happy. I tried talking to him that evening, asking a lot of questions about his family and Bilga, and he seemed to cheer up a bit when the good memories flooded back into him. Maybe he was longing to go back and settle down. I thanked him for the great food and for giving me an introduction to an Indian family. I told him that I was full of excitement about leaving Denmark and going to India to look for a teacher, and then he was able to share my joy.

II

I will not recount my journey in great detail. I'll concentrate on what is essential for my story and leave out all the funny, strange, sometimes interesting things that happened along the way.

I flew to Istanbul, and there I met three other young people. We agreed to travel together, and cross the border into India as soon as possible. Iran was definitely not a place in which to linger and Afghanistan, although very interesting and very ancient, was not on our list of places to visit. We decided to rush through Afghanistan and Pakistan.

There were no difficulties on our arrival at the Indian border. Everything went smoothly; we were not questioned or delayed by some self-important border policeman, so we just walked over and a car took us the last bit of the journey through no man's land into India. Soon we arrived in Amritsar, our first destination on Indian soil.

We felt a tremendous sense of relief, and thanked our lucky stars that we had finally arrived. The atmosphere was totally different from the other countries we had travelled through: it was like coming home. People were friendly and welcoming, and we heard the greeting *Namaste* over and over again. It was like the gentle andante movement of a symphony.

We felt at home in India.

The journey down to New Delhi on the train was fantastic. We passed through the fertile region of the Punjab, all of us having a window seat, so we sat with our noses pressed to the window, enjoying the scenery. We saw fields with wheat and crops of different kinds, small houses here and there, people working in fields, and the wonderful green colour of sugarcane.

I breathed deeply and peacefully, free of worry or fear; I breathed new air into my lungs, exchanging the old blood and its old memories for new, invigorating impressions.

I was happy.

It was almost exactly one month since we had left Istanbul and during this time, it had become clear to me that the happy-hippie trail – Istanbul, Iran, Afghanistan, Pakistan and India – was at variance with my purpose. It dawned on me that the hippies were out there to have fun, to meet high gurus, as one American had said, smoke hash and meet interesting people. Some would go down to Goa, which surely was the heaven of hippies, and on the way most certainly stop in Agra to see the Taj Mahal. Others would go to Nepal for trekking, or maybe to the holy city of Benares to sit at the river Ganges and watch the funeral pyres and so on.

I realized that they were not here for the same purpose as I was, so if I joined them, I would have to leave my own dreams behind. My conclusion was that I had to go on alone.

III

My first decision was to travel to Rishikesh. According to what I had read, this place was one of the most holy in northern India, full of holy men and women of many denominations.

What met me when I arrived was a surprise: there were hundreds of beggars, more than I had seen on the whole journey so far, more than I ever could have imagined. They were standing in a long line, so I understood immediately that giving something to each one of them would have made me penniless. I had to harden myself against the many empty pairs of eyes that followed me as I walked along the line, trying to feel love for them and bless them silently in my heart, with whatever I had to give from there.

Despite the many beggars, Rishikesh was a fantastic place. There were countless holy men and women and plenty of ashrams all around the area. I saw men walking around stark naked, having painted their bodies white, after they had left everything, including their clothes, in order to serve God. I was puzzled. I was at a complete loss trying to imagine the kind of life they lived. There were also the native people, who worked, washed their clothes in the river and looked quite normal, seemingly undisturbed by the eccentricity of their surroundings.

I picked an ashram out of the many that were available, and asked to stay for the night. This was granted. There was a peaceful atmosphere inside, a solid silence, where not a single sound was heard. For the evening meal, all the monks suddenly appeared, filling the room with their presence, and we ate dinner together. The food was the most simple you could imagine; I think it was a stew of pumpkin or something similar. The monks happily slurped it without speaking, and to me the whole set-up seemed rather primitive. I hardly ate anything, as I was secretly looking around as much as possible, hoping not to attract too much attention. Of course, simple living was not a prerequisite of spirituality, but I had thought that the monks, who dedicated their lives to God, would be more sophisticated in some way.

After the meal, I succeeded in meeting the Guru of the ashram. He was a young man, maybe not much older than me. He had a somewhat sad appearance, as if he was suffering great pain, maybe due to hard physical exercise.

I told him about my search, about my life in Scandinavia, about my troubles in finding a way of communicating with God – not that I did not believe in God, but the hope that God would add a new dimension to my life and give it a direction. I asked him about the ashram, and at what I thought was the right moment, I asked, "Can I stay here some time and learn from you?"

He answered without thinking: "NO. This is not a place for you. Continue your search and find something more suitable."

He was very sure and definite about that, so there was no point in trying again. I asked him whether he could help me, by directing me to some other place, in order to find what I was seeking. He just shrugged his shoulders. He said "maybe" and then nothing else, which was a very strange and unsatisfactory answer. However, I accepted his "no" and the next morning I walked away, to look for somewhere else.

Then I found the Parmath Niketan Ashram – that is what I think it was called – but it looked rather exclusive; it was huge, with a monumental entrance beautifully adorned with carved pillars. It was not the sort of place where I had imagined I would find a teacher. The atmosphere again was very silent and peaceful and in contrast to the first one, it was extremely clean and fresh. People of all ages stayed there, mainly Europeans and Americans, and definitely not monks; but there was no teacher, as far as I was told: only instructors. It was a bit like a retreat centre. I slept very well the nights I stayed there, enjoying my rest, but it was too expensive for my purse, so I found another, much cheaper lodging. It was not an ashram, and although the whole surroundings in Rishikesh breathed spirituality, I still did not feel that I was in the right place.

I spent much time walking, which had become a new habit. I did it mainly because I wanted to overcome my periodic restlessness and after walking for some hours I felt calm and tired, but also happy.

The nature in Rishikesh was very beautiful. The river Ganga came down from the western part of the Himalayas and carried on into the Yamuna River, and finally into the holy river Ganges, running east to Varanasi – or Benares, as it is also called. Up in the hills, it was a delight to just sit and watch life down in the valley; I saw the local women doing the washing on the river bank, using no washing powder but simply wetting the clothes and beating them on the stones which, thanks to the law of gravity, got the dirt out of them. I tried this method later and it worked very well, but the clothes wore out quickly. It was a hard way of treating them.

One day when I was sitting up on one of the banks of the River Ganga, I saw a holy man going into the river. He was brown, suntanned, had long black hair tied in a knot at the back and wore a linen cloth around his waist. It did not look as if he was having his daily swim or simply cleaning his body, but more as if he was performing a ritual. I admired the way he moved his young and healthy body, and the serenity around him. After the ritual, he got up from the water and sat down in lotus position on the beach. I was tempted to walk down and meet him. But should I go down to him? Did he speak English? Would he tell me about his way, because there was no doubt that he was a person dedicated to seeking God?

I argued with myself about what to do. Something said: "Go". And another voice said: "No". Was I afraid to go down there? No doubt there was fear in me. I remember from my childhood that, at times, I was afraid to approach people, because I did not know whether I would be welcomed or rebuffed. The voices in my head started making excuses for my hesitation in going down to him, by saying that this man was not a teacher, so to go down there would be a nuisance. Nevertheless, I suddenly found some courage and walked down towards him. He was absorbed in his meditation, so I sat down a little away from him and waited.

He meditated for a very long time. I almost fell asleep while trying to join his meditation. When he finally opened his eyes he looked straight at me, with a friendly smile on his face.

In broken English he said, "What I do for you?"

I tried to explain why I was in India and I talked slowly so that he would understand me. He listened attentively and then he told me that he had been with a teacher, but was now on his own, following an inner teacher. There was something about him that made me feel calm and happy. A light was shining from him; his eyes were radiant and his look penetrating.

"Would you teach me or tell me where to go to have some guidance?" I asked.

He made it clear that he would not be of any real help, since he earned his living from begging, did not have a permanent abode; some days he did not even eat. To be responsible for me, as my teacher, would not be possible. He said this in a compassionate tone of voice, almost apologizing for not being more helpful.

I persisted: "Where can I find the ashram or the teacher you spoke of?"

He threw his arms out in a gesture of resignation. "I very, very sorry, my teacher far away on other side Varanasi, in the mountains. Sorry, sorry."

I sighed, and understood that there was nothing he could do; even so, he most certainly was a very helpful and considerate person. After a little while he gathered his few belongings and walked away.

There was a bridge over the river Ganga. It was not for traffic, cars or scooters, but you could walk over to the other side. The bridge hung between two huge pillars, one on each side, and it was only a couple of metres wide. The planks on the gangway were fastened with wire on both sides and the whole construction stretched out over the river, swaying a little as one walked over. Many people passed back and forth and when I looked down from the bridge, I became slightly nervous.

The scenery from the bridge was magnificent. The slopes of the mountains were covered with vegetation, including shrubs and trees that I had never seen before, and many small houses or cottages were scattered here and there, like gems in a piece of jewellery. Further up, there were no trees, just bare mountain, which in winter would be covered in snow. At the other side of the bridge, I walked along the river passing houses, ashrams and statues. I remember one particular place where there was a statue of Buddha. He was sitting on a lion skin – the head coming out under his feet – in a position facing the river, and he looked as if he had conquered worldly existence, calm and eternal. I sat down opposite him and sort of talked to him. He was at least three times my size, made of stone, as was the lion under him, but it gave the impression that it was going to roar at any moment.

"My dear Buddha," I said, "I don't understand anything right now. I don't understand why you are here. This is a Hindu place. You must excuse me. I know you started your search here in India, but these many ashrams are neither for you nor for me. On the other hand, you are all so tolerant in this part of the world, so I suppose that they are for everyone who wants to meditate or find peace. As far as I can see, this is not a place for me to seek God. You know, all these hippies, they go trekking; they go to famous places where they meet other hippies, smoke hash and feel groovy, then some pseudo-teacher will appear and they will all think that they have met the real thing in holy India. But I do not believe that to be true. Am I being too harsh on them? Sorry for judging them. In the end, I might not be any better. I just happen to have so many high ideals."

I paused a while, trying to concentrate, but I could not be silent inside. I continued: "We all opposed authority, you know. We all left our parents and universities, and turned our back on the church, which had forgotten to renew its message, and was still using language that was two thousand years old, and we found no alternatives. The hippie movement is great, but it is based on opposition to wars, to politics, against the bourgeoisie, against organized religion and in the end, is full of empty values. *Make love, not war* is in itself good, but just an empty phrase. We have found no solid ground, nor a rock to stand on, like the lion you are sitting on. And that, my dear Buddha, is exactly what I want to do. Do you hear me, Buddha? Where shall I go? Where can I find truth?"

I paused for a moment. Then I said: "I feel that the history of the economic boom that developed after the Second World War in Western Europe and America made all of us young people feel that everything was suddenly possible, without us having to make any effort. I want to have to make an effort and so move forwards. Rishikesh is wonderful, but I feel strongly that I do not belong here in this exotic environment. I'm not at home."

Then my mind cleared and, as if I suddenly knew where I was heading, I said: "I think I know what I want. I want to meet someone who knows me, who calls me by my name, and loves me; someone who can teach me to love him back. Is that too much to ask for? Whether it is or not, it is exactly what I am longing for. I can at last formulate what it is I want. I want to be welcomed, recognized and loved for what I am. I know that an incredible creative power exists, the source of all there is, but I cannot find communion with this power unless I have someone who can lead me there. That would be the teacher I long for. I have to go on and search, but thank you for listening."

And then I left the Buddha.

As I was leaving the place, I made up my mind that I would try to find the Kumar family in Bilga. It felt as if the Buddha and his lion had granted me answers to my questions.

Chapter Nine:

KRISHNA

November 1973

I

When I reached Jullundur, I knew I was not too far away from Kumar's village, Bilga; I found a bus and, when I arrived, alighted at the station, a little way outside the village. I started walking towards the centre and, after a while, came to an area where there were more houses and narrow streets, with open gutters on both sides. I had seen similar drainage systems elsewhere; I was told later that they were cleaned out daily.

I did not have an address, only Kumar's family name – Ram Praesher – but by a miracle, I happened to find the place. A man who spoke a few words of English showed me the house. From the street, it was like a typical Indian shop. An old man was sitting there, but I do not think he saw me, or at least he pretended not to, so I walked round the back and in the yard there was a small area surrounded by white walls. I looked over the wall and understood that this was the toilet area, which was "furnished" with a hole in the ground and a bucket of water. A woman in her fifties looked up at me in surprise; she also looked slightly fearful, but as soon as I said the name "Kumar" she lit up.

She shouted for Shakti, who turned out to be Kumar's younger brother, and who fortunately spoke English quite well. I told him who I was and how I had come, whereupon he said to me that Mr Kumar had sent a letter to them, explaining about my possible visit. (They always referred to him as Mr Kumar, perhaps because he was the oldest son and would someday be the head of the family.) Then a beautiful young woman came out from the kitchen and greeted me in the Indian fashion; she was Kumar's sister. They all seemed happy to see me, and I was shown to the living room of the house. The house was small, with only a few rooms, of which Shakti had his own, whereas his mother and sister slept behind the kitchen. There was no furniture and the fireplace or stove was an earthen construction on the floor, so Kumar's sister and mother would squat while they cooked. In the kitchen there was a picture of Shiva, and each morning the mother of the house would pray using a mantra, *Om Nama Shivaya*, repeating the same words over and over.

In the alley where the house was situated, the family's little shop was in the front room, which was what I had first spotted, and it was here that the grandfather lived. The shop had some kind of sliding doors at the front, which were closed in the evenings and at night. I had no contact with the grandfather for the two months I stayed with the family. He sold pictures of the gods, cigarettes, candle lights, nuts and grain. I can't imagine that it was a profitable business, because there were quite a few similar shops down the alley.

Kumar's mother and sister were interested to hear about Mr Kumar. His sister spoke a little English, his mother none, so Shakti translated what I told them about Mr Kumar – that he was my friend and was doing well. I knew that it was not true, but it was exactly what they wanted to hear. I asked about their father and they told me, in a somewhat sad tone of voice, that he worked in a factory in New Delhi to make money for the family. He did not come home while I was there, but later I paid him a visit in the factory in Delhi. He was only allowed to talk to me for about five minutes. It was like a prison and he looked like a prisoner, with a sad, hopeless expression, without a glimmer of happiness or passion, which had been vanquished long ago. I felt very sad and depressed by the sight of him, but I politely answered all the questions he asked about his family, and then a well-dressed person showed up and asked him to go back to work.

From the first day, Shakti and I occupied the living room. We ate there together, while the women had their meals in the kitchen on the floor; the grandfather ate in the shop. Shakti was a great guy. He introduced me to people in the village, and after a few days we had invitations to visit all the important people of Hindu society, for instance the music master, who was some kind of official representative in all legal matters.

II

One day Shakti brought me to the priest of the village. It was in the evening, just before sunset, and the whole western horizon was glowing red. The priest was standing outside with an enormous seashell and when he blew in it, a strong vibrating sound was produced, which sounded like a call or a cry to the universe; although it was done at sunset, it was a wake-up call. He also made it in the morning, but it did not signify his magical power of making the sun rise or set; rather it was a ritual call, reminding the inhabitants that there was an ever-present God watching over them.

We waited while he performed his 'call', and when he had finished he asked us to come inside.

He lived in a little hut made of wood and straw, with only one room, and slept at the back. There was a fire in the middle and a bamboo curtain covered the entrance.

Of course he knew Shakti, who often visited him, and he bade us come in and sit down with him around the fire. The priest sat with his back to his sleeping area, and we sat opposite him. He looked young, but judging from the grey beard he was definitely older. Shakti said

he was seventy, but anyway, he was strong, muscular and fit, and had a very powerful and positive appearance. His hair was black, which puzzled me a bit, but Shakti told me that he coloured it with a plant dye. There were many stories about him in the village and people said

he was like a fakir, and could stand on one leg for a whole month. He had been known to fast for several months, and was revered by the Hindu people in the village.

When we sat down, he did not say anything. Shakti introduced me and the priest said *Namaste* politely. Then we sat in silence again, feeling not the least uncomfortable, because the priest was able to make the atmosphere uncomplicated.

His monkey suddenly came running from the corner of the hut. It jumped up into his lap and squeaked many "words" that were not understood by Shakti or me. The priest caressed it and then it jumped to one side and lay down.

"How do you like India?" he finally asked.

I knew that I was supposed to say that I liked it very much, which I did. Then he smiled and said that it was good to talk to a person who was speaking the truth, although I had hardly said anything.

I told him my name, in case he had not understood Shakti's introduction, and I asked him what his name was.

"My name is Krishna, the Shiva priest," he said. "That's what I am."

He spoke good English, although he pronounced the words "Shiva priest" with a strong Punjabi accent, perhaps intentionally. After that, the conversation once again came to a dead end. No one said anything, but this did not bother the priest as he tended the fire in front of him with slow, concentrated movements.

I had to say something, and the only thing I could think of was telling him why I had come to India.

"I am looking for a teacher in India," I said.

He looked up and nodded in affirmation.

"But I have not found one yet," I continued.

"Do you think you will find someone?" he asked.

"I don't know."

He made no comment, but scratched his beard and yawned, which in my opinion was very impolite, but in a way it was an answer. He did not want anything from me, and he let me be myself, not engaging in a conversation for which I was not really ready. I regretted having been so direct – telling him about my search as the very first thing – but I had a feeling that I was welcome, in spite of the lack of conversation. It was like living with James. We did not speak to pass the time or to cover up the fact that it could be uncomfortable to just sit around without talking. Our priest seemingly did not need to defend himself, and I had the same feeling, so we just "were".

About an hour later we left his humble abode. He got up and followed me outside, saying, "Come any time you like. You are most welcome."

Then we walked home.

III

A few days later I went back to visit Krishna. Shakti was doing something else, so I went alone. It was in the middle of the day, but he was at home: I wondered whether he ever left his hut except to blow in the shell. He sat on the floor and asked me to come in; this time he started speaking immediately.

"Have you found your way around the village now?" he asked.

"Yes, I have."

I decided to be a little more personal, because I was curious and I wanted to know about him.

"How come you speak such good English?" I asked.

"Because I studied in England."

"Which subject?"

"Archaeology."

"That's interesting. I know a person back in Denmark who used to be an archaeologist. He used to take part in excavations in Israel, but that's a long time ago. He is not that young anymore."

Suddenly I was a little ashamed, talking to him in such a familiar way, as if we were old friends. I was just about to apologize for my rudeness by explaining what I actually meant by "not so young anymore" when I noticed a new expression on his face – something like surprise or curiosity.

"What's his name?" he asked.

"His name is Carl Hansen," I said, at the same time not understanding why he wanted to know. What difference did it make? But my priest started nodding his head repeatedly, laughing and clapping his hands on his thighs.

"This is marvellous," he said. "You have come all the way from Denmark and you know an old friend of mine, Carl. Amazing!"

"Did he send you here?" he went on.

I was of course as surprised as Krishna to learn that Carl, the prophet, was a friend of my Shiva priest. Carl had, in passing, told me about a friend in India whom he had met in Israel, but he had not said much more. What a coincidence!

"No. He did not send me. I remember Carl telling me about a friend from India, that's all."

Krishna did not comment on the extremely unlikely coincidence that had just been revealed. Instead he went on as if nothing had happened: "How is Carl doing these days? Is he well?"

"I don't know how he is; I have not seen him for quite a while. He is with a teacher of his and I have not the slightest idea where, but it's in Denmark, I suppose."

"I have heard about the teacher. I met him once, very briefly, in Denmark when I visited Carl, but that was many years ago."

At this point, I was trying to give some structure to my thoughts. Was my Shiva priest in contact with the teacher in Denmark? In that case ...

"Do you know where he lives?" I asked carefully.

"Do you mean the teacher?"

"Yes".

"No," he said, "I don't. But recently Carl sent me a letter telling me that he was going to sell his house in Denmark and work with his teacher. That's all I know at the moment. I am sure Carl will contact me again someday."

At that moment, I had a strange feeling that everything in my life was pre-arranged. Krishna had asked me if Carl had sent me, and as far as I knew he hadn't. But there was a connection between them, so why would I end up in the same little village in India where a friend of Carl's was the priest? It was incredible. And where did Kumar fit into the picture? Did Carl know him, and in that case, how could he have arranged a meeting between us in Charlie Brown's Discotheque? Carl did not know that I would frequent that place in Copenhagen, long after he himself had left his house. It was too good to be true, but despite my many doubts the fact remained that I was here with an old friend of Carl's.

"Would you please tell me some more about your friendship with Carl?"

"We met in Israel. At the time I was known by the name Chris, not Krishna. My colleagues were all from the west, though some of them were local; for the people in the team it was possibly too much for them to work with a Krishna, since it might have given them some strange associations. On the other hand, Chris is the same as Christ, and there was a person in our team from Spain whose name was Jesus. So there you are – why not Krishna?"

Before he could go on, I interrupted:

"But why did you come back here, having been educated in England and worked as part of an international archaeology group in Palestine. Why? And another thing, how were you able to keep in contact with Carl?"

"One thing at a time," he laughed. "Patience, please. To the question why I went back to India, I can only say: Because I had to. I love these people, and I am a Hindu. You see I was sent to England to study, as many young Indians were, especially from the upper classes. My parents were very rich and they could afford it. It was in the twenties, India was English but later on Gandhi came and changed everything. I met him once, at the end of the thirties, before the war and he really did inspire me, especially because he was making India into a country for Indians. I then decided to stay here and be a priest."

I could not restrain myself anymore. I burst out: "But then you have renounced all the wealth of your family, you have given up all the glory of the world and you are just serving a little community in an unimportant little village in Punjab and you are, as far as I see, happy with your life. Excuse me for putting it like that, but ..."

He laughed at my surprise. Then he said, "Why do you want fame and glory? Is there anything more valuable than God? I have God. So what more do I need?"

I was speechless. I waited for inspiration to strike, but maybe there was nothing to say.

Then the curtain – the door – in the hut opened. Five or six women came in. They were carrying vegetables and other food, and prostrated themselves on the floor in front of Krishna. He took their gifts and blessed them in the name of Shiva. They talked a little with him in Punjabi, and finally they left.

Afterwards Krishna looked at me and smiled a very confirming smile.

"You see?" he said. "What else do you want? I love these people. I pray for them, I bless them and I try to be an example to them. For them I am a representative of God and that's the way it is in your country as well, although I understand from Carl, when he visited me some years ago, that people there do not believe as much in God anymore. Well, that was possibly more than twenty years ago. Time passes quickly, you know, so things can have changed."

I wanted to assure Krishna that nothing had changed, but he got up from his place and asked, "Do you want some tea?"

"Yes. I would like some."

He put an iron tripod over the remaining embers and kindled a new fire, then hung a kettle under the tripod. When the tea was ready, it was served in large cups without handles.

After a while, I continued our conversation.

"Why do you blow the shell each morning and evening?"

"Because it is a ritual."

"But the sun does not rise or set because you do that."

"No. It does not. It is a symbol, like all symbols, in every religion. There might be people who take these symbols literally, but symbols are only symbols. You people in Europe think we are stupid, you think that all people in the third world are ignorant and imbecilic, but I can assure you, we are not. You also have symbols in your religion and their function is to unite people, to bring them together and to share."

He continued: "You eat the body and blood of your Christ. Is that sensible? How can you do that in an age of enlightenment, of science? Are you cannibals?"

Now he laughed very heartily, but he did not offend me. He was just stating a fact.

"So," he said, "we are all the same, but we have different ways of expressing God and worship."

"I am sorry," I said. "I know you are right."

He offered me some more tea. Later, we walked outside. His monkey was hopping around in the bushes, and he talked to it like you talk to a child. Then it came to him and jumped up into his arms.

When I was about to go, he said, "Come back soon."

"I certainly will," was my reply.

At this point, I said to Peter that I found it incredible that he should go to India and meet a person that was connected with his life in Denmark – and furthermore that he had gone not because Carl had sent him but because he had met a young man who happened to be in a discotheque one evening.

Peter said that things like that happened to him all the time. He told me about an incident down in Southern India.

On my travels I met a young man who wanted to accompany me on to the South. He had ideas about what to see and where to go. He borrowed money from me. He said that he was expecting a large sum of money, and each time we came to a major town, he went to the bank to check if it had come.

He always asked me to wait outside, and after some time he would come out and say that it had not arrived. He repeated this exercise many times, going into branches of a particular bank, and each time he then asked to borrow more money from me.

We shared a room in Pondicherry, and one morning he was gone. Then I realized that I had been duped.

Later, when I was back in Delhi, I ran into him in the middle of a crowded street. I was dumbfounded and I challenged him, but of course he could not repay me.

The incredible thing was that in a country with 600 million people – a vast country the size of Western Europe, and one thousand kilometres from the place where we had parted – we should meet again after several weeks. Was this just a coincidence?

I think that people in our lives – not all, but some – are connected to us in an amazing way, which it is impossible to explain.

Chapter Ten:

IN THE HUT

I

I spent the next few days with Shakti. There were so many places to see: the village was spread out over a wide area, with many fields. Bilga was a farming community with a few small industrial plants.

One day he took me to a sugarcane factory: it was really a small family business, and the old man had his sons and their sons working there. It was situated far out in the middle of the fields. Four oxen were walking in a circle, attached to a pole in the middle which was rotating the press. It was a very clever arrangement. When the oxen, on a platform above the construction, rotated the pole, the sugarcane was crushed and the juice dripped into a big cauldron underneath. The collected juice was heated to produce the final product of brown sugar lumps, which could then be crushed into granulated sugar, but often as not the lumps were sold just as they were.

I noticed that the desserts after the main meals were often dishes made with sugar, milk and rice. They were very tasty and sweet, and Shakhti's mother was an expert at making them.

We stayed the whole afternoon with the sugar people, and then we walked home over the fields along tiny paths which Shakti knew as well as the insides of his pockets.

II

When I visited Krishna again, I said, "I want to ask you some questions. It is important to me to ask them."

"You are welcome".

I started to ask what was on my mind: "Do you know about the group that Carl is involved with?"

"Not really. I told you, but let me explain further. When Carl and I parted in Israel, before the war, I gave him my family's address in India and he gave me an address for his parents, which was how it was possible for me to visit him a couple of years after the war. I only stayed a few weeks, and then I travelled on to see other parts of Europe. That was most interesting and I learned a lot. As for the group, I only know that at that time when I was there, a house was purchased somewhere on the north coast; Carl only told me that there was a man he was going to work with on spirituality. I met this person only once and I do not even remember his name. Later on, Carl visited me here in Bilga, and he said that there was a group developing over there. That's all I know. We spent the time together here in my place, meditating and talking."

"Thank you, I just wanted to know," I said. Then I changed the subject totally.

"Can I ask you what you think about your religion? I ask because I have had strong doubts about the Christianity I was brought up in. You said you were a Hindu. I read a lot about Hinduism before I came, and it seems that you have many gods, but also that there are people on an intellectual level who do not worship a multitude of Gods. Is that right?"

I think he was a little annoyed. Maybe that was just my interpretation of his silence, but then he willingly started to tell me about Hinduism.

"Long, long ago the Vedic religion was inspired by people who were close to the spiritual mind. I choose to put it like that, but as happens in all religions, it became formalized and the rituals became the core of worship. Whenever an enlightened being initiates a teaching of truth, it will, in time, degenerate: the dogmas, the organization and the rituals become its very centre and then, in a way, the original idea is forgotten. That has happened in Hinduism, Buddhism, Judaism, Islam and Christianity, and in any religion you can think of.

But underneath the official worship, there is always an undercurrent that keeps the original message alive. This is termed esoteric, which means inner, and the formalistic expression of the worship would then be called exoteric. I think this is exactly what you have realized, and you are at this point now."

I had realized that, or believed that something like that had happened.

"About your question of the many gods, I should like to say that from the beginning they were not different entities in the sky or in the heavens that should be prayed to or worshipped. The many gods are expressions of the different parts of our very complicated psychology. We all have many different personalities within us, each of them looking at the world from its own perspective and governing us in the belief that this or that personality knows the truth. The idea of many gods is that they are the 'idols' inside us. We have a Shiva, a Vishnu and a Brahman at the highest level and this is almost like your trinity, whereas the many others correspond to human traits. There is a Parvati, a Ganesha and so on, almost like the Roman Catholic Church has saints. If you see them as gods, you lose the whole idea. The Indian and later the Greek and the Roman mythologies took over these gods and goddesses, not understanding that they were a key to the different aspects of personality and that through the mythologies one could begin to understand what kind of people we are. They also exposed the mechanisms that are at work in our lives in space and time. When Uranus is eating his children, it means that time is swallowing up our lives and making them meaningless.

"That the original idea always becomes distorted is due to the law of gravity, or habit, or inertia or lack of a deep desire for truth. The esoteric side keeps holding on to the first truth, but even these groups or schools have to reformulate the truth over and over again, because times change."

He looked at me to see if I understood. I nodded and he continued.

"These esoteric groups often live within the established religions. There might be a priest in your church who does that, but it is as a cover from suspicion and 'witch-hunting,' if you understand my metaphor. At other times they have to work underground, like in the Soviet Union, or in the Middle Ages in

Europe. Otherwise everything would have been destroyed and vanished from civilization. That, by the way, is why these groups hide from the searching of journalists and other news media: ordinary life does not understand the purpose, the message of these esoteric school teachings, which would be destroyed if it was treated as general news. Either the next day the idea would be forgotten, or the groups would be hunted down and treated as potential criminals, as happened in the case of Jesus and many others."

He stopped and looked at me. His words were comprehensible. Esoteric teachings would not be some ephemeral piece of information that I could soon discard, and what he said was exactly what I had thought many times in my talks with John – even the prophet had said something similar.

Krishna added: "Do not judge anything. Just look, and observe and find the place within where you are receptive to the golden truth of life."

Then I came to think of my search, the reason for being in India and my longing to find the truth. I couldn't help asking: "Krishna, could I stay here with you and become your pupil?"

He looked down, as if pondering the question. He was motionless for a time; then he looked up and said:

"Yes, you could. But there is something you should know. I spend most of my time here and I only go out when a person is dying and wants me to come and help him or her to the other side, as one says. I spend hours in the company of my monkey; I chop firewood, clean my home and make food. And as you've seen, I do not even go shopping – everything is brought to me. So in order to live here with me, you must learn to be calm and rest entirely in your own being. That will need some training and discipline. At the same time, you will be much 'alone' in my company, because I do not talk all the time, not even inside my head. I am at peace; I am together with God. You will not have many theories or theologies from me, but I can show you the way to God. Whether you reach your aim or not is entirely up to you, or rather to the grace of God, but you have to make 'room' in order for it to come in. But please, come and stay if you wish."

Without any further ado, I accepted his offer and acquired a mattress from Shakti, as Krishna had only his own sleeping mattress. Shakti thought I was out of my mind.

"You do not know what you are doing! He is a very holy man; he was once standing on one leg for a whole month. Could you do that?"

"I don't know, but I could practise," was my ironic answer, but I was shocked that Shakti believed such things, so without arguing with him I went and stayed with Krishna.

"Is it true that you were standing on one leg for a month?" I asked him on one of the first days.

He laughed heartily. "There is one thing you need to know about Indian people, and that is that they always use large, round numbers. When they tell you about the Indian civilization, they say it started 50,000 years ago, and anyone who is a little educated knows that it is impossible; so when they say thirty days they may mean anything from three to ten. You see, people here are sometimes unaware of their own age, as no one wrote down the date and time of their birth, so no one has a birth certificate and the authorities may not know of their existence. If you need a passport to travel, you go to a person in authority, for example a music master, and he makes one up for you. The date of birth must be believable, and this has nothing to do with lying; it is simply a matter of convenience, since it is easier to remember the figure 1000 than 783."

Then, still very amused, he added: "Anyway, what does it matter if I stood on one leg? Does it bother you?"

It did not.

From then on, I stayed in Krishna's hut, my mattress being placed along one side of the room. After the evening ritual, we meditated for an hour – he gave me instructions on how to do this – and in the morning we meditated again after the ritual. At first his little monkey was more interested in me than I appreciated, but after two days he had already become accustomed to my presence and did not bother me.

Very soon I saw the truth in Krishna's warning. It was difficult to sit there day in and day out doing absolutely nothing, and I became seriously anxious and stressed. Krishna asked me to go out and chop some firewood.

"That will be useful for two reasons: firstly because it is needed for the chilly evenings and for cooking, and secondly it will do you some good."

After a week, I started questioning my ability to be rooted in myself, as Krishna put it. I helped him with the cooking and the cleaning and all the while he just sat there observing me, shaking his head at my impatience. Then he asked me to sit down and listen to him:

"I am resting 'in' the Self, and the Self cannot be described in words because it is far beyond any explanation; it cannot be observed but 'is,' one could say, experienced when you are 'in' the Self , but at the same time, you are the Self and everyone is the Self. All other things you can observe, both inside and outside your person – every little thought, emotion, sensation or sentiment – these all come and go. All these you can be aware of and observe, but that which can be observed cannot be you, therefore the thoughts, emotions, and so on are not you, but they become you when you identify yourself with them. When that happens, you are no longer at peace and strictly speaking, you no longer exist. It seems a very strange thing to say and I could talk to you about it for hours, but it will not have any meaning for you until you start to have a feeling for the Self; so for now, you have to accept my explanation, in order to understand why you cannot sit in peace all day long. You are constantly moving along the line of time and space and there, peace or freedom cannot be found."

"But how do I get there, to the Self?" I asked.

"You must start by observing which 'I' in you is the active one and let it go. It does not mean that you cannot perform the daily tasks, but you are, in a way, looking at them while they do what they do, and you enjoy the game of living, have your favourite meal, drink your beer and whatever you fancy, but it is like a play and ephemeral; it never lasts but will, from moment to moment, be exchanged with something else. This is my religion, but there are no dogmas and beliefs; just a few rituals, which I carry out mainly for the sake of the people I love, and everything I do is done without attachment. I rest 'in' my Self."

I came to understand that I had to undergo long training in order to be like Krishna, although he said that the Self is here, right now; so in theory, I could be it. Apparently there were many things that I had to give up, but not in the way I had thought – it was not just giving away my earthly possessions; I had to give my inner possessions away as well. Consequently, Krishna advised me to continue my search and to try to understand what was preventing me from approaching the Self. In a serious voice, he asked me to cease being his pupil.

"But these days with me have not been wasted," he said. "Don't forget what you have learned because you have realized something very important that will be helpful in the future."

I brought the mattress back, and Shakti was relieved.

III

I still visited Krishna in the hut or temple, as he sometimes called it, and we often just sat there united in a beautiful state of contemplation. His company became very precious and valuable to me and he created an atmosphere in which I felt calm, giving me a more confident attitude to my life and all that might come.

One evening after the ritual, he took down from a high shelf on the wall – placed out of reach of the nosy little monkey – a bowl with incense. It was probably made of gold, ornamented in an old-fashioned style and very beautiful. He lit the incense, placed it in front of him and asked me to close my eyes and just open my senses. The fragrance transported me to a place far down in my mind, to some distant heavenly place, and I felt as if I was levitating. It seemed that my body ceased to exist and a profound peace enveloped me. He had to wake me at some point, and smiled while saying:

"Now you have activated the realm of your soul, which is on the way to the Self, and you know for sure that it exists."

I protested that he could have done that earlier, while we were together, but he answered that it is not possible to get into such a state permanently with the incense. It is just a help, a tool; in the end you have to find it through your own efforts, by clearing out the rubbish inside you and waiting for the grace of God.

Krishna was a wonderful person, a wonderful teacher and a man of God. I loved him deeply.

On the last day of my stay, we walked around, I said goodbye to everyone and, of course, I had to see Krishna one last time.

Shakti had told me that Krishna could tell the future from reading your palm, so when we went to his house to say farewell to him, I asked whether he would tell my future. He agreed and I sat down beside him. He took my right hand and looked intensely at it for a minute, then he wanted to see the other hand and did the same thing and after a little while he said, "You will never be happy unless you seek God and try to do his will."

At first I was a little disappointed, but afterwards, in my heart, I thanked him for his words. What else could I wish for?

Before we left, Krishna blessed me. Once more I thanked him profusely, with tears in my eyes, but he only smiled and, in the end, he hugged me. He held me firmly to his chest and a wave of warmth permeated my whole body. Then he said to me: "Since you are here in India, and if you still have money, take the chance to travel around. Go down the west coast and up the east, up to Varanasi. Then you can go on to Delhi and decide where your journey should take you."

I followed this wise advice.

In the morning, I bade farewell to Shakhti's mother and sister. They actually cried, and I felt that this display of emotion was sincere. I tried to catch a glimpse of the grandfather, but he hid behind the sliding doors in the shop. On the way down to the bus, I saw Krishna's house in the distance. And I knew that I was parting only from his physical presence, not from his love.

Chapter Eleven:

JUDE

1975

I

In the summer of 1975 I moved to York.

I had followed Krishna's plan and travelled all the way down south, staying a short time in Bombay, spent Christmas in Bangalore and arrived in Pondicherry, where I stayed for more than a month. My journey continued up the east coast to Varanasi and from there back to New Delhi, once more over land to Istanbul and back to Copenhagen.

During my trip something matured inside me, a certainty that told me that I wanted to go home to Denmark – having no other place to go.

I was convinced that I had not wasted my time going to India. My meeting with Krishna had shown me that I was on the right track. To go all the way to India and meet a man who was connected to the prophet was a sign that I was still connected to him and consequently also to his teacher. My travels had not been a deviation from my search to find the truth, and had confirmed to me that going to India was a part of my preparation. Where my travels would lead me from now on, I did not know; how my future would unfold was something I had to quietly leave in God's hands.

But one thing was sure: I did not want to stay in Copenhagen. While I had been away, John had found a job in an office; his wife worked at the hospital and so they were well off economically. They had no children yet and were not intending to have any. I think John had hoped that I would come home with a guru or teacher, but now he wanted to see if there was the possibility of joining some spiritual group or other.

Then there was Jim and my family, whom I loved, but having no wish to have their kind of life I had to find a life of my own, not associating with the same people as before. I visited my parents and told them I had found God, which made them very happy; I gave no further details. I told them that I had no definite plans for the future, but was confident that something would turn up.

However, there was no future for me in Denmark. I wanted to leave.

I talked with James and told him of my dilemma. He suggested that I move to York, at least for some time. He could introduce me some friends of his, and for a kick-off I could stay with them.

And thus I travelled to Yorkshire in August 1975.

II

York was a beautiful city, with white walls all around and a cathedral so huge and magnificent that it filled me with wonder. I spent a lot of time there.

I found myself a job in a hospital as a porter, and more or less my only duty was to wait until the "beeper" sounded and I was called. There were three other porters and we sat in the porter's lodge making small talk all day long. I withdrew from the gossiping and started to bring a book with me, and as time went by, I brought more and more books. This way, I became almost invisible and they accepted me sitting there reading all day long, only interrupted by the beeper. I was given the nickname of "the Dane with the books". I do not know how many books I went through, but I often went to the library on my way home.

I started to meditate regularly each morning, as long as I did not oversleep, using the method Krishna had taught me. It gave me some peace and mental muscles, and I was grounded in the firm conviction that from now on I would not deviate for any whim, but continue day by day, trusting in God's guidance.

I met some people at the hospital who, in turn, had other friends, and I was becoming a "member" of a loosely constructed group who met at the pub, or in their homes, playing cards or discussing world issues.

Although daily life was dull and boring at times, I tried to make the best of it, playing my classical music on a brand new stereo system, reading my books and looking forward to Friday evenings, which became the highlight of the week, although they ended sadly and abruptly at 11 p.m. when last orders were taken.

The first year passed without leaving a deep imprint on my soul, apart from the meditation which gave me a kind of stability.

III

In the spring of 1976, something happened.

It was a Friday. I had a day off and in the early morning I walked to the city centre, enjoying the fabulous weather and looking forward to whatever the day had in store for me. In the evening, I was going to meet the usual crowd, as I had started to call them. I entered the park near the library and sat down on my favourite bench, which happened to be vacant. I was watching the peacocks strutting around in all their glory, trying to impress the peahens. These birds were so funny: someone had told me that they even destroyed beautiful flowers, to eliminate all competition. I was in an unusually pleasant frame of mind, feeling free and in good spirits.

I went to the pub around seven o'clock. Within some fifteen minutes, we were all there chattering as usual. I spotted a man at the bar who looked familiar. I had seen him before. When it was my turn to go and order he was still there. I stood right next to him. He looked at me, and I saw the greenish eyes and knew who he was. I said in Danish: "How are you?"

He was surprised, and did not remember me. I had seen him when I was sixteen or so and I had, of course, changed. He, on the other hand, was just as I remembered him. It was Hans, or Jude, the prophet's son.

I told him who I was and that I'd seen him at the prophet's house many years ago.

"Aha!" he exclaimed. "You were the one flirting with Maria, while she taught you to play the guitar."

He gave me a smile indicating that he was teasing me.

"That's right," I said. I tried not to overreact to his remark about flirting, and honestly, I was not aware that I had flirted with her, since I did not know at the time what the word "flirting" meant.

"Can I buy you a drink?" he continued.

"Thank you, but I am with some friends and I am just going to order ..."

"That's all right," he said. "No problem. By the way, how is Maria these days?"

There was something about his attitude and his whole demeanour that gave me the feeling that he was not being entirely honest. It was possible that he was joking, but I thought that he was trying to make me feel inferior to him. Surely he knew that Maria was with the teacher – or at least if he was still with the group he would know – and therefore I could not have seen or met her for ages.

I pulled myself together, and said straightforwardly, "I would like to meet you, if possible, since both of us ..."

I stuttered. I was not sure how to say what I wanted to say, but I knew that I wanted to meet him. I felt that Hans was a mystery: what little I had heard about him was surrounded by vague suspicion, uncertainty and doubt. But why should he be willing to meet me? He'd only met me once, and probably did not know more about me than my name, if that.

"Can we meet soon?" I asked.

"Oh, yes, of course. Let me invite you to dinner. Do you know the restaurant at the north entrance of the city, just outside the walls? It is a nice place, so let's meet there. Shall we say Tuesday, at 7.30 p.m.?"

I was surprised: he had been so quick to invite me that I became suspicious, and uncertain as to whether it had been a good idea to ask to meet.

"By the way," he said, "what was your name again?"

I knew it. He did not remember my name.

"My name is Peter."

"Right, Peter, we will meet on Tuesday."

He went over to a table where some other people were sitting, and did not even say goodbye or turn around.

I went back to my friends with the drinks.

IV

Jude was already in the restaurant when I arrived. He had chosen a table in a corner near the window. I went over to him and he got up.

"There you are! Nice of you to come. Have a seat."

I sat down. He looked at me intensely for a second, and then he said, "Are you hungry?"

"A little, I think."

He beckoned the waiter to bring the menus. Then he continued: "I do not know why you wanted to meet me, because I hardly know you and you cannot know me very well. Was there anything you'd like to ask me?"

Then I had an almost telepathic insight: he had agreed to talk to me because he wanted to know where he had me, so to speak. Maybe he was curious about my relationship with Maria. He did not wait for me to answer his question, but called the waiter back to the table.

"I forgot to order drinks for me and my friend here," he said in an exaggeratedly apologetic tone of voice, and turning to me: "What would you like?"

"I'll have a beer, please," I replied.

"Good. Two beers please, Carlsberg if possible."

I could tell he was enjoying showing off; I really did not like his arrogance.

"I suppose you like the good old Danish beer," he added, "coming from Denmark."

Although there was no reason for him to be out of breath, as he had been sitting with me all the time, he made a noise as if he was catching his breath, sighing deeply, inhaling and exhaling in order to relax himself. Then he seemed to become very calm and relaxed; he took the napkin from his plate, unfolded it carefully and placed it in his lap. Afterwards he examined the fork and knife, and even the spoon, and as if they were exceedingly important, and lifted the side plate and looked underneath it, presumably to see if it was a costly piece of porcelain. He did not look at me once during the whole of this operation. Then his eyes wandered around the room, as if searching for something. His attention seemed to be constantly drawn to some couple or other, who were either arriving or leaving the restaurant. One minute he looked anxious, the next he became absentminded; but I could not make out what was going on inside his head. I wanted a chance to catch him off guard. I wanted to know something about him, so that he was less elusive. I interrupted his train of thought by saying:

"Tell me a little about yourself. I hardly know you."

He looked startled for a moment, but quickly regained his composure and began to answer my question.

"I suppose you know that I am an accountant. I have a degree in economics, qualifying in 1959. After my degree, I found a job in Denmark with a multinational firm and learnt a lot; in 1963 I was offered a job here in England, which is why I moved from Denmark. I am in charge of the finance department in this company here, a member of the board and an adviser to the chairman. I know a lot about the stock market, and my task is to invest our assets in such a way that we can grow economically." He looked at me with a questioning expression.

"I do not think you understand finance. But money grows all the time when it is well invested. I tell you that I am very clever." He looked extremely confident.

"I have a sixth sense about where to invest, which is why I get huge bonuses, and which has allowed me to purchase a large estate, where I live alone."

"So that's what you're doing," I said, somewhat impressed. I then remembered something that would enable me to prick his sense of self-importance. I thought about the letter that John and I had found at George's house while sorting through his belongings: "I want to warn you about Hans" and so on.

I bluntly asked: "Do you know George, the schoolteacher?"

That shocked him. I had knocked him out of his financial sanctuary and his complacency.

"Isn't he dead?" he replied.

"Yes, he is." I hesitated a little about how to proceed, but then said, "I suppose you know JC as well, and the group he is working with."

His mouth dropped open and with a furtive look, round the restaurant, he answered: "Oh yes, I know him."

"Good. Are you a member of his group?" I continued, now determined to dispel any remaining arrogance.

"Why do you ask these questions?" he countered. "It is none of your business."

"Maybe not," I said calmly, "maybe not. But it so happens that a friend of mine named John – we went to high school together – had a father, George, who probably was a member of this group, and we would very much like to know more about it."

I knew the prophet had told me that Hans was a member, and he regretted that he had introduced him to JC.

"Since you say you know him," I said, "then ..."

"Stop. OK, I am a member," he retorted angrily.

"You say you *are* a member, not that you *were* a member?"

"No, I have been a member since 1960. My father – or Carl, as he is not my real father, so let's just call him the poor old man – took me with him once. He was very stubborn and said that I was ready over and over again. I don't really know what that means, but I was accepted, and I have been a member ever since."

The waiter came to take our orders. Apart from the food, Jude ordered a whisky for himself and a glass of red wine. I also ordered wine. But I had no intention of changing the subject, and so I continued: "But after you moved to England, you couldn't have continued being a member of the group?"

"I am still a member and I've been over to Denmark a few times."

He continued: "You see, my job is not a nine to five job. I travel a lot, Hong Kong, Tokyo, Frankfurt, New York and so on. So I have time to spend a few days in Denmark when there is nothing important going on."

He was still acting a little nervously; his eyes were not calm, but flickering from side to side like a candle fluttering in the wind. He didn't look me in the eye, although I could not see what there was to frighten him in the restaurant. I had a sudden insight to his state of mind: it showed that he had something to hide. We think that we can hide what is going on inside us, but this is a great mistake. People always sense when we are agitated or nervous or trying to hide something. They may not be able to articulate clearly what they see, but the emotion is registered subconsciously at least, and will leave a feeling of uneasiness.

I disregarded his uncertainty and went on.

"So what do you think of JC?" I asked.

He lit up as if a miraculous wand had struck him.

"JC is marvellous, simply outstanding. There is nothing like him on the surface of God's earth." Then he stopped himself. "But I am not supposed to talk about this. For the time being, JC wants to be rather – let's say – anonymous."

"Why?" I asked, remembering very well what Carl had told me.

"Because people would not understand, and his time has not yet come."

"I do not think you need have any worries about telling me: my friend Carl is there and Maria as well. They trust me, and had I been around more before the house was sold, I would have been invited to the group; Carl always said that I would come someday."

"Oh no, not that again – you talk like Carl. He could be mistaken, you know; he took me there, but afterwards he started to treat me like a schoolboy, and then we quarrelled a lot when he wanted me to leave, but JC allowed me to stay. He is a wise man."

He sighed his special sigh again, but I insisted that he tell me about JC.

"I can tell you about JC. He is not like most of the miserable students – JC calls us students – who do not understand what he is doing or what the whole plan is about."

"But you do," I interrupted sarcastically.

He chose to ignore the sarcasm.

"Let me tell you something. I am an economist. I have got insight into the world economy and I know what I am talking about. In the sixties there was a boom, and all the economies in Europe prospered, one of the consequences of which was that foreign labourers came to Scandinavia, mostly from Turkey. But one day there will be a recession and then there will be unemployment, and we will have to pay for all these people, who, in the meantime, are bringing up second-generation foreigners and we do not want them. They never assimilate or adapt to the country, living together, never integrating and the women do not even speak Danish, but only their own language. They should go home, but the governments are so afraid of being accused of racism. That is one thing. Further, the whole stock exchange is rotten and it is only making a few people richer and a lot of people poorer."

He read my silent conclusion.

"Yes, I am a socialist. And I know that JC will bring about a change in the whole of Scandinavia, maybe even in Germany. He will someday make all the poor miserable sheep willing to fight for him."

"Excuse me," I said. "How do you think one person will be able to change a country?"

"You do not know JC," he said brusquely. "He is not like you and me and he has helpers. I am one of them and I shall help him as soon as I join him at his place. I have saved a lot of money from the enemy, so to speak; I have used the market to make myself rich and I will be at his disposal when the time is right."

He had worked himself up to a state of enthusiastic anger. He was burning with conviction for JC and the plan, as he called it.

"So you go to Denmark occasionally?" I said this very cautiously, so as not to feed his anger more than necessary.

"Where I go is none of your business, but I will shortly join JC."

I changed the subject. I started talking about England, comparing the way of life with what I had seen in Denmark and India.

He went along with the conversation, finishing his whiskey. After about fifteen minutes the waiter brought our food. We ate in silence to start with; then I brought up the subject of JC again.

"What is this JC like? You seem to have a rather high opinion of him, but tell me more."

He put down his knife and fork and looked me straight in the eye for the first time that evening.

"I've told you already. He is different; he doesn't belong to any category you can name, even if you have a well-developed imagination. When one is near him, one feels his energy very strongly: it is almost like being near the sun; one seems to become transparent. He sees directly through you, knows what you are thinking and, with a simple look, can tell your whole life story. He can make people think what he wants them to think, he can do anything he likes. He is skilled in practical matters, building and farming, and he has an intellectual capacity in comparison to which you are just a five-year-old boy."

He sighed again, a deep sigh all the way down to the depths of his being.

"And I am sure he sees the future and maybe even arranges it."

Now he smiled.

"I would like to meet him," I said almost casually, not to provoke any suspicion. "Do you think that would be possible?"

He looked a little hesitant and blinked his eyes a couple of times, seemingly measuring me from top to toe. Finally he said: "I don't know if I should do that, but since you know people who are there, then ... I could give you the telephone number of someone in Denmark. Then if they want to meet you and introduce you to JC, I suppose it would be all right; they can decide whether you will meet him or not."

"Really?" I exclaimed. I was no longer interested in testing him; in that moment, I thought my search was over. I would meet JC at least, and whether or not it would take me any further, only the future would show.

"But don't let them fool you," Jude warned me. "Don't be a stupid fool, like all the other meek sheep that just obey, but try to learn from JC and let him use you."

"But," I protested, "there must be someone else who understands him too. You couldn't be the only one, could you?"

"No, of course there are others, but the majority are old hippies, and they know nothing of importance. Trust me."

I thought to myself that I should fit well into that category, but all the same, I did not really care and I definitely did not trust his judgement. The prophet was a member and he was a very intelligent and wise man, nothing like a stupid sheep, and John's father had probably not been stupid either.

I asked Jude: "When was the last time you were in Denmark?"

He did not answer me. Somehow, he had isolated himself on his side of the table, and did not utter another word, which was rather strange for an educated man. He ate his food, drank his wine – the whiskey had been consumed during the more heated points of our talk – so we both finished our meal, very quietly, and at the end he paid the bill, and gave me the telephone number of someone in Denmark.

Then we parted. He shook my hand in farewell but did not look at me.

Peter and I talked all that evening. There were so many things to ask him. For many years I had been devoted to scientific investigations into my subject, and suddenly a person had turned up who gave me totally new information about secretive esoteric groups that only accepted people when they were ready. I had never heard about such things before. It was incredible.

After he told me about Jude, I could not help saying, "But that person seems to me to be insane."

"Yes, but I saw many other sides of him in later years. In the end, I understood him fully, and knew the reasons for his despair and longing. Even his love!"

"But at that time in England when you met him, you must have been very confused, since you knew the prophet and he was dear to you, so what Jude said must have been total nonsense, or megalomania," I insisted.

"It was, and at that point I didn't have much else to judge him by, but the most important thing to me was that I finally had a way to make contact with JC's group."

Chapter Twelve:

SELF-REMEMBERING

Autumn 1976

I

I called Denmark the next day and arranged a meeting, bought a ticket for the boat from Harwich to Esbjerg and took the train across to Copenhagen.

The meeting was to take place in a coffee shop, just outside the city. The others were already there when I arrived. They welcomed me and introduced themselves. They were rather young, a man called Matthew and two women named Mona and Anna.

My first impression was that they seemed to be sincere. They had an aura of calmness around them; they did not fidget but sat quietly and relaxed, hands resting in their laps, listening and answering my questions. They did not try to convince me about anything. They gave me the impression that they would be happy with whatever outcome transpired. I understood that no matter how much I longed to meet JC, who had become something of a myth to me, it would be useless to try to force a decision. But one thing was certain: I had come to a decisive point in my search.

They told me that the core of the teaching was that "man is asleep" and that one has to realize this. Man is a "stimuli-response machine" and being a machine, we act mechanically. This was important to understand.

I asked them what they meant by that.

Matthew explained:

"Let me start by telling you about a state of mind which is not mechanical. Most people, possibly everyone, have experienced this state of mind. Imagine you are sitting looking at the sea, watching the sunset, listening to the seagulls, feeling the gentle breeze against your skin and smelling the fragrance in the air;

then suddenly you are filled with wonder. You are calm, present and everything around you is peaceful. At that moment, you are close to the divine, to real love. You are 'remembering yourself'. A similar state can happen when you are in love, when you hold a newborn child in your arms or when you rest after a long day's work, having overcome obstacles, and are now satisfied with what you have achieved. You will notice that in such states there is pure emotion involved, and this is the closest you come to what we call self-remembering, as opposed to what we call sleep."

The first thought that came to my mind was recognition. I had experienced these states a number of times in India. When I was with Krishna, at the beach in Pondicherry, looking at the children shouting for joy in the water and in Varanasi when watching the funeral pyres. I had not been able to explain why it happened, and used to call it "grace".

"I would like to know how I can experience these states more often," I said.

They answered that it was not possible to control higher states of mind; we experience the state of self-remembering very seldom, so from that point of view, most of the time one is asleep. Anna then said:

"We think that we are creating our lives but we are not. Of course we do everything necessary to function; eat breakfast, go to work, earn money, pay bills, use spare time for fun, have worries, problems, marry, have children and educate them, get old and die. Sometimes we are important people, sometimes not. We can engage in politics, become managing directors of companies, work in factories or sweep the streets. We have good days and bad days, but from one point of view it does not matter, because we are like machines and, depending on our circumstances, using the endlessly inherited patterns of behaviour. Such a life is dull, like the difference between night and day, when compared to the beautiful state of self-remembering, where impressions are vivid and we have the feeling of being truly alive. It was not the intention of our creator that we should live with the mechanical state of mind, as if living in the cellar of our houses, when in fact we have mansions at our disposal. When approaching the state of self-remembering, we realize what the meaning of life is and we enter into relationship with a higher dimension which is divine. Therefore, the aim is to remember ourselves, but as we said, we cannot do this without help. We need someone who has realized self-remembering and can teach us how to acquire it."

They made it clear to me that the teacher was such a person and that he represented an esoteric teaching, which was not new, but had been handed down through the ages. Depending on the society it served, it changed its outer appearance from time to time, but the inner aim had always remained the same: the awakening of man.

I asked whether it was the teaching of Jesus, and they said yes and furthermore, it was the core of the teaching of the gospels. They asked me if I was familiar with the bible. I affirmed that I was.

"Then try reading the gospels from that point of view and use them as a means of awakening."

I recalled the book of Isaiah, and the strange part in the gospel about being put to sleep, so I asked them why we are asleep. They said: "The whole of humanity is asleep. We cannot explain why immediately, as it needs practice of the teaching in order to understand."

Although I agreed with much of what was said due to my many struggles, I still had some doubts and badly wanted to know why humanity was asleep. Why didn't God just create us in an awakened state? And how can one say that we must try to remember ourselves and at the same time say that we cannot remember ourselves?

I was just going to mention my doubts when the person called Mona smiled and told me that it was not possible to use the ordinary intellectual or logical part of the brain when trying to understand this idea. She called it the *formatory* part of the intellect, which understands only yes and no, and has no discrimination. It is a registering apparatus, which sorts information into pigeonholes and works by association, but it cannot think. She stressed that word. It cannot *think*.

"Don't waste your energy trying to understand things theoretically. It is not useful to find an answer to 'why humanity is asleep'; the fact is that *you are asleep*. That is not theoretical, but a fact, which you will have to verify for yourself, and in order to do that, you have to use your emotions. Otherwise you will not really understand. You have to discover something that, somehow, you have known all along, but have forgotten. That is why it is called self-remembering – to re-member, to become a member again; namely to find that capacity within yourself once again, a capacity that was always there. The whole teaching is inside you. You were born with it; everyone is, but we forget and 'dis-member' ourselves. Now it is time to re-member.

"Try to make it your aim for some days to remember yourself, then you will realize that you cannot and that you need help from above to learn how to do it. Then you need to try as hard as you can, to practise it. When a child of six months tries to walk, it cannot; it needs help and practice, and then one day it takes its first steps. There is no contradiction in that."

She made a strong impression on me, of someone very rooted in herself and with an amazing presence. I think she convinced me without even trying to, and she also spoke to my inner capability which all along I have called my seed. I did not any longer have to find what the real teaching of Jesus was about. From now on his teaching and The Gospel of Thomas would not be found in my mind but in my heart. My search had come to an end.

There was going to be another meeting in a few days' time, but they told me that I could not meet the teacher, JC, as he was not in Copenhagen at the moment. I was given a book to read in order to familiarize myself with the concepts of the teaching. They accepted me as a student and I was welcomed into the group.

After the next meeting I decided to join, although I had yet not met JC.

II

I went back to England to prepare for my new life. Once again, I had to leave everything behind and move on to something new, which, at that point in time, I hardly understood. But I was supported by a number of "high" inner states. The sound receded, the light changed, and I saw a glowing radiance around people; I almost looked through the physical objects. This was self-remembering.

When I entered the pub on the next Friday evening, I told my friends that I was moving back to Copenhagen.

"Wow! But why are you going? Why have you suddenly decided to go back? You always said that there was nothing for you in Copenhagen."

I had to admit this, but I said that I had a strong feeling and longing to go back.

And as Anglo-Saxon people always react, so did they. "We will miss you so much," they said.

Finally I arrived back in Copenhagen. I went to stay with John, and told him what had happened. He was eager to hear everything.

"Do you think these people are real?"

"Of course the people are real."

"Sorry, I meant, do you feel that they are genuine?"

"I think so," I said.

"Good. Could you introduce me?"

I promised that I would, and a few weeks later, to my great surprise, John became a student too.

Chapter Thirteen:

THE TEACHER

Christmas 1976

I

We were sitting in a circle, about 20 of us. Once we had gathered, everyone introduced themselves to me and John and welcomed us. I could not remember any of their names – the only one I knew was John, who was sitting next to me, and the people from the coffee shop. For both of us everything was new, and John whispered in my ear: "Have you met him?" He meant the teacher.

"No, I haven't."

"Neither have I," he confided.

The room was full of expectation, with an intense uplifting energy. I suppose it was not just something taking place inside me. I had been looking forward to meeting the teacher so much and had spent much time in intensive preparation.

He arrived at the appointed hour for the get-together and just sat down. He looked young, maybe not much older than me, but he was in reality much older – around sixty. I was told this later.

And then I saw Maria. She followed him in and sat down beside him.

At that moment I wanted to get up and greet her, but instead waved my hand discreetly and she answered it with a smile.

The teacher started to speak.

"I see we have some new people here today." He asked us to say our names. Then he continued:

"It is important that you do not believe anything, because to believe leads nowhere, except to new beliefs which then become a substitute for the old beliefs, carrying them along, side by side with the new ones. That makes the burden you carry even heavier, and the sack on your back will force you to go walk your knees."

Everybody laughed a little at this analogy and he smiled, almost chuckling, holding his hand up in front of his mouth. He went on:

"You must verify everything you hear for yourself, for otherwise it will not be useful, neither for you nor for me. The teaching, as written in the books, is theory and it is all right to acquaint yourself with the theory, but some of it, about the universe, you will not be able to verify. So just register it, but try to verify as much as you can through observation. As your teacher, it is important to have trust in me. I will also teach each one of you individually, in which case my teaching is not just theory but direct communication with you. Follow me as far as you can in that, and whenever you ask for advice or help, you need to take my advice and put it into action."

When he said these words about teaching us individually, I believe he turned his head and looked at me, and I knew I had found my teacher.

Directly after this introduction, he went on to speak to all of us, not just to John and me. He talked about personality.

"You have by now verified that personality is a mask. We say that there are two parts of it, a false one and a true one; however, personality is personality, but there is a difference. You know very well that true personality is needed, as one must be able to organize one's life, for example one has to pay one's bills, keep appointments, shop for food, etc. All that is personality, but you must understand that this is not your real higher self. The higher emotional centre, as I call it, does not need food, or pleasant afternoons with friends with a cup of coffee or a drink. Still, the aim is not to avoid these earthly pleasures of food and drink. This teaching is not an austere way, where you have to sacrifice everything and practise abstinence from worldly things, but you must learn to discriminate and find out what is useful for you. The needs of the body are necessary and must be met, because they sustain our life here on earth, and it is true personality that takes care of your physical needs.

"The so-called false personality, on the other hand, is totally non-existent and more than anything else, it is imaginary, something invented, but believed to be true. Perhaps you know the story of 'Alice in Wonderland'. She met a knight who told her all the time that his totally absurd devices were his own inventions. That's what false personality is: A totally absurd invention that governs you all the time."

He paused in his talk, and stood up.

"If I now say that this chair is stupid, that would be false personality, because the chair is just a chair, but we all get cross with things and events for no apparent reason, and we insist that we always have good reasons for becoming upset or negative. If I cannot open a tin can, I become irritated and am ready to curse the thing, saying that the can is stupid. But in reality this is nonsense. It is the same in relation to other people. Maybe someone says: 'You are an idiot.' When we take that personally, we get very upset and produce all sorts of reasons and arguments as to why this person is wrong. But the fact is that the person calling you an idiot is as stupid as you in believing that something real has been said. It is all false personality, and since it is imagination, it does not exist for real, only in your imagination.

"Personality, then, is in part useful, especially if you want to walk home from the pub, because you must remember how to get home; but personality is also in part useless, because it allows you to carry a lot of impressions that made you react to situations – for instance, what happened at the pub that evening, when someone said you were an idiot.

"Personality dies when the body dies and does not even know that it has died or where it 'lived'. Memory is of some use, especially for the true personality, but only while you are living; afterwards it has no function. The only thing that continues to exist is the amount of, or the power of, our ability to remember our true selves. Please understand that this remembering has nothing to do with 'memory'. Self-remembering, as it has been explained to you, connects us upwards and creates a soul that is vibrant and that is eternal life. All the rest will disappear."

He paused and looked around. Nobody said a word, but they listened attentively. Then he said:

"All this is no big deal, as long as it is theory. You know about self-remembering, but it is not enough if you do not put it into practice. If you do, it will have an effect, and you will start to move on from where you are now. You will thoroughly change your perspective in relation to yourself, how you see yourself, and other people."

After some time, the teacher asked if anyone had any questions. I cannot recall much of what was asked or the answers, because I was burning inside, and my cheeks were warm, but I was delighted. Still I remember some questions about how to remember oneself and about negativity, which appeared to be a very important issue.

"I shall come back to this subject many times, because it is the largest hindrance in our daily lives to remembering ourselves. When you are negative, grumbling, complaining or criticising, you do not remember yourself."

After a couple of hours the meeting ended. Then sweets, coffee and wine were served. The teacher sat on a sofa talking to students. I quietly approached him and, to begin with, he seemed not to be aware of me, but somehow I knew that he was. Suddenly he turned and invited me to sit down next to him; it was like being in the sunshine on a summer's day, just as Jude had told me. He looked at me with a gentle smile.

"Well," he said. "So you are new?"

I agreed. Then he said something very startling:

"I think that you should finish your studies."

"What?"

How did he know that I had been studying and had left my studies? He went on:

"Maybe it is good to end the 'octaves'."

I asked him what he meant by "octaves".

"Yes," he said. "You know in the books about the teaching, there is a lot about octaves. For me, an 'octave' is the full unfolding of an activity, whether short or long; the completion of everything it includes. There can be difficulties at certain points of the octave – we call them 'intervals' – but whenever you manage to bridge the interval, you are approaching the end result. This can be very useful, and that is why I think that you would benefit from completing your studies."

"But," I insisted, "I have at least a year left, maybe more, and I want ..."

"It is all right. That is not much. Will you do it and then you can come and live with me?"

It was strange, and although everything he had said was more like a suggestion than a command, he spoke with such authority it was impossible to say 'no'. At the same time I knew I could easily have said 'no', but he suggested the idea in such a way that, for me, it became the most natural and obvious thing to do.

"Yes," I said, "I will think about it."

And he smiled again, in a way that confirmed to me that I had been accepted completely.

"Yes, I think I will do that," I repeated.

I recalled Jude once more: meek sheep, always doing what they are told. All right, I was one of them.

Then the meeting was over. He got up and left with another student. I saw Maria going with him, but she did not look in my direction and they disappeared.

I was certain that JC was different from anyone I had ever met before in my life. Of course, I was very happy to have had a conversation with him, but afterwards I could not understand how it had happened that I had agreed to finish my studies at university. Incredible!

Later that evening, people started leaving, and I felt that, even though I barely knew the names of any of them, I suddenly had a lot of new friends.

II

Peter stopped for a moment.

"I think I must give you some information as to how the school – as we called it – was organized."

"Please do," I said.

"There were groups living in Denmark, Norway, Germany and Sweden. The students were living in communes, sharing everything and taking turns regarding cleaning, shopping and cooking. We always referred to the different groups as 'Centres'. And in each one JC put one or two in charge. Of course I met many students during my time in the school, but I cannot recount everything. It would be a deviation from the core of my story. Anyhow, I have to mention some of them – not portraying them in such a way that you see them before you. But I mention them because in the end JC gathered twelve students around him and gave them the task to continue his teaching. It is almost as described in the New Testament."

Then he continued.

Over the following weeks, John and I attended meetings in the Centre. There was a weekly meeting on Saturdays, and quite a few students not living in the Centre came to these. JC had put Matthew and Anna, whom I had first met in the coffee shop, in charge of the Centre.

Matthew was born in Hungary, but had come to Sweden when his parents fled following the 1956 uprising. He had been with the school for some years, although he was still very young, about twenty-three; he was a photographer and many of his pictures were on display around the Centre. He was tall with black hair and piercing, deep, dark eyes, like an eagle, which gave you a feeling of being pinned to the spot. I felt he was the right person to be in charge of the Centre.

Anna was small, with blond hair, even though she had Italian roots. She had been born in Italy but had come to Denmark with her parents as a child and was now studying at the university. What I noticed most about her was that she moved quickly – not only physically, but mentally too. She grasped new ideas with great speed, and though you sometimes had the feeling she was not listening to you, she was preparing her answer while you were talking. She was charming and lovely to be with: sometimes her Italian temperament showed, as when she was in an argument, but she could change in the blink of an eye and become calmness personified. She and Matthew balanced each other well and created a good atmosphere in the Centre.

Matthew was very good at chairing meetings. He was always in a positive state of mind, very gentle and pleasant even when he corrected you, which he did when he pointed out your weaknesses. During the meeting he would say to someone: "Now you are in fantasyland. You are dreaming. Try to be in the present."

Then the person would try to defend himself or herself, saying that they were not dreaming, just thinking. Matthew would just look at them silently, and then say: "Try to remember 'yourself'." And that was the end of the discussion. There was no need to try to justify, excuse or defend oneself, as Matthew said:

"We are all poor musicians in the orchestra of the Lord, so let us try to play our parts well."

I enlisted at the university again, which is how I came to stay in Copenhagen for almost another year.

III

My parents were happy that I had come back to Denmark. They had many questions about my life and wanted me to tell them about my plans for the future.

"It is good that you have found God," my mother said. "We are so happy that we could help you a little to travel to India." Then she looked at me and continued: "But I hope you did not forget it all when you lived in England."

I assured them that God was an important part in my life, more than ever. They both smiled and looked happy and pleased with me. My mother said, "It makes me glad that you've found

God. I have been praying for you daily since you left home, and the Lord has been good to you, I understand."

Then my father wondered about my studies at university. I said that I had taken them up again, and I think he regained the hope that he had lost some years previously; maybe his son would become a priest after all.

"I have joined a Christian group of people." I stopped and wondered how I should explain to them about self-remembering and the teacher.

"Is it like our people?" my father asked.

"No, it's not."

"But what kind of group is it then?" my mother said.

"Baptist," my father suggested, "or Presbyterian?"

They tried every denomination they knew about, and I realized that I had put myself in a difficult position by mentioning the Christian group. In the end, I simply had to invent something and I told them it was a totally new teaching, but that it was Christian and that we prayed to Jesus. That seemed to satisfy them, especially my mother.

I had been warned not to talk about the teaching to friends and family and people I met. I understood now that when the prophet told me not to talk about the group, it was because it was not possible to explain what it was about. It was as I had entered on a path where ordinary standards did not apply. I could not say to my parents that they were asleep and had to try to remember themselves. That would have been rude. If people showed a genuine interest, I could tell them what I knew, but otherwise it was simpler to say nothing.

Consequently, spending time with old friends and family became difficult, as the inevitable questions would always come up: "What are you doing? What kind of group is it?" and so on.

From now on we, more or less reluctantly, had to leave all old relationships behind. Maybe that's what Jesus meant when he said to "leave everything behind and follow me". It was, as JC had said, not a question of forsaking people or things, but it depended very much on why you did it. I had no further contact with the old group of hippies I had known before, and my relationship to my family also weakened. Over the following years I saw my parents only a few times and each time, I was bombarded with questions and their worries about my so-called useless life that did not seem to be leading anywhere. I was like a prodigal son, whom they would have loved to have back – the son who should have become a priest, to give them honour in their little congregation; to come with them to church, to have a "normal" life, which to them meant marriage, children and a well-paid job.

I could not fulfil any of their dreams. All I could do was to love them for who they were, forgive myself and forgive them for our common past mistakes, and, from now on, walk in the newness of my new life. It was sad in a way, but simultaneously I felt liberated and I was becoming free of the past.

The result of it all was that people considered me strange. They started to say that I had joined a sect, and then, shaking their heads, they happily left me to my "sad condition". But for the first time in my life, the words of Jesus in the gospel meant something real to me. It was time to wake up and be healed, from the illusion of false personality, which was a mask to take off or put on, a veil between me and the world or a curtain that could be pulled aside to let in the light from the sun. The truth could not be found out there, but only deep inside me.

I studied hard at university. I was determined to finish as soon as possible and I no longer cared about the subjects, the theories, the dogmas or the theology. I just did what I needed to in order to get my degree.

Still, for me orthodox Christianity had become a mystery. I knew now why I never could find what I was looking for in Christianity, because I wanted insight, not faith. Faith for me was to believe in an absurdity – that Christ had died for me; that God had sacrificed Jesus, his son, to compensate for humanity's disobedience to God. It was the Semitic interpretation of the events around Easter in 33 AD, based on the practice of daily sacrifice in the Temple of Jerusalem.

Sometimes I thought that my mother was the last real Christian. She believed that Christ died for her, and her faith never wavered. During the last three weeks of her life, she gathered her four children round her. On one of her final days when we were sitting with her, she said:

"Look, can't you see? He is standing there. He is stretching out his hand and saying: 'Come, I will help you over the threshold.'"

And she had this glow in her eyes, an expression of great happiness, for now she was going to be together with her master and teacher, the carpenter from Nazareth, the Christ.

She died peacefully, willing to follow her saviour to the end.

IV

I passed my exam in philosophy, and the only thing left was to write a thesis on New Testament exegesis. It was to be an interpretation of St John's writings, the Gospel and the letters, relating to Gnosticism. By now I had a job in an office and, as I wanted to finish my thesis by Christmas, I needed to commit totally and do the enormous amount of work that was required. After my degree I would join the teacher, or, as he had said: "come and live with" him.

We continued going to the group meetings in Copenhagen. So far I had been living with John and his wife, but now I managed to get a room in the Centre and was living among students.

John often visited me, not only on the days we had meetings. He was talking about divorce and joining the teacher in Sweden. I did not offer an opinion or suggestion as to what he should do. I was sure he would find the right path for himself, but one thing I could understand was that it was very difficult for two people to live together when pulling in different directions.

John told me one day that he had talked with my English friend James and one of his friends, Phillip, about the school.

"Are you sure that is a good idea?" I said.

"They are both interested," he replied.

Thinking about James from the time we had lived together before, I felt that much of what we had done fitted well into the way we arranged our lives in the Centre, so why not? But Phillip was an active person, a carpenter, an extroverted, talkative type. Could he be interested in the teaching? John said that he had met Phillip many times and talked about religion and philosophy. That made me wonder why I had never visited them. I was somehow isolating myself, while trying to learn a new way of thinking and acting, and I was probably a little afraid of being drawn in undesirable directions. This I could not deny.

It turned out that they were both accepted as students and joined the Centre in Copenhagen.

Chapter Fourteen:

A Midsummer's Night

June 1977

I

At midsummer, there was going to be a party in Sweden, far away from Copenhagen, somewhere in the countryside. The only parts of Sweden I had visited previously were Malmö and Helsingborg.

JC sent invitations to all of us in Copenhagen, and I was told that similar invitations had gone to the groups in Germany and Norway. Naturally the Swedish students would be there, and I was really excited about meeting them and seeing where JC lived. It was called "the Farm".

We were a large group of people, 25 in all, from Copenhagen. We rented a coach and left Copenhagen two days before the midsummer party, which was to be on a Friday evening. John and I sat next to each other on the coach, talking about the wonderful landscape we were driving through. He told me that he and his wife had finally decided to separate.

"Where are you going to live then?" I asked.

He did not know, but would try to find somewhere near the Centre in Copenhagen or, if possible, move to the Farm in Sweden.

We finally arrived at the Farm in the evening. There were several houses spread out in front of us. The main house was the farmhouse: it was situated on a hill with a view over the river. There was a huge barn and smaller sheds where tools and machinery were kept. I was told that between 40 and 50 hectares of land was attached to the Farm, and local farmers also rented land to us.

A mountain rose up behind the farmhouse, with woods stretching far up the sides, and from the house a pathway led some 100 metres up to a fairly large bungalow, where JC lived.

The first time I walked to the top, I saw a magnificent landscape laid out beneath me, with houses on the slopes and the beautiful valley far below, where the road ran alongside the river. On the other side of the river there were more houses and also workshops, where all kinds of handicrafts were produced. Later I would get to know the area very well indeed.

I had the good fortune to be accommodated in the main house sharing a room with John. The person in charge of the Farm and farmhouse was Mona, whom I had met in the coffee shop in Copenhagen. She was very firm and sure of what she was doing.

Following breakfast, we were each assigned a task. It was not what I had expected, which was that we would sit around and listen while JC was teaching. Mona and her helpers gave instructions to everyone about what needed doing over the following few days. As we were a large group of people there was much to arrange for the party, as well as all the normal jobs around the Farm during the middle of summer.

I was in a group designated to bring in the hay. On the Farm there were many sheep, which stayed in during the cold winter months, so there was a great need for hay with which to feed them over the winter, and this was the right time of year to make it. We set off to some big fields on the other side of the river. The guy in charge was Michael. He had probably once been a farmer, since he seemed to know about hay and farming. He had a baler attached to the tractor which packed the hay into bales of about 30 kilos; another tractor with two trailers then collected the bales. I was on one of the trailers, stacking bales that were thrown up, and when the wagon was full we went back to the Farm and unloaded the bales into the barn.

It was very warm work. After eleven, the heat made it even more difficult; I remember looking for some shade, but there was none in the middle of the field. After some time, the sweet smell of the hay was the only really enjoyable sensation. Sweat was running down our faces and bodies so that dust and grass cuttings stuck to us, causing an unbearable itch. Things only seemed to get worse.

At lunchtime, food and drinks were brought out to us and we could eat, drink and rest. We walked to a little clump of trees and finally we sat in the shade. But this blissful interlude did not last. The work continued in the field, and by 2 o'clock the heat was so unbearable that it reminded me of hellfire or other possible torments of body and soul.

Even the evening meal was brought to us. It was delicious and I could not help but admire the way that everything was organized, so that there were no problems and no time wasted.

We worked all day, welcoming the weak breeze that blew up during the late afternoon, which cooled our tortured bodies. I was exhausted, as I was not used to this type of physical work, but each time my strength seemed to fail, it was miraculously renewed – I know not how or from where it came. It was late evening by the time the last wagon load of hay was in: Michael had wanted us to finish this part of the field, and have all the bales under shelter.

Our little group of five were lying flat on our backs on top of the loaded cart. The summer evening was fading into night; the stars were appearing, as well as the moon, which meant that it was at least 10 or 11 o'clock. I noticed the Plough, which reminded me of the time when I passed through the Khyber Pass on the way to India. The same stars at that time had given me a feeling of trust, and once again it was a good omen. Now I was at the teacher's place, had been working all day, and was tired, with the feeling that my body could move no more, but I felt a peace beyond understanding. My mind was empty, but not a void. Happiness and peace were creeping over me and I was present, in the here and now: I could not have been any more present than I was at that moment, remembering my-self, having no thoughts about anything whatsoever. I just was. Maybe the phrase is "I am", because this moment is now, and now is not something that was; it has no extension in time and space, but exists for ever.

When we arrived back at the barn and started unloading the last wagon, I suddenly understood what this work was about. The teacher was making us work with practical things, such as on the Farm, to enable us to give up our resistance or to obliterate the old self-complaisant false personality, which always wanted things its own way, and to make us ready to receive on another level of reality.

I remember lying on top of the hay with empty hands and an empty mind, ready to be filled with the blessing of some higher power. It was surrender and it was wonderful.

II

While we were unloading, another student came and asked for Peter.

"That's me," I said.

"JC wants to see you."

I left the bales and walked up the hill to the bungalow. The door was ajar, so I went in and entered a large, well-lit room, tastefully decorated as if designed by an architect.

I stopped and listened. There was silence. Then I heard JC's voice from an adjacent room.

"In here," he said.

I walked across the floor and looked into the room. JC was sitting on a mattress on the floor, with only a candle lit in front of him.

"Come in," he said, "and have a seat."

I sat down beside him on the mattress.

"I was just sitting here thinking a little," he said, almost as an excuse. "Sometimes I think I have to go out and meet people. Life is about people, you know, and without people there is nothing. No life at least. It is people who have taught me everything I know, for without them I would have spent my whole life sitting on a pillar in the desert, looking out into nothingness and never understanding what life is about."

He looked at me to see if I had understood the message.

"Now, come. Let's go out into the kitchen."

The kitchen was large, and I smelled freshly brewed coffee.

"You do drink coffee?" he said, and without waiting for my answer he took two cups from the cupboard.

"I'll show you how to drink schnapps – the Swedish kind."

He took a bottle from the fridge.

"Firstly, put a coin in the bottom of the cup." He took out two coins from his pocket.

"Then you pour in schnapps until the coin is covered." He did that.

"Then you pour in coffee until the coins disappears." He did that too, and then he said, "Now you add schnapps until you can see the coin again, and finally you add coffee until you cannot see the coin."

After doing this he took out the coins with a teaspoon. He added sugar because, as he said, that made the essence of the drink more easily absorbed into the bloodstream.

Then we drank the brew and sat down again while the drink made my body swim around in space. After a few moments he looked at his watch and said, as if a thought had just crossed his mind, "We'd better go to bed. It is going to be a long day tomorrow!"

That meant that the audience was over and I staggered to the door, said "thank you" and "goodnight".

When I came out into the beautiful starlit night, I was intoxicated but not drunk. I was in a strange floating state, and did not know what to think about my first day on the teacher's Farm.

Walking down the hill, my head cleared and I was smitten by a sudden inspiration.

He had shown me myself, the way I had been sitting at home, becoming sad and gloomy. The talk about meeting others reminded me how much I had isolated myself from people, even friends and family. He had attached no blame or guilt to my way of living, nor had said what was right or wrong, but like Socrates, he made me understand myself and that I needed people – in the real sense of needing. What an amazing way to teach. He had released an insight, which I somehow had already had, but which now became conscious and as clear as daylight. He was like a midwife, helping to bring forth what was unborn. That was the first time I experienced his extremely advanced teaching method.

John was already asleep when I lay down. I fell asleep within seconds and suffered no bad dreams.

I said to Peter that I hadn't done much physical work in my life. Working all day, from morning to evening, would have made me leave immediately.

Peter interrupted me and said:

"You must remember that I had prepared myself for a long time and I could not give up just because of a tough day. Little by little, I found out that my strongest enemy was my own resistance. This first day was no exception. We often worked hard, in summer and winter, sometimes under difficult conditions, like when we took timber out of the woods in winter. It could be extremely cold and I would dream of a warm room, sitting in front of a fire with a coffee or a drink.

"I must tell you that the thoughts that constantly come to the surface of the mind, we called 'I's' – sometimes saying, I don't want this, I want that instead, or something different, and so on. As soon as opposing 'I's' came into my mind, the resistance increased and then a battle would take place within. That made it almost impossible for me to continue; it left me feeling negative and just wanting to forget the whole idea. Peace of mind was restored when I gave up resisting and surrendered.

"JC once said that we have a spirit that is eternal, and that is the nearest we can come to God. And we have a body which is mortal, and that is the tool we must use to the best of our ability in this life. But we also have a soul. It is an embryo, and needs to grow. It is the seed I have been telling you about, and each time we can surrender and make the body follow, give up its self-will and resistance, an atom of soul is created. So we need a well-developed soul to make the connection with the spirit. That's why the right use of our bodies is so important."

III

The following day everyone took part in the preparations for the midsummer party. It seemed that people came from far and wide, and I had only seen a few of them since my arrival, mainly due to the day in the field. I understood that Mona was the main person responsible for the organization, with a leader assigned to each individual group. I was placed in a group whose job it was to decorate the area to be used for the party. I did not know anybody there, and we had to speak English so that everyone could understand. I guessed that a large number of nationalities were represented; in our particular group, there were students from communist countries such as Poland and the Soviet Union. I was amazed at that. How could people from behind the Iron Curtain be allowed to come and work here?

The party was to be held in the barn; there was a fairly large area that was empty, next to where the hay had been stacked the day before, and the smell of the new hay was amazing. We swept the floor and took out hay bales to sit on, and the whole building was decorated with midsummer flowers. Outside other students put up the midsummer pole. It consisted of a large cross, which lay on the ground while it was decorated with green branches and flowers. On the arms of the cross were hung two wreaths of grass and flowers, and then it was raised.

The dance around the pole started in the late afternoon, after the arrival of the neighbours, who looked a little shy – probably because of the many young people, or maybe because they were not used to seeing so many people of different nationalities together. Around the pole was a huge lawn, so large that everyone fitted into just two concentric circles. I was in the outer and we moved in opposite directions.

The fiddlers were playing different tunes – children's songs, slightly melancholic Swedish folk tunes, but also happy, joyous polkas. I saw many faces passing by while dancing around the pole; I caught a glimpse of James and suddenly I also saw Jude – I think he noticed me, but pretended not to. In both rings, during the dance, we were holding hands and I had a strong feeling of being part of a big body moving rhythmically around: the usual feeling of being an individual faded as the dance went on.

After what seemed a long time, the dance stopped and we went over to the farmhouse, where a big marquee had been put up. Here the food was served on long tables. The main dishes were the traditional midsummer food of new potatoes, pickled herrings of many varieties, sausages, sour milk, vegetables and bread and butter. A long queue formed itself into two rows and when you had picked out what you wanted, you found a comfortable place to sit, anywhere. The weather was the same as the day before, warm and sunny.

While we were eating, JC joined the party accompanied by Maria. She was once again dressed in red. She was so beautiful. She fetched food for JC and they sat next to each other on two bales. I was sitting on the ground in the grass, and suddenly Jude came towards me and sat down.

"So you came," he said.

"Yes, and I am glad that you introduced me to the school."

"You are in Copenhagen, right?"

"I am. I am trying to finish my studies in theology."

He shook his head.

"What are you going to do with your degree in theology? Why didn't you study something like I did, something useful like economics?"

"Because I have never been interested in economics."

He started eating his food. I tried to enjoy mine, but there was something about Jude that I did not like: I had the same feeling as I had had in York when I met him there. I could not put my finger on it, could not define what I felt, but just his way of speaking annoyed me, mainly because of the exaggerated self-love in his voice.

"JC has put me in charge of the economics of the whole school. Maybe you don't know it, but we have a shop downtown, on the main road where we sell the produce from the Farm and the handicrafts; I have my office there, in the shop, and I take care of all the accounts, incomings and outgoings from the shop and the Farm, and I am even the accountant for the other Centres. JC has also made me responsible for investing the money in a good way. You see, economics can be very useful and necessary."

"I know that. Good for you," I said in an unnecessarily sarcastic way.

"You still don't like me, do you?"

"Well, I suppose you are all right. I think it is good that you can be of service to the organization." I swallowed. "Excuse me for saying this: although I had only seen JC once before yesterday, the impression I get does not seem to correlate with what you told me in York."

"Meaning?"

"You know very well what I mean. You talked about the country and the future and all the imbeciles following JC like meek lambs."

"That's your problem. As you say, you don't know him. Wait and see."

Then he changed his tone, as if wanting to change the subject, and said, "But come and visit me down in the shop one day."

He looked around and suddenly changed again. Something within him hardened; he got up abruptly and left me sitting there, and he almost bumped into a young man. (I was told later that this was a new student. His name was Richard.) Jude grabbed him by his arm and literally pulled him aside. I do not know why, but I followed them. I saw them standing some distance away, Richard with his head bent down, not looking at Jude. Jude was talking rather loudly and from his gestures, it was clear that he was upset about something. I could not hear what was said, but Richard was trying to get away and Jude was preventing him from leaving.

I overheard only one sentence. It was when Richard at the top of his voice shouted, "I know nothing," and then Jude let him go.

IV

After the meal JC gathered everybody in the barn. He sat on a chair and took out his guitar while the students and guests stood and sat all around. He told some funny stories, and then started to sing; admittedly his guitar playing was not the most advanced technically, but when he sang, he did made a strong impression on us – a feeling of wonder, a feeling of being at home. He sang many songs and talked in between and made us laugh. Then he told a story:

"There was a man who had two sons; both working at his farm. One day the younger asked his father if he could take out his share of the inheritance in advance, because he wanted to travel the world. And, he said, it is, after all, my elder brother who will one day take over the farm. So the sharing was done, and the son left his father's house.

"Many years later he came back. Life had been hard on him, he had lost all he had, and couldn't think of any better solution than to return home and see whether his father could give him some work on the farm – not as a son, but as a hired hand. When his father saw him from afar, approaching the farm, he became exceedingly happy. He ran towards him, kissed him and took him back as his son.

"The other brother was angry. He thought it was unjust, which in a way it might seem, and even though his father tried to calm him down and make him understand that he would have done the same for him, he left in anger."

JC looked around on all of us and then concluded: "This is the story of the school. Try to understand what you hear." Then he sang "Amazing Grace".

After that there was silence. Of course everyone knew the story he had told – some even thought that it was not a good story – but I learned later that JC had a way of saying things that at that time in your life seemed unimportant or strange, but later made a big impact because you remembered and understood.

JC got up and went over to "the musicians". Then the dance started. The music was everything from the fifties to the present day, and the students danced with great energy. While they danced, Michael, the farmer, stood next to me.

"Have you met JC?" I asked.

"Oh yes, many times," he said. "I live here."

"What's he really like?"

"He is not like any of us," Michael answered. He thought a little. Then he said:

"JC is a person for whom other people's opinions mean absolutely nothing, not because of lack of interest in others or because he regards them as nonentities, but because he cannot be hurt or flattered or anything like that; he is just not attached to anything. What he is doing is teaching, seemingly not in order to have fame or credit, but only because his task is to teach."

"I am looking forward to meeting him again," I said, "but I have to go back to Copenhagen tomorrow."

"Perhaps you will live here one day," Michael said in a comforting way.

V

When JC left, it was late and people were going home. Some had the difficult task of clearing up after the party, while others had to make breakfast for a lot of people next morning. It was all well organized.

The barn was almost empty and I was about to go to my room when I suddenly remembered John. I had not seen him the whole evening, and yet I was sure he had been in the dance around the pole. While I was wondering about him, Maria came into the barn. She came straight towards me in her red dress, now with a shawl over her shoulders.

"Do you want to go for a walk?"

Of course I did. We walked down towards the river.

"It is so good to see you," she said.

"I am very happy to be here," I replied.

"How did you get in touch with the school?" She asked.

"Hans told me. I met him in York."

"I didn't know that. Do you talk to him sometimes?"

"Not much. We are not really close," I stated.

"He sometimes tries to get close to me, but I do my best to avoid him."

Maria then said, as if it was a confession, "You might not know that he was in love with me once, when we lived with my father, and he ..."

"I have heard. He tried to force himself on you," I said quickly to spare her going into details.

"Yes, and even now, he sometimes takes me by the arm and wants me to listen to him. But I feel no tenderness, only a strong violent reaction. I do not like him, but I suppose he is as he is."

She continued: "But there again, here it is not a question of liking or disliking. We are training to remember ourselves and we want to develop that part of us which is above likes and dislikes. What we are trying to observe is what we think about the world, what we think about other people and how we feel about them, not to change them or the world. The question is why we are constantly identifying ourselves with everything we perceive. We are victims of what happens, of other people's opinions and of our own shortcomings. One day, we shall be free and learn to love. In love, there is no dislike and no judging."

"But you just said that you did not like ..." I interrupted.

"Yes I did, but I also immediately corrected myself," she quickly replied. "To stop thinking in terms of like and dislike does not mean that we should fall under other people's dominance without trying to put a stop to what we do not want to take part in. That is why I stop Hans."

We walked down over the field leading to the river.

"Have you heard anything from your father recently?" I asked.

"He is here."

"But I have not seen him."

"No. He did not want to be around so many people, but he is fine. He goes to Denmark sometimes, to the coast in Gilleleje. You probably know the place."

"I don't, but I have heard about it and even tried to find it once."

"He is very close to JC. They talk a lot and I know that JC appreciates his support."

"How is he getting on with Hans?"

She shook her head a couple of times, as if she did not have any definite answer to this, but said: "They don't talk much together because he is not in step with Jude, as he often calls him. Do you know about Hans's points of view?"

"He told me a lot about them in York."

"Well, I know that he is useful to JC. Someone has to look after the finances, now that it has become a very large organization. So JC accepts Jude as he is, and makes use of him; otherwise I don't understand why he keeps him here. I have asked him, but he won't answer the question."

We stopped at the riverbank. It was rather late. The new day's light was dawning in the east, almost the north-east, and we both stood looking out over the water. On the other side, some fishermen were putting a boat into the river. A haze drifted south over the water, which gave the landscape a mystical quality – a real north Scandinavian paradise in midsummer. I imagined fairies and trolls moving in the half shadows behind the shrubs and trees, and I heard the music of the spheres and the sound of oars from the boat on the far side. Silence with heavenly music, and the cool sweet smell from the grass, flowers and water filled my senses.

I put my arm around Maria.

We stood motionless. Then we kissed each other gently and started to walk back towards the houses up the mountain. I said goodnight to her when she left me on the pathway to go to the bungalow.

"Goodnight," I said again, when she was some distance away.

She turned and gave a slight wave full of love.

My heart was beating faster, but calmed down when I looked out over the valley. Midsummer was a blessing, and a profound peace filled me.

VI

I think many of us slept until 10 o'clock. After breakfast, it was time for our departure. I told Mona that I would like to speak with Carl from Denmark but she said that he, JC and Maria had left earlier that morning, so I would not see him this time.

We drove all the way back to Copenhagen. I asked John, "Where were you all the time last night? I didn't see much of you."

He smiled with an air of secrecy, as if saying, "If you only knew!"

"Come on, tell me, don't be like that."

"Well," he started slowly, making me even more curious. "At the beginning of the evening, I was with at the party, as everyone else ..."

"And ..." I waited.

"But later in the evening, I was with JC as he just wanted to say something to me. He talked a lot. And the wonderful news is that he asked me to come and live at the Farm. Isn't it fantastic?"

It was fantastic, but at that moment I almost cursed my studies in Copenhagen.

"I want to move to the Farm as well," I said a little sulkily. "When are you moving?"

"As soon as possible. I have to clear up things with my wife, but I think we will have a divorce with no hard feelings towards each other."

Over the following months, I concentrated intensively on my studies. My final exam was set for the beginning of December.

Autumn was knocking on the door and I was reluctant to "open" it, because I never liked the days getting shorter. In

October, the darkness had taken over and the days became rainy and dull, except for the odd sunny ones. I especially loathed the rainy days, when the sky was grey and it was impossible to extract any energy from the daylight.

My thesis for my final exam was finished by November; after that I still had to go through some of the New Testament writings in Greek, but that was easy. My thoughts about St John became much tainted by my new ideas of Gnosticism. I tried to use what I had found out at the teacher's place, but my thesis was close to being failed due to these new ideas. I could not help using my knowledge of the new system in my work; however, my teachers at university did not find it scientifically grounded. There were too many assumptions about what should and what should not be, too many conclusions that the texts did not allow for, and that was not accepted in science.

Finally they passed my thesis, but made it clear that what I had written was not good: in fact, it was barely acceptable. Anyway, I was very happy that I had finally left university with a degree in theology. I was now a Master of Divinity, a title that made me laugh a little – imagining telling JC that I was a religious master!

VII

Before the final exam, at the end of November, there was another invitation from JC to all of us – to a Christmas celebration, this time in Germany.

We flew from Copenhagen to Frankfurt and from there to our destination. There were only three of us – Matthew, Anna and I. It was expensive, but I had found a better job in December at the central post office, just behind the main station. It was cold and a little snow fell around the middle of the month, so I had to buy good gloves because I was distributing the post by bike. Some days my ears threatened to fall off but, in the midst of my misery about the cold and the wet, I looked forward to the visit to Germany.

The Centre was situated a fair bit outside the city. Around 20 students were coming to the celebration, but as the Centre was in a small house, most of us were staying with students and friends in the neighbourhood and the celebration was more like a family party.

The day before Christmas, we went to the Christmas market in the city with JC. He showed yet another side of his complex character, spending a lot of money by buying lunch for us all and shopping wildly. He bought lots of things – perfume, wine, chocolate and clothes – as gifts for students at home. When we returned to the parking lot where we had left our cars, we were loaded down with everything he had bought. I admired JC's way of handling money, as if it was worthless paper, which, at the same time, had a value. He did not seem to worry about money, and Anna said to me that he had a magnificent way with it. She did not know how he acquired it, but often he was with friends, presumably rich ones, and we guessed that they and many others donated large sums to his school.

On Christmas Eve after dinner, JC asked me to sit next to him. I finally had the chance to tell him – proud as I was – that I had passed my exams.

"Fine," he said. "Now you will train for ordination, I suppose?"

I was shocked, as if I had been hit over the head. "Not again," I prayed inside my head.

"What? Ordination?"

"Yes. Wouldn't you like that?"

"No."

Quite frankly, it was the last thing I was thinking about.

"I had hoped to come and live with you. That is what you said, wasn't it?"

I felt like Jacob, after working seven years for Rachel and then being given Leah. I was just about to consider it as treachery when he stopped me by saying, "Sure. You shall come and live with me. Come to Sweden, to the Farm. But still I think ordination would be useful."

"But I suppose you know what the church is like? I haven't been to a service for many years."

He looked as if he doubted the truth of what I had said, and then I remembered I had been to a service in Bombay during Advent some years previously.

"Well, maybe not so many years, but still ..."

He smiled knowingly. I had noticed before that it was impossible to lie to him. Earlier in the day, when we were walking around, I had had some strange thoughts. He was walking next to me and I felt sure that he knew what I was thinking, as if I had become transparent when close to him. He "radiated a light": he made me see myself, become aware of the whole body, inside and out, and it felt difficult to find something to say at times.

"Come to Sweden," he repeated. "It will not take long for you to be ordained; I can arrange this for you. Of course the church is a special organization, but the important thing is to give everyone what he or she needs. There are people who need to take things literally, fundamentalists who need safety because of their fear, and there are people who wish to be woken up, to be drawn out of repetitive liturgical worship, who want to break free of a pattern. There are people looking for understanding, who want to go deeper into themselves, people who need to pray, and so on. Each one has a place, and they are just as right wherever they are on their journey, and if they want to continue as they do, support them; if not, show them alternatives. There are most certainly people who would join the school who are attracted to esotericism, who feel that there is another way, and who have what I call a magnetic centre, but have not yet found a group. They are waiting for you. Do you see what I mean?"

I did. But I had never thought about the church like that and I realized that JC had a respect for people, an acceptance of them as they were, and did not seek to change them. He was showing a tolerance that I thought would not have been possible when one knew the truth, but now it seemed that the truth for JC took on many faces and aspects. Then he added:

"At the same time, you will fulfil what you were destined to be. You will be what your father prayed for – a priest."

He looked at me quizzically, wondering how I would react. How did he know about my father's prayer and his wish? Then he said:

"But of course, it's up to you."

"I will think about it," I finally said.

Chapter Fifteen:

THE FARM

1978

I

After New Year, I put my few belongings in a bag and travelled to the Farm, where the midsummer party had been held.

JC was not at home when I arrived, but Mona had been informed about my arrival. She showed me to my room, which had a window facing the pathway up the mountain; from there I could see the bungalow where JC lived.

John was already here. At first he had come to live in one of the houses further up the mountain, but very soon JC had put him in charge of the shop down on the main road. He had a room behind the shop, Mona told me.

Now the hard work really began. My day was planned from early morning to late evening, which was a good, but tough, form of discipline. Now and then I had to go down to the shop, bringing things for John or Jude. I met Jude often and, remembering what Maria had said about likes and dislikes, I tried and even succeeded in changing my attitude to him. I answered his greetings, but we mainly exchanged small talk and never became close.

JC, Maria and Carl arrived back in late January. I had not talked to Carl for a very long time – I hardly remembered the last time we had talked – but I wondered how he was getting on. Maria had told me that he often stayed in Gilleleje, a place he loved and used as a retreat. He was not really interested in meeting many people: as he put it, he wanted to spend time just thinking and meditating on the absurdities of people and life. I met him only occasionally, when he went out for a walk; otherwise he spent most of his time in the apartment in JC's bungalow: he did not seem to want company.

A few days after his return, JC invited me to go out with him. He drove over the bridge, further on down the road, and up onto the other side of the river. The road was icy, but the water had not yet frozen this winter. We arrived at a large building on a hill, where we parked the car.

On the ground floor, there was a large carpentry or joiners' workshop, with all kinds of machines for processing wood. There was also a large store of planks, which I was told came from our own forest.

"This is where you are going to work," JC said.

"But I do not know anything about working with wood."

JC again gave me one of his looks.

"Well," I corrected myself, "I did work for short time in a joiner's shop while I was studying, but there again ..."

"You will learn. Just do your best. Tomorrow Gerhard will be here and he will teach you." (Gerhard turned out to be a German, who had been working in the joinery for the past year but would shortly be returning to Germany on another assignment.)

I now remembered JC's talk about ordination.

"But then I cannot be ordained," I said, almost with relief.

"Oh. So you have thought about it. Good. Yes you can; I'll arrange it."

"But I thought you wanted me to," I said.

"It was only a suggestion."

He said it in a tone of voice that sounded as if it had been only a suggestion, but since I now brought it up, it was my own wish too. Then he laughed heartily.

"Don't worry," he said. "You do as you please, but while you are living here with me, I want you to learn about joinery and then, later on, take charge. This is part of my plan, but I hope it does not put you in an impossible or inconvenient position."

"No, no: it is OK. I would like to learn about carpentry. As a matter of fact, there are joiners and carpenters in my family, so I probably have some of it in my blood."

I was surprised at myself, coming out with ideas that I was not even aware of.

When we were driving back, I suddenly realized that I was about to become an apprentice in a joiner's shop in an esoteric school, and I would be ordained as a priest sometime in the future. I must admit that my life seemed to be changing – things were happening outside of my control.

The next morning, I started my work in the joinery shop.

II

In February, I had to leave the joinery for a few days. We were felling trees up on the mountain, partly for firewood for the following winter but also for our building activities. This wood would not be used until next spring, which meant that for the coming summer projects there was already a plentiful supply of timber.

I walked behind the timber wagon all the way up the mountain, together with six or seven others. Michael was driving the tractor. It was cold, there was snow on the road, and at times it was difficult to drive up over the hill to the plain where the pine forest was. That day Michael had put chains on the tyres to help to cope with the conditions.

Suddenly I saw Carl coming down the mountain – perhaps he was just out for a walk. He was an old man now, and no longer took part in the physical side of our activities. When he came nearer, my heart started to thump. He stopped and looked at me with great joy.

"It's so good to see you," he said. "I knew you were here, but understood that you were too busy to see me."

I hugged him and was very happy.

"I have been busy – of course I would have come to see you, but there are so many new things to take in and sometimes I feel a bit overwhelmed, and at other times, you were not at home, and ..."

"Don't explain anything," he said. "I was glad when I heard you were coming. I know Maria talked a little with you earlier on – that's good."

He took me to one side while the others continued upwards. "Now," he said. "My prophecy has come true. You have travelled a lot, you have prepared yourself well and one day you will bring the teaching to other places."

This sounded strange: it almost made me afraid.

"How do you know that?" I burst in.

"Because it is your destiny."

"But Carl, please wait a little. If that's the case, you could have told me a long time ago."

He shook his head. "No, I could not. That would have interfered with your free will and your decision making. I knew there was this possibility, because it is destiny, but there are always choices to be made, including the 'wrong' choice, which leads one astray and brings unhappiness and unnecessary suffering. Still, there is the possibility that you will make the right choice, even though it can take a long time."

He looked at me intensely.

"Now I know that you are on the right path, and this makes me happy. There will be many difficulties and hardships, but you will be given the strength to carry on."

He put his hand on my head and blessed me. Then he continued his walk, and in my bewilderment at this conversation, I stumbled many times while trying to catch up with the others.

Some days later, JC asked me to come to his house. I knocked on the door, which was opened by an unknown student. Like a maid, she showed me the way into the living room, where JC was sitting in an armchair, smoking a cigarette.

"Have a seat," he said.

I sat down. I had developed a respect for him that was not fear, but I recognized that he was in charge, and when meeting him I felt a strong sense of security – a feeling that nothing in the world would harm me, as long as I worked with him and for him.

"I have arranged for your ordination. A friend of mine knows the bishop. I had a talk with him the other day and he has agreed to ordain you next month. He wants to see you a couple of times to talk things through, and then he will ordain you. I told him you were a suitable candidate, and he took my word for it."

I could not help thinking that everyone took his word for whatever he wanted them to do, when he wanted them to do it.

"But how do I get there – to the bishop, I mean?"

"You can borrow my car, or if I have time, I'll drive you."

I felt honoured, and thanked him.

Then the talk ended, so I got up and started towards the door.

"By the way," he said, "you are doing well in the joinery, so I'll soon be sending more people over."

As I was closing the door, I heard his voice again.

"One more thing – it is time we found you a car."

I thanked him again and left. I repeated to myself: He is going to give me a car. And for the first time I saw the use of having acquired a driving licence.

III

JC drove me to my first meeting with the bishop. We went into the city; it was a very strange feeling going there, as I had not been in a city for some time. Life at the Farm was so peaceful; the surroundings provided a calm, gentle atmosphere, no matter what happened outside. Although we worked hard at times, we also had time to rest, especially on Sundays when we visited other houses. Generally I got on well with most of the students, though some I liked more than others. Being human, we all felt more attracted to some than others; however, we were constantly reminded that love and respect were more important than any personal likes or dislikes.

The city, on the other hand, was noisy and busy. People seemed to drift aimlessly around, although they probably knew where they were going, but I was sure of one thing: they did not know each other. They were strangers that just happened to be in the same city, each with their own story, whereas at the Farm we all shared the same vision, and therefore were all going in the same direction

JC dropped me outside the bishop's residence. I rang the bell and was shown into the bishop's office. He was a middle-aged man, wearing a red shirt and his clerical collar. He was amiable and spoke in a compassionate but matter-of-fact voice. He asked me about myself: what I had been doing and what I believed in. It was difficult for me to speak about my years at university, when I had turned my back on the church. When I showed him my exam papers, so that he could see what subjects I had done, I was worried that he might not like my thesis on Gnosticism – not a subject much appreciated within the church. He looked at my papers for some time, but made no comment. At no point did he cast any doubt on my integrity.

He had a very high opinion of JC. He told me that they had talked a lot together, and that he thought he was an extraordinary man.

"He is like Christ come back," he said laughing.

When I left, JC was waiting for me.

"How did it go?" he asked.

"Fine," I answered. And then we drove home again.

I met the bishop four or five times during that spring. By the time of the next meeting, I had my own car for the first time in my life, and at the last meeting the bishop agreed to ordain me. He arranged for me to be the sole ordinate, as I had not trained with any other candidate priests.

The ordination took place in the cathedral on 11 June , which, according to my father, was the birthday of the devil. Now I had fulfilled my father's promise to God.

JC was not present at the ordination, but he met me on my return to the Farm.

"Well done," he said. "Now it is time to be a student for real. Now you are to live with me, and, as I promised, you will be my pupil. Isn't that great?"

I agreed, but my mind was full of images and thoughts from the ordination, and I was somewhat confused as to what it meant to be an ordained priest.

"Don't worry," JC said. "You'll find out."

A party had been arranged, with just a handful of people. Much to my surprise, Carl was there. I asked him if we could meet afterwards, which we duly did.

IV

Carl had a small flat in the bungalow where JC lived. We sat in the big, comfortable armchairs.

"Now," Carl said, "what do you want to talk about?"

I told him that I had been thinking about our perturbing conversation in the forest. He smiled when I used the word "perturbing".

"People usually want to know the future, but when someone tells them, they become afraid, even when the future looks bright and promising."

I then remembered Krishna, who had read my hand and had reluctantly shared his insights with me. He had definitely seen more in my hand then he had thought wise to tell me. He had summed things up in a vague way, painting a picture of a life without shape and the fact that I should only be happy when I had found God.

"Tell me honestly, why is it that people called you a prophet?" I asked.

"Because in a way I am," he replied.

"In what way?" I asked.

"I was born with the gift of seeing; I could not answer questions on command, about things people had lost, or similar requests, but sometimes I could see events that were to happen before they happened. I mean I 'had seen' events, which then happened, and at that point I realized I had the gift. The first time was about my grandfather. One day, when I was playing with the other boys, something inside me showed me my grandfather in bed and asking us to be with him, because he was going to leave, as he put it. I walked, or rather ran, home and told my mother that grandfather was dying. She did not take it seriously and patted me on my head, saying, 'Sure, he is old, maybe he will soon die.'

"But I insisted and said that he was dying now and, I suppose, because of my strong conviction, she asked me how I knew. When I told her what had happened, she believed me. We went to grandfather, and sure enough, he died that afternoon.

"Similar incidents took place many times, and that's how I was given the nickname, 'the prophet'. At first I was not happy about the name, since I was not religious, but little by little it stopped bothering me, so if people wanted to they could call me that."

"Does it mean that you know how your life will be, when you will die, how old you will become, and things like that?"

"No, I do not control this gift of mine; I cannot predict everything I want to. It works in unforeseen ways: suddenly something takes shape in my mind, which I cannot explain to you; I simply know when it is a prophecy and more often than not, I tell no one."

"But you told me," I argued.

"Yes, I had my reasons for that. Don't be afraid, but remember that you are going to carry out a great task, so let that be a help to you when things are difficult. For you have an important role to play in this life. It is already written."

My mind started thinking wildly about destiny and free will, but I managed to control my thinking and a mantra came to me, which said, it does not matter that I cannot understand; with God's help, it will be as it has to be.

Carl changed position in the chair, crossed his legs and smiled, saying:

"I did 'see' JC before meeting him. He was standing in front of me, as if in a dream, if you like, and I knew that I was going to join him. And so I did."

The prophet was full of self-confidence, and seemed almost a little smug, like a schoolboy who had given the right answer to a question; I did not remember seeing him like that before.

"You said you saw JC standing in front of you; how did you meet him then?"

"I met JC at the end of May, after the war ended. In trying to deal with my deep sorrow, I often walked down to the graveyard, to the same place each time, thinking about my dear ones. Suddenly, one day, a man stood in front of me. I was sitting on a bench and at first, saw only a shadow on the ground, then I looked up and there he was. That is how it started; he became a great help to me from that day, comforting me but also telling me about a system he was going to teach."

Now the prophet told me about the teacher and the school.

"JC is younger than me; he was born around the end of the First World War. He had met a teacher who came from Armenia, but who lived in Russia until the revolution in 1917 created total chaos in the country. The teacher left Russia with a few students, travelled through Turkey and finally settled in France, where JC joined him. He was a young man and a quick learner, and after some years he was sent to Denmark, where he started building his school straight after the war in 1945. That was when I met him. In the beginning, there were only the two of us, but soon JC had other students. He managed to buy a house in Gilleleje, which was like a refuge for all of us – it is still owned by the school. We held meetings there and gradually things expanded. The teaching spread to Sweden and Germany and later to Norway. JC then moved to Sweden."

JC had told him that it was an ancient teaching, going back to Jesus and his disciples. Although the teaching had been around for a long time, it had been hidden, but had been directly transmitted from teacher to student from the time of Christ up to this day. In the early middle ages it survived in the monasteries, beginning with St Benedict, and on through the so-called Dark Ages. And so it had been from the beginning of the Christian era where the mainstream Christianity developed, while the esoteric teaching was carried on in smaller groups of which we know nothing. This is the reason why the disciples of Jesus simply seemed to disappear into history without any account of their work.

"Today we know nothing about them, where they went or what they taught, and only Peter and James, the brother of Jesus, and John are mentioned. And their function cannot be discerned from the New Testament, but surely they founded schools in different places.

"The Freemasons were most certainly part of the tradition. During the building of the Gothic cathedrals, they were handing on the teaching. It has been adapted to the different circumstances over time, but it has always focused on the idea of self-remembering and the creation of 'a conscious soul'."

I recalled my very first meeting with JC, or rather with the students he had sent to the meeting, and their talk about becoming conscious. Almost from the start, I had understood that the word "conscious" had a different meaning from the usual one. When we talk about being self-conscious, we mean feeling embarrassed or uncertain of oneself; this is the polar opposite of what it means in the teaching. Self-consciousness in the teaching is a state of mind where one is fully present, or could be present, whenever one wished to be. Carl assured me that since we had not attained that level, we could not really know what it was like; but we could imagine. The proof of self-consciousness in this context was right in front of us, when meeting JC. Without a doubt, he was a most unusual person. A "conscious" being.

Something new and unexpected always came up when I talked with Carl, and that day was no exception. He started telling me that when JC introduced him to the system, he had had only a small amount of preparation for spiritual practice.

"I was not brought up in a religious milieu, and did not think of God or Jesus or anything of that nature, but when I was in Palestine, during the excavation I met an Indian man, Krishna, who made me start thinking about the other world, as he called it."

The name "Krishna" rang a bell – the "sound" immediately flashed through my mind.

"Is this Krishna a priest in a little village in India, a priest for Shiva in the Punjab?" I asked.

He stopped, and remained motionless for a moment.

"Yes, he is. How do you know that?"

"I met him in Bilga. He told me about you and your work in Israel, and he said he had visited you in Denmark."

"He did."

"I have to tell you that when Krishna told me about you, I thought you had told him about me and sent me to India – because you had said that I would go there – and even arranged with Kumar to introduce me to his village."

"Oh no, none of that happened. I know who Kumar is. I met him one day in Copenhagen, and since I had been to India and reckoned that he was Indian, we talked a little and to my surprise he was from Bilga and knew Krishna. Of course I was surprised, but there again, it fits in very well. People who are connected stay connected. I know that now. But I did not arrange for you to meet Kumar; I just felt that it would take place somehow, and it was in my mind when I was telling you about India – a prophecy, one could say."

A whole new universe opened before me: human beings from all over the world were meeting each other because they were meant to, and I remembered the guy who cheated me out of my money in India and the fact that I met him again hundreds of kilometres away. So yes, it was possible. But how?

Carl perceived my astonishment, and said:

"It is not the general rule, but I think that most people relate to certain circumstances involving certain people in their lives, and the whole picture includes a long line of events that seem to be more or less accidental. But seen from a higher level, a higher perspective, it is what was meant to be – or let us say most likely to happen. Do not become fixated on this idea; it is just a theory, but looking at my own life, I feel sure everything was planned from the beginning. It is like walking through a landscape. You approach a hill and you do not know what will appear on the other side; then, to your astonishment, you see a wide, beautiful plain with grazing sheep and a shepherd boy tending them. You walk further, sometimes deviating from the path, but sooner or later you reach the end of the path and, of course, you realize that the landscape was already there before you walked through it. Maybe it is the same thing when we think about time. It is a dimension, and the distances in time are perhaps just as real as in three-dimensional space, so that we walk through time and meet what is there for us. But please do not become entangled in too many theories, like the one I have just told you about – just take life as it comes and ask yourself, 'what do I have to do at each turn in the road?'."

He stood up and asked me to follow him outside.

We walked down towards the river. On one side there was a pasture where a horse and foal were grazing. We sat down on some big stones and looked at them. They were peacefully eating, moving forward a little after a few mouthfuls of grass. The mother horse walked as if she was alone, but it was clear that she was very much aware of her foal. The little one, on the contrary, seemed to be lost at times. It would suddenly look up and, seeing its mother further away, would rush over to her for a reassuring feed, so that peace was re-established until the next time.

I had never really observed the interplay between horses and the relationship between mares and foals before, so I perceived it to be a beautiful, perfect creation of God.

"Do you see?" the prophet said. "They [meaning the two horses] need no theories to function harmoniously, and so, sometimes, looking for intellectual explanations leaves you worn out and, at the end of the day, you realize in your soul that it leads nowhere. It is like science. When the atom was discovered, one could have been satisfied but then the intellect wanted to know more, and so came the idea that there were particles within the atom. To this day, the search continues and I am sure that the scientists will continue for ever, or at least until the prevalent paradigm runs into a dead end. Then a new one will be invented and so it will go on, because for every answer, two new questions will arise. This is the nature of science. It is like the fairy tale of the sorcerer's apprentice. These horses were created as you see them today, so that they can pass on their seed."

Maybe he chose to use this word intentionally, but I almost felt a sting in my heart. The mere sound of the word "seed" made me remember a promise from long ago to develop my seed, and certainly that was exactly what I was doing now. I had a great task to carry out.

Chapter Sixteen:

A CHAIROS TIME

I

My new car was fantastic. The only problem was that I had to fill it with petrol, and I did not have any money. Since my arrival at the Farm, everything had been provided for me, and my old clothes and shoes were still in reasonably good shape, but the need for money became urgent one day when my car ran out of petrol. Luckily a passer-by helped me with a few litres, to enable me to drive back to the main building.

Since Mona was in charge of the daily organization of the Farm, I had to go and talk to her and straighten out my problem. She told me that although we all worked without pay, our personal requirements would be taken care of.

"But where does all the money come from? I wonder how the whole school is financed, because I talked to Jude and he gave me the impression that astronomical sums are involved, and from what I can see, it seems unbelievable that the small amount of sales from the shop would be enough ... although I do not know how many people shop there, but considering the Farm and machines here and there and ..."

She interrupted me.

"First of all, I do not know exactly how things are financed and it is not my problem to figure it out. I know that students donate money, and it appears that JC has sources which we do not know about. I do not think it is that important. We all do as well as we can and if there were problems, I am sure JC would solve them, therefore do not listen to people's suspicions. There are some that say JC is making himself rich, but he does not own anything; all that you see belongs to the foundation and the only liberty he takes is to be able to travel around, to dress and have his most important needs covered. My job is to distribute money to students as needed and to organize the shopping for the household, and that's it."

"I thought that was the case, but you know how people talk: they think we are being indoctrinated; they tend to think of us as slaves, working here without pay."

I had overheard a conversation along those lines somewhere. I concluded: "In other words, the foundation is like a company or a business. Usually every business is liable for tax. So is it what Jude does?"

"The school is a foundation," she repeated. "A non-profit organization, which means that all of us work without pay. We support the foundation, and in return there are tax regulations which specially favour such organizations."

She looked at me as if I was being slow and naive. Why was I wondering about such things? Could it be because of Jude and his comments in the past, or was it that I was uncertain of my role in the organization?

Mona said that it was OK to ask. "There are no secrets in the organization, but there are students working in each area to help JC with the various regulations, and Jude is one of them."

"OK, but then I should also contribute," I said.

"If you can."

"But at the moment I have nothing, so I would have to raise some money."

"Don't worry," she said. "You are working in the joinery and thus paying for your stay. More important than the money aspect is that you are working on yourself and trying to remember why you are here. All the same, it is also good that you are showing an interest in how things work – not everybody does that. Once again: you should not worry about the state of the finances or about the organization. We are all well taken care of. Trust in that, and if you need something, you are welcome to ask me."

"Do you mean for personal things like clothes and ...?"

"Yes, anything you need personally. Food and accommodation is, as you know, paid for, and in case you need money, come to me."

I finally brought up the reason why I had come: money for petrol. She had already guessed this; she asked how much I needed monthly, told me to get receipts every time I spent money and then fetched the amount I had asked for.

With that our chat ended, and I felt I knew a little bit more about the organization.

II

John was away for some days, a young man in the shop told me. The young man was from Eritrea and spoke Swedish with difficulty, whereas his English was much better – he said that John had been sent to arrange some property matters, but he was not aware of the details. We talked a little and then Jude opened the door to his office.

"Would you like to come in?" he asked.

"Of course," I said.

He shut the door behind me. On his desk were piles of papers, and he seemed to be in the middle of some work.

"A cup of coffee?" he asked.

I thanked him and he showed me to the little side room where the pantry was. I sat down at a round table in the corner, and after a short while he handed me a mug of instant coffee and sat down opposite me.

"I heard your voice out there and remembered that for a long time, I have wanted to show you something. Would you like to see it?"

I became alert and curious as to what it could be: I was amazed that Jude was actually going to show me something. Today he seemed like a person transformed – not like the angry, hot-tempered man I'd met before. I nodded.

He opened a cupboard, took out a large album, asked me to move my cup a little and placed the album on the table in front of me.

"Please, open it."

It was a stamp collection, but only of Danish stamps, neatly arranged and, as far as I could see, consecutively numbered, according to a stamp catalogue. I turned over the pages and noticed that there were empty spaces here and there, and instead of a stamp, the number of the missing item was written.

"What do you think?" he asked.

"It is very beautiful," I remarked.

"It is more than that," he replied. "It is almost complete. I am collecting only Danish stamps and I have nearly all of the issues since 1851, when the first stamps came out. The missing ones are rare and expensive, but sometimes I come across one and buy it."

For the first time I saw a side of him that was mild and soft, as if the stamp collection, which he was proud of, was a creation sprung from his soul. He was like a boy who was showing the most precious thing he had in life.

"Where did you learn about stamps?" I asked.

"It was Carl who taught me. When I first arrived to live with him and his wife, I was in a bad way and very restless. I do not remember my first few days there, but I know I was confused and frightened because of all that had happened previously in England. So Carl tried to interest me in something, in order to help me to concentrate. I am grateful that he was good to me."

I tried to forget what Jude had previously said about Carl.

"As time went by, I became captivated with collecting stamps. I made it my goal to collect all the Danish stamps ever issued."

He was still standing in front of the table, while I continued looking through the pages of stamps.

"It is perhaps childish, but I do like to look at them now and then," he excused himself.

"I think it's great," I said, with no pretence. I had heard a little about his childhood from Carl. Since the opportunity to ask had arisen, I said, "I would like to hear about your childhood before you came to Carl."

He sat down and rested his head in his hands, as if it was painful to recall these memories.

"Very well," he said. "I can give you a flavour of my life, but it is not a nice story – something I am almost ashamed of." And then he started to tell me.

"My parents were both alcoholics, and mother was also addicted to drugs. Of course I don't know how it all started but I have found out a little from what people have told me. But I clearly remember how it ended. I was seven when I moved to Denmark, having earlier spent a lot of time alone in the flat, being beaten up many times, and even left chained to a radiator for days. I did not dare to scream or shout, which would have attracted the attention of the neighbours, so I just waited. The feeling of hunger is one of the strongest memories, the constant gnawing in my stomach; the thirst that made my mouth so dry that, when I finally decided to call for help, I was not able to make a single sound.

"When my mother returned from wherever, she tried to be nice and compassionate. She sent me down to the shop to buy some food with the little money I was given; the shopkeeper noticed my bruises, and called the police and set the whole machinery going. I was transferred to an orphanage, where life did not seem much better. I have many sad, sad memories of the orphanage and clearly remember the harsh discipline and punishments. You must remember that this all happened in 1938, when hardly anybody was aware of how badly orphaned children, or those taken into care, were treated."

He paused and sighed, that special sigh I had noticed during my earlier meetings with him, and I was reminded of how careful we must be not to judge.

Then he continued:

"One day, a distant member of the family came to see me. He lived alone, travelled a lot all over the world, but after hearing about me he wanted to see for himself how I was getting on. He understood that things were bad, and since he knew Carl well, he contacted him and arranged for the adoption. It all happened very fast, and late in 1938, I arrived in Denmark."

He got up, made some more coffee and sat down again. His facial expression changed to one of anger, but then he regained his composure and went on with his story.

"Actually, I have told few people about my childhood because it is impossible to describe the number of times I was mistreated.

It is my secret, but now I am sitting here telling you, because I suppose I feel calmness in your company. Anyway, it was good to come to Denmark, and when Carl and his wife, Miriam, had their daughter, Maria, I was happy. I loved that little girl from the beginning. After the war started, she started walking and making funny sounds, which no one really understood but they were so full of love. I liked to kiss her on the head; I played with her and tried to teach her words. She objected to being kissed so often, so I had to control myself, so as not to annoy her.

"I had no thoughts about Jews, all that happened later, but I do know that when I was twelve – she would have been four that summer – the Nazis were trying to get rid of all the Jews in Denmark, as well as elsewhere. I had heard the story of the Jews in Europe from Carl, but in contrast to him, I developed an anti-Jewish attitude. It was then, at the beginning of puberty, that I became a socialist. I read certain books, and came to the conclusion that the Jews were to blame for the evils of capitalism, which gave me a monumental dilemma. Maria was Jewish and I loved her very much, and I could not imagine someone killing a wonderful girl like her.

"I hated the Nazis because of their campaign against socialism and communism, so I certainly did not sympathise with them. You know, they sent the entire membership of the communist party to concentration camps."

He sighed again. I felt deep sympathy for him.

"When they – Miriam and Maria – left, I was very sad and didn't know what to do, but when the little girl came back one day, I couldn't believe my eyes and was overwhelmed. Later, when she became a teenager, I fell in love with her, and I have been in love with her ever since ... yes, and one could say that some strange things happened."

He crossed his legs and seemed to change inside, from the mild, childish Jude to the grown-up, tough version of himself. It happened so quickly that I expected a sudden outburst of his anger.

It didn't come. Instead he sat without saying a thing, and I racked my brain trying to find something appropriate to say in order to express my understanding of what he had suffered. Now I regretted encouraging him to tell me about his dreadful experiences, which had provoked the sad memories. I had felt I had to ask him: not out of curiosity, but out of a sincere interest in him as a person.

Suddenly he got up and said brusquely, "I have to get on with my work."

And that was his way of saying the chat was over. I could not reclaim his attention, so I rose and left the room.

III

"Could you join me for a little ride?" JC asked. "I'll drive and we'll go to my favourite restaurant in a nearby town."

I was taken by surprise, but agreed without thinking. It was a Saturday evening after the weekly meeting; I had been absentminded the whole way through and hardly remembered anything that had taken place. I had come to a standstill. I was beginning to question my abilities and my usefulness.

We walked to the car and suddenly, he changed his mind.

"Perhaps you would like to drive?" he asked.

I started the car and we drove off. It was dark as dark can be, with heavy rain – a nasty, windy October night. Whenever we met another car, I was blinded by the oncoming headlights through the cascade of water on the windscreen, but in some miraculous way I stayed on the road while the car passed. JC sat calmly in the passenger seat with his arms folded across his chest, and sometimes I caught a glimpse of him, looking at me in admiration.

"You are a good driver," he said.

We arrived at the restaurant and by now I was anything but absentminded, rather somewhat shaken and not a little relieved that we had made it through the awful weather. It was late, between eleven and twelve, but there were still a lot of people around. There was live music, and couples were dancing. JC chose a table where we had a little privacy and were less "disturbed" by the music, which he seemed to enjoy. The place was very exclusive and fortunately I was properly dressed for such an occasion, as we were usually asked to dress as smartly as possible for the meetings. JC used to say that we had to present ourselves to the "higher" world in a fine manner, but I had never been to such a high-class place as this before.

JC looked at me and took out a handkerchief. He held it up in front of his face and said:

"I can see through the veil."

Then he lowered it and smiled one of his mischievous smiles, as if he had done something completely out of place.

"But it is true," he said. "I can look through the veil of physical existence; it is like a 'cloth,' but behind it is reality. Do you want to see reality?"

"I suppose so," I mumbled.

"I have observed you over the last month and noticed that you have become full of doubts, have many questions about where you are heading, what you have to do and whether you will get what you want. This is quite a normal stage to reach, after some time in the teaching. You start out as a novice, full of optimism and enthusiasm, but then after a while you reach the point you are at now, which is leading you to despair and hopelessness and so, you tell yourself that it is not worth the struggle."

I listened, and what he said was true.

"Please tell me what you want to aim for, but it has to be achievable, not something out of reach," JC said.

"I would like to be rid of the fears and doubts and the feeling of hopelessness, and I do not like cold and rainy autumns," I said, sounding a little naive and stupid.

"Oh, that's not really a very achievable aim."

"Why?"

"You'll never get rid of autumns." He laughed. "But the other things are also too great to achieve, until you realize that you cannot achieve them on your own: you need help from above. Nobody creates their lives: they happen. You have forgotten that when you came to me, your desire for guidance was strong; you were full of enthusiasm and wanted so much; but now, there is this setback. Now it is important to ask yourself: What is it in you that says, it is not working? Listen carefully and you might discern a voice saying: 'I do not want to lose control. I do not want to give up everything I have, so I do not wish to change. It is too painful.' You must want to get rid of the veil."

"I have had instances when I have let go," I said defensively.

"Yes, but the taste for it must be stronger. The more thirst we have, the more we look for water. I can tell you that behind the veil, there is a universe so incredible that if you saw it, you would be out of breath – maybe even out of your mind. You see, if you try to sit for one moment, and just be, leaving aside thoughts of tomorrow or yesterday, then you will be in the moment, and, as a matter of fact, that moment is eternity. I don't mean a moment in passing time; I mean the 'Now'. You probably don't believe it, or you cannot grasp it. But it is so."

"How long should I sit there without thoughts?"

"Forever," he answered.

"But that is not possible."

"No, I was joking. I said for a moment, but it is not a matter of how long or how far. It is just now. I can tell you that I am there; or rather I can position myself there whenever I want to. This 'Now' is called the eternal now. It is the crack in the timeline where escape into eternity is possible. There is no other place to reach, only now."

"Tell me about this place," I said.

"OK. When you are there, this world disappears. Sometimes it is in the background, like the sound of a radio playing in the room next door. You, however, are not in space and time, but outside it all. You can go deeper, and there is probably no limit to how deep, or high you can go if you want to; there are no ordinary thoughts, no future and no past. The thoughts are of a different density. They are not pulled down by the weight of words; they are pure thoughts and cannot be explained in words. It is a paradox to try to tell you about something that cannot be told, because we do not have any appropriate words anymore. It is the alpha and the omega simultaneously. Do you follow me?

It is what, to a normal intellect, is impossible, beyond all forms of logic, and thus discarded by ordinary reason. Still it is a fact.

"It is the movement between the different levels of reality, all as real as the one you came from, but still with a new and unexpected dimension to the eternity of God. You know this will never end, and it does not matter, because you are no longer longing for anything. You are in a perfect state of bliss and pure joy. You are participating in the cosmic dance of God and all the time, you are full of divine love.

"What do you think of that?" he said.

"I would like to be there."

"Then try to give up your doubts, your negativity and self-control, and follow me. Develop trust."

From then on, things changed. Again I felt confident in JC, and tried to follow his advice as much as possible.

IV

November arrived, with its rainy, dull and foggy days getting shorter and shorter. I was about to complain, as I had done every year of my life, when struggling to cope with my depressive autumn moods, but I remembered JC saying, "This is a difficult aim."

Instead I tried to be thankful. Thank you, Lord, for the grey, dull and ever shortening days. Thank you for being able to work indoors in the joinery, smelling the wonderful pinewood and teaching the new young students how to work with wood. Thank you for this moment where your reality is behind the veil.

One day I went to the shop. John was there but Hans was not.

John said that he now tried to keep the shop in good shape, ordering things that were out of stock and keeping reliable account and stock books. He felt that the most important thing was to do the things assigned to him, and to try to stay out of negative emotions.

I told him of my evening in the restaurant with JC and about the veil. He was amazed, since he had had similar experiences himself – coming to a point where initial enthusiasm diminished, after which the effort became more and more arduous and finally stagnated. That was the reason he had been away, the last time I had tried to see him.

"The young man in the shop said that you had gone on an assignment looking at property projects."

"That's only partly true. When I came back, JC told me what was going on inside me and explained it with the help of octaves and intervals.

"He told me the theory I had read about in our manual, but apparently the importance or even the meaning of it had slipped my mind. The whole universe is governed by a law called the law of seven, or the law of octaves. It has nothing to do with music as such, but since the Pythagoreans, an old esoteric school, demonstrated that it works in music, we know it mostly from the musical octaves. There is not the same distance between the notes in an octave. Between E and F there is a lesser distance and as well between B and C. These places are called intervals.

"It does not matter when you play music because you know about it, but practically it governs our everyday lives, although we are never aware of the intervals, which are places where things do not develop by themselves and therefore need a special effort or energy. If you are a smoker and try to stop, you know that after the decision to stop is taken, at first you find it easy, then it starts becoming tougher and it would be easy to start smoking again. You have approached an interval in the octave and an extra effort is needed, using information about lung cancer for example, to give you the strength to carry on. Otherwise you start smoking again and even find good reasons for carrying on. This extra force or energy is called the third force, according to another law, the law of three.

"What JC does, then, is to add this extra force, this encouragement, which gives us the strength to continue and makes us continue pushing forward, and all things become possible. It was a great help to me, and now I know that from time to time, this interval will appear."

At that moment, I knew what was meant when JC said he was working with all of us individually. He did not talk about octaves and intervals to me at the restaurant, and the only time I encountered the expression was at the beginning, when he said it was useful to complete octaves.

"I shall talk to Carl about this someday. I am sure he knows about it, though he never mentioned it."

"Of course he does," John said, "but JC warned me not to become an addict to 'strange' theories. It is all practical. Don't become an esoteric-teaching academic, he said, but as soon as you experience something that was mentioned in the theories, then it is not a theory anymore, it is a fact."

"Yes, I have also been convinced that theories are of no use or maybe useful only at the beginning, as a first step on the way, as JC says. But I feel that it is most important for us to be very vigilant and awake now, to use what we have learnt every time we find ourselves immersed in inner talk and confusion and negativity. We are approaching a *chairos* time."

"What does that mean?" John asked.

"It is a Greek word and it means a time when something very important and decisive will take place. It could be a time of upheaval and final change but it *will* happen: one could say, it has to happen."

John got up and without asking me, fetched two coffees. It became a sort of introduction to another subject.

"How are things with Maria?" he asked. "I mean, are you two ..."

"We are friends," I said. "We have met many times since I came to live at the Farm and we enjoy each other's company."

He didn't go into it any further. Then I asked him about Hans. He said that he'd met him quite often.

"What's your impression of him?" I asked.

"He is strange. I do not understand him. He seems to value my presence here, especially as he has authorized me to sign for his registered mail."

"So what kind of mail does he receive?"

"Letters arrive from all over the world."

I told John about my meeting with Hans some time previously, about his love of stamps and his gentle side, which surprised him. Hans was not easy to understand, he was very complex, but, I said, we should not forget his background. There was a child inside him, full of deep wounds.

"Do you think that JC is working with Hans individually as well?" John wondered.

"I think so."

"But then he too will change."

"Probably."

"But he seems to avoid any questions about JC. There are, it seems, limits to his openness to me concerning JC."

We talked for a long time, probably for hours. While sitting there together, John and I started sharing memories. This afternoon seemed to be a kind of reunion for us. We had not had much time together since we moved to the Farm. We had different assignments and were each developing at our own speed and direction, or so it seemed.

"John, do you realize that we have travelled a long way together, on many spiritual roads, through Buddhism, Christianity, and esotericism? We have walked this road together for more than ten years, and today here we are, working in an esoteric school. Where do you think we will end up?"

"I don't know," he said. "But honestly, we have gone this far and there is no turning back. It must lead somewhere."

We hugged each other and remained seated holding hands, joined in a common purpose of mind, soul and seed.

A customer came into the shop. She saw John and me through the open door, sitting on the couch hand in hand, and we could read the expression on her face. It said loud and clear that we were homosexuals and she was disgusted. Then the rumours and gossip spread and the opposition to the school started. It built slowly over the years, until it broke out with a vengeance.

We were approaching a *chairos* time.

Part Three:

The Fruit

Chapter Seventeen:

GROWTH

1978–1987

I

As soon as we had adapted to a certain work routine, JC would change it. He was absolutely adamant about this; he did not want us falling into a comfortable existence with a daily routine and becoming stuck in a rut. No rest pattern was allowed to develop, and we were constantly moved around to encourage us wake up.

The midsummer and Christmas celebrations were the exceptions, but JC also introduced a party in August, to celebrate an old Swedish tradition of eating newly caught crayfish. Furthermore, we started celebrating Easter for a whole week with eggs and bunnies, but there was a silent day for meditation on Good Friday.

I could not explain month by month how things developed, but will give you a general picture and focus on a few important incidents.

The organization expanded enormously. Around 1985 there were three centres in Denmark and four in Germany. In Norway, a third centre was founded far up in the north, in the land of the midnight sun, and finally three further centres opened in Sweden in addition to the Farm, which was always the heart of the school.

To my great joy Gerhard, who had returned from Germany, brought a new student with him, Rainer, who came to assist me in the joinery. At times there were an enormous number of orders from the different centres, for chairs, tables, cupboards, windows, and much more. The workforce increased and I was assigned two further students from abroad, the first a Russian called Ivan, who had come to Sweden via Poland and Germany. He spoke German, but I never asked him about his past. Gerhard and Rainer helped me by translating my instructions into German.

The second person assigned was a man called Jack, who came from the West Indies and spoke both English and French and was trying to learn Swedish too. He succeeded so well that he was able to pass his driving test, which was a huge accomplishment, considering the hard work needed to learn all the complicated theories in the Swedish driving manual. He was very proud when he showed me his new licence the evening after the practical test. I asked him to become the driver of the joinery car, which had a tow bar and trailer for collecting anything we needed from the hardware store; he even succeeded in learning how to reverse the trailer, which is not an easy thing to do.

During these years, Jude started attending our Saturday meetings. He talked about his difficulties and made important contributions when he shared his points of view. I had the feeling that JC had been working with him. I knew that they often met, but knew nothing about the content of their meetings. It seemed Jude had found a way of dealing with his past, which made me very happy, but in the end I realized how badly mistaken I was.

Matthew, from Copenhagen, was seconded to the Farm. He and Mona worked together, meeting new students who wanted information about the school. It seemed that JC was opening up the school more than before. There was information about the school in the newspapers and posters were put up in bookshops, which was a very different approach from the earlier years, when new students found the school only by hearing about it from those who were already there. JC started sending students out to supermarkets and shopping malls, to sell our handicrafts.

The whole organization became a business, with all the young people working for no wages, and it was the aim that ideally no profit was made on the crafts sold. We became quite popular wherever we went. Many new people were attracted to the teaching. In the years up to 1987 many students came and many left; some stayed for a month, others for a year, and the result was that the teaching was spread around a great number of people. During this period, a few students gathered around JC and were taught intensively; I was one of them. So the deeper message of the teaching was carried on in "secret" behind the smokescreen of the business activities. He thus established the circle of the twelve.

Simultaneously the school seemed to be reaching out to an ever widening group of people, which was crucial and turned out to be part of the higher plan.

II

In the Gospels there is a parable about a seed. Jesus says:

The Kingdom of God is as if someone would scatter seed on the ground, and would sleep and rise night and day, and the seed would sprout and grow, he does not know how.

JC quoted the text at a Saturday meeting, and afterwards he asked me, "What do you think this means?"

I didn't know. To me it was so simple and straightforward that I couldn't detect any deeper meaning.

"It has a very central place in the Gospel," he continued. "It is exactly what my teaching is about. Think about it." Then he turned to some of the other students and didn't give me any further explanation.

Some days later, I travelled to one of the centres in the south of Sweden to look at some furniture that needed repairing. JC was expected in the afternoon, and when he arrived, I happened to be in the hall. I opened the door for him and when he entered, he looked like a poor beggar, creeping around looking for mercy or alms. I immediately shook my head, wondering what on earth he was doing. I judged him to be in bad shape, not coping with his mission; but then he straightened up and was self-confidence personified, saying, "There is vanity in you; it wants to judge and thinks you are better than others."

He walked past me into the house and I stood there somewhat bewildered, not understanding that he had been playing a role. I had seen him do this before. He was a master at playing roles, often using them as a way of pointing things out about oneself, but he only did it for teaching purposes; he was successful, as I now understood a facet of myself that had hitherto been hidden from me. He had made the point much more effectively than if he had merely spoken to me about it. Now I should have to acknowledge the fact and change.

I worked at the house all day and had to stay over. JC also stayed, and after dinner, he asked me to join him for a walk. This particular house was in a beautiful area, surrounded by forest and with a lake nearby.

We walked down a path towards the lake. I remember it was spring because we could hear the birds singing their "evensong" most lustily. For a long time, neither of us said anything, but when we came to the lake, he stopped and looked towards the horizon, as if expecting something to appear. Then, without turning towards me, he said, "Do you know that vanity is selfishness?"

"I suppose I do," I answered.

"Then you know the effect it has; it means that you don't really care about others, being not the least interested in them. Selfishness means that you only care about yourself and only love yourself: not your real self, but the picture you have made up and which you call yourself."

This was a shock. I looked across the lake to the other side. Some seagulls were screaming loudly and I wondered for a few seconds how they could travel this far inland, since they were seabirds. Because JC was standing there, looking at me with a love I had never experienced before, it was impossible to deny my lack of interest in other people. It had never occurred to me before; I had never thought of myself as selfish, but then I recalled the past and I started to cry: not out of self-pity, but because of my sadness at my ignorance.

After a while, he suggested that we return. I felt a strong impulse to hold his hand, but didn't dare, then all of a sudden, I felt his warm hand in mine. It was as if, I had a father again.

The next morning, when I came down for breakfast, JC had already left. I was in a strange mood, feeling empty, but not angry or negative. I was at point zero.

Over the following few days, I experienced something extraordinary. Back at the Farm I saw all the people I knew well, including the ones I did not like very much. At work, I was very polite, but without being friendly, so as to avoid any possibility of becoming closer to them. But one day at dinner, a student I really did not like sat down next to me, and I turned to him and asked, "How are you today?"

He looked surprised, and answered, "Fine, thank you." What he did not know, and what probably no one at the table knew, was that I was not deliberately trying to show off that I was a good person, above the petty human likes and dislikes: not at all. It was a completely spontaneous gesture; I had turned to the student with kindness.

Similar situations arose many times over the following few days. It was a miracle. Why was I suddenly so nice and kind? Why did I suddenly appreciate these people all around me, even those I had usually tried to avoid? I did not know the answer, but it happened. Was this the meaning of the parable: that I would sleep and rise, day and night and the seed would sprout and grow, and I would not know how?

I asked JC about the parable. He took me to his flat in the bungalow, and when we were seated he started to explain it to me.

"When I pointed out to you that you were selfish, you did not defend yourself or deny the fact, but you observed yourself to be selfish; you saw, with your inner eye, the many situations where you had been selfish. They flashed through your mind at that moment; it was painful for you to acknowledge the truth, but you did, and that was growth.

"Most people never think of themselves as selfish. We usually take it for granted that we are good and well-meaning people;

admittedly, selfishness exists, it is always out there, in others, so we project it onto others, in order to hide our own selfishness. This is the story about the speck in your neighbour's eye and the log in your own. It is always easy to see fault in others, but we are all selfish, and as long as we live on this planet we will never be totally unselfish, because the body is selfish. That does not mean that the body is bad and should be denied; I have often said that this is one of the unfortunate misunderstandings that certain religions practise. No, the body must be selfish because it needs to survive and there is nothing wrong in that.

"The problem is that we learn to conquer selfishness in the wrong way. In early education, we tell our children that it is bad to be selfish: you must share the cake with your sister, not thump your little brother on the head, and generally be kind. In this way, we cover our selfishness with a layer of morality, and unconsciously accept that selfishness is a defect of our being and must be repaired. But it cannot be repaired in this way. Some religious teachers have said that moral education is a remedy for our broken and sinful nature, like a painkiller that makes the headache disappear without knowing why there was a headache in the first place. Do you see what I mean?"

"Yes, I think so. On the other hand people must grow up to be good citizens and treat each other with kindness and respect, so morals are needed."

"They are necessary to allow society to function in an orderly manner, but we all know that in everyday life, people cheat on each other, steal from each other, even hurt and kill each other, no matter how much morality is preached. So, as I said, education creates a personality, which enables us to function on a human level, but it is only a remedy. Moses brought the Ten Commandments to Israel and these laws were given in God's name, to give them authority, but we know that they cannot change human nature. That is why Jesus spoke of the 'whitewashed tombs' which on the outside look beautiful, but inside are full of the bones of the dead."

At this point, JC stopped; then he asked me if I would like to go for a walk, and so off we went. I had by now realized that

JC often preferred to teach while walking. We went down to the river and followed the narrow path along the stream, walking with difficulty sometimes due to the encroaching shrubbery. JC continued talking and I had to concentrate hard on what he was saying in order to be able to follow him.

"Once I met a man on one of my travels. He was rich and, as he became interested in the teaching and the school, he decided to donate a large sum of money. He was talking about the bad state the world was in, with its lack of morality. He was also appalled by the evil that had happened from time to time during the course of world history. I told him then that evil was not something, or someone, running around out there creating trouble; there is a capacity for evil within all of us. At that point he became very upset, because, he said, he was not evil, and he left, taking back his promise of a donation. I sort of knew that he would do that, but at the same time, he had such a strong belief in his own righteousness that I thought it would be useful for him to realize his apparent lack of this particular quality. He didn't understand it at the time, but perhaps he has later on in his life."

"But from what you tell me, there is not much hope for humanity," I said.

"You have proved that is not so. When you were confronted with your selfishness, you let it go; or at least you removed a little bit of it, by seeing it within yourself, without rejecting or projecting it onto someone else.

"Of course selfishness and evil are a matter of degree. But the teaching gives you the possibility of observing the different aspects of yourself, and when you acknowledge and accept all that you have in your personal make-up, when you accept everything in you and see it as it is, not suppressing anything, then you will grow and start approaching the Kingdom of God ... *as if someone would scatter seed on the ground, and would sleep and rise night and day, and the seed would sprout and grow, he does not know how.* The seed will grow, but your part in the growth is your willingness to prepare the ground."

We turned away from the river and came up to the road past the Farm. We walked back to the bungalow in silence. When we were sitting in his room, he broke the silence and said:

"You surely understand that growth is developing the essence, or the seed, as we have said. And we have to use different metaphors to understand what it is about. A human being who has undertaken the work of spiritual development can also be likened to a walnut. The shell is the personality, and when it is green it is impossible to remove the shell without damaging the kernel. Shell and kernel form an inseparable whole. After a certain drying-out process, however, the shell becomes brittle and separated from the kernel. Then it is possible to break the shell and the kernel is revealed in its perfection."

He looked at me and added, "One day we shall have to break your shell. Then you will be free."

III

Occasionally the prophet asked me to join him for a game of chess. Having white, I often opened with e2–e4, a very common first move for white. He responded with the Sicilian opening, which I had difficulty handling, and the prophet usually won.

After one of these games we were both in a pleasant mood. Carl made coffee and he even served a glass of brandy. We talked about the past, my childhood and the first times I visited him in his shop. Then I remembered one occasion where we left my question unanswered.

"Do you remember when I was at High School? One day I asked you about a text in the Bible, the one that said God had put humans to sleep. Has God really put us to sleep in order that we should not be saved, as it is written in the gospel text and in the book of Isaiah? You promised me long ago that, one day, you would explain it to me."

The prophet nodded. "You're right, I did."

He tried to concentrate and then spoke: "Let's start with something simple. Have you noticed that everything you are able to observe is developing upwards or downwards? Have you heard about the universal laws, the law of seven and the law of three?"

"John told me about them recently. We need a push or an extra force at certain points to carry on a line of work. JC had told him that this push, or extra effort, was called the third force."

"Good, then you know. It is not useful as a theory unless we can observe it at work. What I mean is this: we all can see that when someone starts a fire in a house, it could burn down in a matter of hours; it just needs a starting agent. The burning house shows that there is a downward or descending development. But to build the house would be the ascending version, because it cannot build by itself, whereas the house needs no help to burn down, once the fire has started. It takes much more thought to build a house, to overcome any problems. The same can be said for our developmental path when we reach what is called the 'interval'. That is due to the law of seven."

He looked at me, to see if I was still with him.

"But I like to use myths instead of theories," he said.

"Why?" I asked.

"Because there are so many things that we cannot understand: to learn explanations and theories makes us believe that we know, but we don't. The world we see around us and our life within this world are so complex and mysterious that all we can do is surrender to the unfathomable. That is why I like myths: because they are not explanations but still they give us some kind of understanding without taking away the mysterious."

Then he fetched a Bible and read from the second chapter of Genesis, about Adam and the creation of Eve.

So the Lord God caused a deep sleep to fall upon the man, and he slept; then he took one of his ribs ... and the rib that the Lord God had taken from the man he made into a woman.

He closed the book.

"This myth is not trying to tell us that the woman is inferior to man because she was 'taken from' man. That is nonsense. In the Hebrew Bible the man is called Adam, which means the one who was taken from the earth and the woman is called Eve, meaning the 'life giver'. So Adam and Eve are not names of two people; they are two principles joined together into one being, a human being in which matter is filled with life.

"The Bible never tells us when the man was woken up from his deep sleep. So he is still sleeping. God put him to sleep when he was sent 'down' to the earthly domain. And when the human being opened his eyes – still asleep, but in what we call the waking state of mind –he was confused and bewildered because of all he saw around him. He did not know where he was and who he was, but of course started to arrange his life according to the will the Lord had given him. The myth goes on to explain that the human beings ate of the tree of knowledge about good and evil. That opened their eyes, meaning that they became aware of having a will to do good or evil. Their son Cain killed his brother Abel. It is easier to destroy than to build up: the ascending development needs effort; the descending goes by impulse, by envy or hatred, 'by itself'. Now we have come back to your law of seven and law of three."

He smiled and seemed pleased with his way of explaining things in myths.

"But why would God create man like this and a universe with these laws instead of a paradise?" I asked.

"Because, without the law of seven, no change is possible; everything would continue endlessly, up or down. People often say that God is cruel because he did not make a universe that was like a paradise, but what no one ever realises is that such a universe would be impossible. The body would never get old; people would not be able to change their minds, or their emotions. Everything would be the same, always and everywhere; we would be like unchangeable automatons of no possible use. If you, for example, are angry, you would be angry forever – which is impossible. The law prevents this because when the anger comes to the interval, i.e. the point of equilibrium, it will change into something else, so the law of seven guarantees change. When you want to awaken, it is difficult; but it is very obvious that it is easier to live 'mechanically', following your impulses and every little whim. Still, we were endowed with a will to choose between the two possibilities."

He got up and placed the Bible back on the bookshelf. When he was seated again he said:

"The creation, as an emanation from the supreme God, is interestingly used in science. According to the big bang theory the downward or outward emanation cannot go any further than to a black hole, because here, there is no longer any movement. It is not possible to know what could be beyond black holes – perhaps only nothingness. But science says that the universe is expanding and that at some stage, the light would be so 'diluted' that the universe will die or will start to contract and go back to the beginning when a new big bang will take place. I think this is God breathing; it takes billions of years but God exhales and inhales constantly, creating and destroying universes, but he cannot die, because he is all there is."

"Wow!" I exclaimed. "Wow. What a theory." I couldn't help laughing.

"Well, it is a myth, not a theory, because again it does not really explain anything. It is like poetry. It is stimulating and helps us to catch a glimpse of the divine."

Then he summed up his talk.

"So, finally, when Isaiah and Mark say that God has put men to sleep so that they do not hear or see, then in a way, they are correct. He did this by placing them in the downwards-going creation – that is, below the interval – and therefore they could not return on a simple whim; they were asleep but had to discover God's plan. Many messengers were sent to earth to inform humanity about the plan. They said: God is love and we have the capacity to love God, but love cannot develop mechanically; it must be an action of will, of effort, a decision to join with the love from above, and it needs free will to do that. It cannot be accomplished through force or exertion."

I concluded: "From my own experience I know it is extremely difficult to remember myself, to create an ascending octave: the chatter in my head is constantly going on, I react to things around me, become negative and there does not seem to be an end to it. But with the help of JC I intend to accomplish this upwards-going movement."

"Good!" he said. "I know you will."

Chapter Eighteen:

THE SERMON ON THE MOUNT

1987

I

For midsummer 1987, JC arranged the biggest party I had ever seen. He invited all the students from the centres in the various countries, around 200; he also invited the families from the neighbouring farms together with many others, some of whom I had never met before. Altogether, there were about 400 people at the midsummer party. JC bought in plenty of food and drink and had marquees set up all over the Farm. Inside, there were stages for the bands with coloured lights illuminating the walkways in between.

The event was organized down to the smallest detail: everyone knew exactly where they were working and what they had to do so that the party would be a great success. It started in the afternoon, with the customary dance around the midsummer pole – in fact there were a number of poles with music and dancing around each one, although I must confess that the organization, at this point, was not what it should have been and there was a certain amount of chaos. When the dance was over and just before the evening meal was due to be served, JC walked up the mountain, and from a place where he had an excellent view over the crowd, he took the microphone and started speaking.

"Dear brothers and sisters! I wish to welcome you all and I thank you for coming. I want to talk about a matter that is most important to me, so please listen, and afterwards the party will start in earnest. There is food for everyone, and I do hope you will enjoy a memorable evening. In the future, I hope you will look back on this evening with appreciation and joy, and I hope that each one of you will take something from here and cherish it in your hearts for many years to come."

Then he began his sermon.

"We live in a strange world. We are told that it came about by an accident – a big explosion 14 billion years ago – and we are told that life on our planet, as well on all other planets in this enormous universe, came about by accident. We are also told that from the first living cell to the great diversity of organisms we have now, including human beings, our development was accidental, without any aim or purpose; in spite of this, intricate living organism were created. But I tell you, the universe was created by God, the Absolute. It was created for a purpose, as was life; everything was created in the image of its creator and therefore we see his 'fingerprints' in each atom, in every leaf on the trees and the shrubs, in the delicate structure of the human body and in the smile of an infant.

"We are told that humanity once lived in ignorance, but that civilizations through the ages have developed and refined the intellect, so that science today has become master over the physical world and nature, and one day, science will know all the secrets and be able to create life without God. The human body is an automaton that can be manipulated in whatever direction we wish and furthermore, there is no more need of a God because we, human beings, have taken his place. But I tell you that we are all sons and daughters of the most high, God the Absolute and without God, we would not live a single moment, because God sustains all creation. It is in God that we live and move and have our being, and the purpose of man is to be united with his creator, whether he lives or dies.

"The introduction to the Sermon on the Mount, we usually call the Beatitudes. We know the words of Jesus so well; we have heard them many times and the words are both provoking and comforting.

"It is said, I am blessed when I am poor in spirit and that the kingdom of heaven is mine.

"It is said, the pure in heart shall see God and the meek shall inherit the earth. These are provoking because, when seen from the perspective of ordinary human beings, they seem too high, impossible to realize.

"I ask myself, am I poor in spirit, I who know so much and have learnt so many things in my life? Am I meek, merciful, and pure in heart, I, who often reacts to what is said to me, especially when someone criticizes or corrects me? What about my inability to forgive? Is that merciful?

"So if the answers to these many questions are a resounding NO, then all the promises that follow are not within my reach. I will not be filled with righteousness, I will not be comforted, and I will not see God.

"All Christians, including myself, since the beginning of the Christian era, have asked these questions, and have come to the conclusion that it is impossible to live up to the demands of Christ, because the further one reads, the more the demands grow. In the end Christ says: *Be perfect as your heavenly Father is perfect.* So where is the comfort?

"Let me tell you where to start. I will tell you about your room, your inner as well as your outer room, because they are connected. You are sitting inside your own room. The room is full of your things, your personal possessions such as the paintings on the wall, the old clock, and the dining table and chairs that you had from your father. But the room also contains your beliefs, your hopes and wishes, your fears and shortcomings; everything that you have learnt from the moment you were born is in here and your room contains the past, with its joys and happy moments, it contains the sadness and the sorrow, and also the grievances – blaming yourself and others; in your room, there is also every little unforgiving thought and all the questions you have asked yourself a hundred times: Who am I? Why did I choose to go this way and not that way? Could I have done something else and bettered my life? The many questions, torturing me at times, do not lead anywhere. But all you see in the room is yourself, your old self, the same room you have been sitting in for so many years; and yet you are longing for a new life. Where can it be found?

"You knock on the door again and again, but no one opens it – until you realize that you are knocking on the inside of your own door, and you cannot expect anyone to open it. You have to open it yourself and walk out into the new life and let the words of Jesus inspire you to wake up and leave the old behind. Let us go out to meet him.

"And there, outside, he stands, your Christ. He was knocking on your door the whole time from the outside, but you did not hear him, as you were so preoccupied with your own problems. The words of Christ awake a longing in us. The longing makes us silent, and then we can open up to new dimensions.

"I was in the situation many years ago, struggling and searching, but suddenly it dawned on me: Why would Jesus say all these things if they were impossible to achieve? Would he ask me for things that I would never be able to do? No. Jesus is not lying to you; his words seem direct and uncompromising, but they are true. I wanted to compromise, to make things easier, more human-like, and in an attempt to do that, I made things even more complicated.

"Now, in this silent moment, this now, when time is standing still, I am with him, and there is nothing else that I need. Everything is here: the past is gone; the future is unborn, but blessed because of this pure moment, where I am pure in heart and see God. Christ, I beg you, let your kingdom dawn in me, and let me be able to remember myself, because I cannot do it alone, but you can do it through me and in me. He can do it in all of you as well."

JC sat down on a rock and was silent for a little while. There wasn't a sound from the crowd. Everybody was simply waiting for what would come next. JC continued:

"Humanity is destroying nature through exploitation. The other day, when I walked in the forest I listened to the trees and they were sighing heavily under the burden of man. But don't lose hope. God is standing there outside your door.

"There are many upheavals to come in the next 30 years and the world order will change radically; economies will collapse from time to time and ignorance will try to conquer the world. But don't lose hope. He is standing there outside your door.

"And each time you fall and lose sight of your aim, don't lose hope. He is standing there outside your door.

"And therefore he also says: For man it is not possible, but for God everything is possible. Go out of the door, out of your old room and meet him. Go into the silence of your heart, close your eyes and do not think of anything. Just be and he will be there with you.

The Kingdom of God is as if someone would scatter seed on the ground, and would sleep and rise night and day, and the seed would sprout and grow, and he does not know how.

"But it will grow. You have to take the first step. Recognize your longing and open up to your seed. And the Lord himself will take the last step. AMEN."

I interrupted Peter here. The sermon was excellent and I suddenly remembered having heard about the midsummer party and the sermon through newspapers. I told Peter that I'd read some of the articles from that time. One paper wrote about a new prophet who was gathering hundreds of people around him, and printed the whole sermon the following day. (I am now using this article, which I had saved, to recall the wording: Peter was actually remembering the whole sermon, almost word for word.)

Others were indignant and said that this man was dangerous, manipulating young people and using them for his own purposes. He was even employing foreigners, who did not have permits to stay in the country, and they exhorted the authorities to do something about the sect, as they called it.

I recall a Christian newspaper which said that this JC was Christ – in other words, Christ had finally come back. It reported several cases of healing that this master had performed, but some priests and even a bishop of the Swedish church were reluctant to accept the message contained in the sermon. They claimed that this person was working against the church and trying to gather a group of people around him, separating them from the church, by teaching a new gospel which was at variance with the true canonized gospel in the bible.

I didn't take the various statements too seriously, since I am a critical person, but now I find it very interesting. At that time I did not have the slightest thought of one day meeting someone who had actually been with this teacher. It was amazing!

Peter simply smiled.

Chapter Nineteen:

HAPPINESS

I

The 10-year period from 1978 to 1987 was the happiest in my life. I know many of us underwent a growth that was slowly healing all the wounds that life had given us. I personally enjoyed the company of John, Maria and Carl. John and I spent many hours together, and our friendship became so deep that I don't have words for it. Normally friendship deepens when you have a common "history" like a large "memory bank" that you often draw from. For us it was different. We became mighty companions since we shared a common purpose: a deep desire to awaken. And this deep relation we shared with many others, even those we "mechanically" disliked.

My friendship with Carl also deepened, as with Maria, whom I met often. There were the evenings when we played the guitar together and sang. To me, she was still the most precious woman and sometimes when sitting with her, I was so happy and unconcerned about everything. I am sure she felt affection for me and that she loved being with me as well.

Sometimes when we finished a song she would laugh, and her eyes would sparkle with joy; and when we had tried to sing in harmony and it went horribly wrong, she would laugh even more, not minding the mistakes at all. She simply loved the fact that we were both trying to accomplish something together that could be extremely difficult, but nevertheless was worth the effort of trying – the important point was the joint effort, not being perfect. She was not getting any younger, of course, and neither was I, but still she remained young in my eyes, and as she matured into her forties and beyond I think she became more beautiful and my love for her became a cornerstone of my life.

That year of 1987, Christmas was celebrated in the different centres without the usual large gathering. On St Stephen's Day, JC and Carl left for an important meeting. I don't know what the purpose of that meeting was, but JC asked me to look after Maria. I did not really understand why he had asked me, as I knew Maria was perfectly capable of looking after herself. JC and Carl left on Friday afternoon, and shortly after my return from the joinery, Maria came and knocked at my door.

"I would like to talk to you tonight," she said, smiling.

I agreed that I would come straight away and we walked to the house together, hand in hand. There were none of the usual formalities when we met; we knew that we loved each other and were happy together. She served me a glass of sherry, which I found a little posh.

We sat in the living room, I in the deep armchair and she on the sofa. This evening she was wearing a blue dress, not her usual red, which looked so natural on her.

We looked at each other and shared a smile which soon turned to hearty laughter. Then she said, "I have something I want to talk about that bothers me a bit. It is about my brother, Hans."

This did not surprise me, because she was often worried about him and he was often included in our talks.

"Tell me what's worrying you," I said.

She came straight to the point, without any unnecessary explanations, in a way most women seldom do.

"Hans came to me and asked me if I knew why so few people are developing into higher beings, becoming enlightened or conscious? I replied that I did not know, not wanting to discuss such intellectual matters, or argue about right or wrong ideas. Then he said that it is because of the interval. No one can bridge the interval by himself but needs a person who has already done it, a Christ, who is interceding for us in heaven, or a JC. He looked at me as if he had found this out all by himself. Then I asked him what he wanted to tell me. He replied that JC is bridging the interval for all of us, making a new society. Had I not heard the 'sermon on the mount' at the midsummer party? I told him that I did not agree with him, but he said that it would not happen straight away. First the Farm had to change, then the town down the road and then, little by little the movement would spread out across the whole country. Then he shouted at me that JC was going to make a difference, and why didn't I see that?"

Maria shook her head.

"Dear Peter, he is insane. He does not understand, and when I said to him that JC was not going to make a kingdom of this world, he just laughed. He said that JC had told him about the kingdom, and when I asked him to tell me what he had said, Hans continued to talk about the interval. I think he has taken this idea very seriously and, at the same time, given it an interpretation which has no foundation in anything we have learned from JC. I said to him that when JC spoke of the kingdom, it was a kingdom that was not of this world. It was a state that was created inside of us, but he went on to talk about the law of seven and the third force needed to bridge the gap and then, suddenly, he said with great force that I was right – the kingdom is not of this world; it is a new world, a new world order. Didn't I understand? Christ did the same, but after some hundred years it was destroyed by ignorant people, but this time we have a new Christ, and this time it has to work."

She had an expression signifying that she had heard something absurd and ridiculous. Something unbelievable. I moved over to the sofa and put my arm around her.

"I know Hans is confused, but I have seen a good and human side of him as well," I said. "He is a wounded child; he is damaged from what he's gone through, but we must help him."

"Do you know how? He is still in love with me; he has asked me to go with him and leave the teacher. I said to him, if he needed the teacher for his plan, then he could not leave; to which he answered that of course we were not going to leave JC, but that I should live with him and then both of us would join the teacher in the new age to come."

I asked Maria if she had told JC about this.

"Yes, I have. He said I should leave Hans alone and that he would take care of the matter."

"Then everything is all right," I said. "You don't have to worry. JC knows what he's doing."

"I suppose you are right. But I grew up with Hans and feel a certain amount of love for him, so it makes me sad to see his confusion."

"I think we are approaching difficult times. We will have to stand together and have trust. I believe that whatever happens, it is meant to be, but you know that I am with you all the way, if you are in need of help."

She nodded. I kissed her cheeks and caressed her head. She smiled a vague, rather insecure smile, like a child who is unhappy and needs comforting, as if something was threatening our total existence. Then we started kissing passionately, almost violently, holding each other tight. I started to open her dress and felt my hands moving over her naked shoulders and her back. We looked at each other and then I lifted her up and carried her into her room, where we made love on her bed. It was such a relief, and not until now did I understand how my physical longing for her had been unconsciously suppressed all these years.

I got up and lit a candle on her table. Then we lay on our backs, naked, holding hands and looking up into the ceiling. I think we were both aware that it was more than twenty years since she had made love to me the first time. I am sure we each had many questions, but we silently agreed not to start talking now. This moment was holy.

"Everything is going to be all right," I whispered.

I repeated it many times throughout the night, and I truly believed and trusted in what I was saying.

Chapter Twenty:
THE BOAT

Summer 1988

I

We made it through another winter. It was 1988 and I was 41 years old. Maria sometimes slept in my room in the main house, and of course our relationship changed, but it did not develop possessiveness, a clinging to each other, because we had no expectations of each other and no plans for a common, shared future. We took each day as a blessing. She was often away with JC on his travels and every day, I went to work in the joinery with the other students. She told me once that when she met JC, she felt that she wanted to dedicate her life to him and his work. She took care of the house for him, as well as acting as his personal assistant. She arranged the practical side of his journeys, such as booking tickets and sometimes arranging hotels, plus taking care of his correspondence.

But we still met as before, playing chess, singing, laughing and talking. We both felt that events were coming and that we would have to deal with them, which would require all our strength. We were right – from that summer onwards, things moved very fast in unexpected directions. What took place, I could only describe as a disaster. Once I asked JC what he thought. He said:

"Do not ever resist evil. I don't mean that you should agree with it or support it; of course not. But never resist or fight against it, for in doing so, you will simply make it stronger. What we can do is to use it for growth. When we meet evil in the right way, we create a power – a tremendous energy that no one has ever seen before."

One day in late May, JC told me that he was sending some of us to Halden in Norway. One of the Norwegian students,

Fredrik, had bought a fishing boat in Bergen and had taken it down to Halden. It needed repairing, mainly the interior, and I was to lead the work.

We were to go to Halden in June, after the annual midsummer party, but there was a fly in the ointment: Hans was to go with us. I had mixed feelings about him, which were now even stronger after the conversation with Maria. I really wished he could heal the wounds of his traumatic past, but I could not help but be worried, as now I did not trust him. A feeling of dislike entered my mind, but I had repeatedly been told that likes or dislikes are all the same – just absence of love. So this journey was a test, or rather an opportunity to learn to love someone that I disliked.

I had to accept the assignment. JC then told me that the group going to Norway included Richard, Gerhard, Rainer and Jens – Jens being a new student who surprised everyone by progressing extremely quickly in understanding and growth. In Norway, we would meet up with Fredrik and stay in his house, and finally James and Phillip would be around and would help out as best as they could.

Midsummer was celebrated in the usual way; this year it rained all through the weekend, which could have dampened everyone's spirits were it not for the discipline of the students. Good or bad weather was not a cause for negativity; to change the weather was a far aim, as JC jestingly had put it!

On Tuesday morning we set off, arriving in Halden that evening. Jude was driving, sometimes a bit fast for my taste, although admittedly he was a good driver. We travelled in the minibus, so there was space for tools and personal belongings.

Fredrik lived in a big house with several rooms. I volunteered to share a room with Richard, out of consideration for him. Over the past year, I had observed him and had come to the conclusion that he was frail and vulnerable, so I made up my mind to be as supportive as possible. What had struck me most with regard to Richard was the monthly – sometimes weekly – presence of his mother. I suppose Richard was about my age at that time, perhaps a little younger, but why did the mother cling to him like that?

In the evening I talked with him a lot. He was a person with an extremely developed sensitivity. He told me of an experience he had had while walking on the pedestrianized street in Copenhagen, Stroeget. It runs all the way from the Central Square and City Hall to the area around the Royal Palace. I knew from my time in the city that the street is almost always full of people.

Richard remembered that he had not noticed the people walking in the same direction as he did, but those coming towards him had had a strong effect on him, since they gave the impression of being fast asleep, resembling puppets being drawn by a magnet or as the moon controls the tides. He felt that he was being pulled too, but in the opposite direction, and all these people were involuntarily flashing past him. This had made him realize that we are living in a dream, as he expressed it. He said that this was the point when he decided to seek the teacher.

"But how did you know about him?" I asked.

"My mother knew a school teacher who participated in a group: his name was George, and he was a member."

I suddenly felt a very unpleasant sensation and a strong urge to somehow protect Richard from Hans. I remembered what I had seen on that midsummer evening long ago – how Hans was arguing and shouting at Richard, which had somehow indicated that there was a connection between Hans, George and Richard. I wondered if it could have something to do with the letter George had written to Carl, but I did not know the purpose of George's letter.

Richard stopped for a moment, and then he said:

"Do you know him?"

"I did, vaguely, but he is dead by now."

"Well, my mother found the teacher, JC. I knew as soon as I had met the group and then JC that I had to follow him, and then I was accepted." He looked down, which he often did; he had some odd habits such as licking his lips, as if eating ice-cream, then he looked up again. He was a strange man – not quite what I would call a normal person.

But at that moment and on that particular evening, I was happy to share a room with Richard.

II

We worked hard for a couple of weeks. The weather was fabulous, with sunshine every day, which was exceptional for Oslo bay.

The galley on board was renovated and completely refurbished. In the dining room, which was rather small, more like an extension to the galley, we re-upholstered the seats with leather; and over the doorway we put a figurehead, in the old style. It was Richard who had the idea; he also designed and made it, as, much to everyone's surprise, he turned out to be a talented sculptor.

Hans mostly avoided us, even at mealtimes. On most days he left in the morning, without even going to the boat, and went into Oslo. He just said, "I have some business in the City." What his business was I do not know, but he seemed to take himself and his errands in Oslo very seriously.

James and Phillip worked with us. Phillip was the only one who had the nerve to climb the mast, and he assured us that the view from the top was breathtaking. I had always been afraid of heights, and I had no intention of imitating Phillip's "madness".

We behaved like boys at times, and since I was in charge and we needed to finish the boat and get back to the Farm, it was up to me to remind everyone why we were there.

With Hans it was different. I understood that he was with us in one sense, but not because of the boat – for some other reason. I tried talking to him sometimes in the evenings. We would stand outside looking at the starlit summer sky, and I told him what I knew about the stars, which he also appeared to be interested in.

Then, suddenly he would ask me questions about my personal life. I hesitated to tell him too much, mainly because I did not think it was worthwhile. After my time as a student, under JC's influence, it had become unnecessary to indulge in what "had" been, or the feelings or aspirations that had led me hither and thither. It was the now that was important.

Peter stopped for a while and said, "Of course I am telling you the details of my life not because I am still caught up with regrets or anything like that, but because it has been allotted to me to have my story recorded, as a witness, if you like. Please try to write it as if you have put yourself into my life and my situation, and describe how it was then, not now, because now all has changed."

As a matter of fact, it came as a surprise to me that it was my story, about his life, that was to be recorded.

At the time, I did not understand the changes to which he was referring. As I touched upon earlier, I felt he was relating events as if he had a distance from them, or as if he was talking about someone else. It was only much later, after he had recounted many astonishing events about which I had not the slightest inkling, that I understood.

He continued:

I, in my turn, questioned Hans. He was still a puzzle to me and aroused much speculation in my mind. Why did JC confide in him and entrust to him the complexity of the organization's economic affairs? And what about the ideas I had first heard when I was in York? I asked him bluntly: "How is your ambitious project going?"

He looked at me with an expression bordering on suspicion, which he was right to do. By now the ice was broken, and he knew that his answers or reactions might lead him further then he was willing to go. He asked, "What do you mean?"

I kept him on tenterhooks. I knew he would have to give me a straight answer and not be evasive.

"Oh, come on," I said. "You know very well what you told me about the revolution, about the meek sheep, the students; about the plans that JC would one day realize for overthrowing the existing order and then establishing a new one, or maybe even a kingdom, and about the interval."

He was alert now. "Have you been talking with Maria?"

"I have, and ..."

He looked up into the sky in such a way that it was clear he was preparing what he was going to say. When it came, I was shocked.

"You are a stupid idiot. I do not know who you will thank for that, maybe your parents or even the creator. Who cares? Don't you know that I have observed you, how you follow the teacher, gathering up every nugget of information, every so-called pearl of wisdom? Do you think that he cares one bit about your miserable life? He is just keeping you passive. He knows that you do not understand what, in reality, is going to happen. Why do you think he has given me authority over the all the finances of his school – or rather, let's call it the operation? Because he knows that I am capable, that I am made of the right stuff. He sees into the heart of all of us and he knows exactly what is going on in there."

He paused and then said in a loud voice, "Maria is absolutely none of your business!"

Clearly, for him, I had crossed the line into his private life, where I had no right to be.

I must admit that for a few seconds I was quite taken aback, but I regained my composure, and remembered something I had heard long ago: instead of going into attack or defence, simply give the person credit for what had been said. So I said:

"Very interesting. There is probably something valuable in what you say."

"I don't believe you," he sneered.

"Possibly, but nevertheless, I find it difficult to understand what it is you want. What are you trying to accomplish?"

He became a little calmer. "I told you all that long ago. It was my mistake, but I don't think you have betrayed me yet."

"I would never betray you," I replied. "By the way, to whom would I betray you or what is it that I could betray? I don't understand."

For a moment I think he believed me and trusted me. But then his suspicions returned.

"What about Maria?" he asked with a cunning smile on his face.

"Maria told me that you are still in love with her, and ..."

"And that's a fact," he interrupted. "And I also said that I do not blame JC for taking care of her; but I think that his plan has nothing to do with her. He will easily put his plan into action, no matter what."

Then he asked, "Why not betray me and say that the plan is unfolding secretly? You would be a hero."

I refused to accept his suggestion, and I explained to him where I stood in all this.

"With all I have learned from JC – despite what you think about me and my relationship with him – I can, without any doubt, say that he has taught me to trust him and not to judge or resist violence, but to forgive every person I meet. Therefore I would not instigate rebellions or trouble or betray him in any sense. And since he has given you the position you have, I am not the one to question that decision, and whatever it leads to has a purpose."

He was obviously relieved by my statement, but I think he could not read between the lines, because the word "purpose" has many meanings, and must always be seen in its context, and the level it is seen from. But I did not expound on this any further.

"You see," he said, "there are things that must be put right and I know that I have to do them with the help of JC. I don't know the end result, but I still have confidence in the teacher, so let us leave it at that."

I noticed the word *still* and tried to lodge it in my memory.

I stretched out my hand and he took it.

III

After we had finished the work on the boat, Fredrik wanted to take us out on a trip through the Oslo fjord into the archipelago. James and Phillip stayed behind, having other things to do.

We set out in the morning and after coming round the South Coast, we reached an area with many small islands and we anchored near one of them. We used the rowing boat to reach the island, due to the shallow water.

Gerhard and Rainer had prepared lunch for us and we really enjoyed ourselves, relaxing after all the hard work on the boat. It seemed that everyone was in a very good mood; we talked and joked, and walked round the island looking at the fauna and flora. There was a rich bird life and we even saw a rabbit. We laughed for a long time while trying to work out how the little fellow had made it to an island in the sea, and came to the conclusion that apparently he could swim!

Jens, the new student, told funny stories, of which he had a large supply; some of them were so funny that tears ran down my cheeks. Then Gerhard, using the rowing boat, fetched the stilts he had made. They were very high, with two different levels, so you could start on the lower level, then when you were proficient you moved to the higher level. It was not as difficult as I had imagined, and walking up there, high in the air, you had the feeling of being a child again, playing and enjoying life, using the simple things at hand. Even Jude tried the stilts, but he never managed level two.

Later we went swimming. The sea was warm and everyone except Richard swam and splashed around in the water. I asked him to join us, but he said he could not swim and he just paddled around at the edge of the water.

Afterwards we lay naked on the hot boulders, enjoying life fully. Gerhard had brought his guitar and after dinner, we sat around a bonfire, singing well-known songs. Richard sang with all his might, although a bit out of tune, and even danced, whirling around until he fell flat on the ground.

It was getting dark and the sunny weather came to an end; the sky became cloudy. We rowed back to the ship and sailed further out. When night fell, I was standing with Fredrik on the Captain's Bridge and he showed me the secret of navigating at night. On the coast there were red and green lights and when we approached a light it would change from red to green, or vice versa; at that point it was time to change direction. These lights were marked on the nautical charts, and the information from the lights helped ships and boats to avoid shallow waters and plot the right course. Fredrik's plan was to get back to Halden in the morning.

Later that evening we anchored up, and went to sleep in bunks in our cabins. What a wonderful day it had been!

IV

In the middle of the night, I woke up on hearing a scream. I scrambled out of bed, and rushed up on deck to find the gate to the gangway wide open. Screams were coming from the water and I realized it was Richard, who must have fallen into the sea through the open gate. I looked round for a life buoy and glimpsed someone disappearing round the bow of the ship, going towards the starboard side. At the time I did not think about or act upon it, only registering it in my subconscious. Fredrik and Gerhard came up from below, still in their pyjamas. Fredrik quickly found the buoy, fastened it firmly and threw the ring down to Richard. Now no screams were heard.

Gerhard stood as if petrified for a second, and then, without warning, he threw himself out through the open door and into the water. I heard the splash, but it was difficult to see anything in the dark. By now, Rainer and Jens had arrived. We all looked down into the water, trying to make out what was going on. Then Gerhard shouted that he could not find Richard.

"He's gone! He's gone!"

We started pulling Gerhard up, and in the middle of our efforts a fully dressed Hans appeared.

When Gerhard was back on deck, Fredrik ran up to the captain's bridge and called for help over the radio. Gerhard was shaking all over, and went down to get dried and dressed. We all looked at each other. No one said a word, until Hans asked, "What happened?"

The waiting was horrible. It seemed most likely that Richard had drowned. There was nothing we could do for now – just wait and think and imagine. The coastguard arrived about half an hour later and started searching the area around the ship. The light from the lanterns swayed over the surface of the relatively calm sea, but nothing was seen. The police arrived later and came on board. We were all questioned and felt as if we were under suspicion.

Finally, the ship was escorted back to Halden and we were all asked to come to the police station. It was morning now, but we were not aware of our tiredness.

Richard's body was recovered some hours later.

When we arrived at the police station, we were interrogated one by one. It was probably the open gate that gave rise to the suspicions. Why would anyone leave it open? It was out of the question that Richard had dived into the water in order to swim in the middle of the night. This idea was so absurd that it could be discarded straight away, as he could not swim.

I only know what I told the police. They asked me where I had been at the time; I told them that I had been in bed asleep, had heard someone shouting for help and had rushed upstairs straight away.

They tried to reconstruct the incident from beginning to end, and it was suggested that Richard could have committed suicide, since the gate had been found open. They had examined it, and it was in such good repair that it could only have been opened deliberately, and not by the wind. What was my view on the matter, they asked. I answered that I could not think of any reason why Richard would take his own life. To me, he had seemed happy and in good spirits the evening before.

They went on asking questions about him and I gave them all the information I could think of, but I suddenly remembered that I had seen someone vaguely, when I first came on deck. Now I felt sure that it was not imagination. Had someone been with Richard and possibly pushed him? Or had he lost his balance while struggling with someone? But no, the gate had been open – something was wrong here. Then I remembered that Hans had been fully dressed when he came up on deck, which led me to the conclusion that there were only two possibilities: either Richard had taken his own life or he had been pushed into the water; the only person who could have pushed him was Hans. However, I kept my suspicion to myself.

It was afternoon before we were all allowed to return to Fredrik's house. James and Phillip were there, and we told them what had happened. Needless to say, we were all strongly affected by the incident.

The next morning, we returned to the boat in the harbour to fetch our things and then drive back to the Farm. Imagine our surprise at the sight that met us: the ship had sunk. Only the mast was visible above the water. It was only a few days later that I realized my grandfather's watch was on board.

V

On the way back in the car, we became painfully aware of the consequences of our boat trip. When we stopped at the first filling station on the Swedish side of the border, the newspaper placards told us the story we knew so well: "Young man drowned in the Oslo fjord. Police suspect crime!" The news was flashed all over the country, especially in the tabloid papers which excelled in dramatic stories.

It was as usual, in the words of Isaiah: *Blind yourself and be blind. Be drunk, but not from strong drink!* That means, enjoy the scandal and bathe in the misery of others; magnify the horror, drink the wine of horror and pain, and say to yourself: how terrible the world is. But we, the readers of the papers, are not like that; criminals, thieves and all the rest! No, we are good common people, a little special of course, but still, thank you Lord that we are not like all the others. And what about the poor young man who was pushed into the water and drowned? Horrible! They had probably had a party on the boat, been drinking heavily, maybe even taken drugs. You must be careful with these people; besides, they come from a sect and that explains everything. We have now located the centre of this sect, where people work for hours on end without pay. It is time the police and people in authority put an end to all this.

There was even a picture of Richard on the front page, and smaller pictures of us. I wondered from whom they had received their information, but it was all there. Sadly, we began to understand what we were returning to. The media was blind drunk on sensation and the urge to make people feel indignant. In their minds, they were doing their job as well as they possibly could.

A feeling of anger took over my whole body. When this had happened before, I was aware of how the feeling started, but being aware also allowed me a choice to draw back and control the feeling. The choice was surprisingly easy to make: almost like choosing between apples and pears.

I observed Hans while he was driving. He displayed no emotion, and from what I could tell, he was a very good actor, or totally innocent, or incapable of showing his feelings.

The police were able to identify Richard from the papers he carried, so we did not have to identify him. They had already informed his mother. We felt bad about leaving him behind, but we knew that the undertakers would take care of all the formalities. It was a weird drive home, digesting everything that had happened; we felt we were fleeing from the situation and anyway, at the time, we could not make sense of it. We stopped several times on the long journey and all the way, we were met with the same message. I almost started feeling guilty, even suggesting to myself that I had killed him. However, I quickly ejected these thoughts from my mind.

I think Gerhard, Rainer and Jens had similar feelings. They did not speak much because they had also seen the placards and knew what was awaiting us.

When we pulled up in the parking space at the Farm, the main house was surrounded by reporters and photographers. Mona was trying to calm them down by answering their questions, which was difficult for her, as she was not really aware of what had happened. Her common sense told her that, in their somewhat insane world, the press were not interested in the truth, only a good story.

As soon as we got out of the van, the reporters ran towards us, almost trampling over each other. The cameras were in position and now it was my turn to be grilled by them. I saw that Gerhard had succeeded in escaping into the main house, whereas Jens and Rainer were trapped and for once, looked like silent sheep.

I saw Hans talking to some reporters, leisurely leaning against the car, answering questions. He looked as if he was enjoying all the fuss, which at that moment bothered me greatly.

I was asked about the accident and the reporters insinuated directly that the victim had been pushed. I was inwardly repeating my mantra to myself: Remember yourself. Remember yourself. Try not to become upset and get involved in this circus. Stay calm. And then I felt the presence of JC. It was the same state that I had experienced so many times before; the sound receded and I saw everything in a beautiful light, felt deeply present and full of joy.

The anger that had been simmering under the surface all day disappeared, like the mist over a meadow on a summer's morning evaporating through the power of the rising sun. I no longer needed to defend myself, as I knew that the play had been written, the actors were in place; the reporters, photographers, etc. were all fulfilling their allotted roles. They could play their roles differently, but I realized that how they played them would not affect me. I was free of anger, I just stood there with them indirectly accusing me, but I forgave them; I blamed no one; I was just concerned and serious.

I said that none of us knew what had happened.

"But you were there, weren't you?"

"Yes, but it happened while we were all asleep."

"But could it be that ..."

"Stop it," I said in a very calm voice.

I was almost surprised to hear the calmness in my voice, but I knew that JC had said that such a situation could be used for growth, if it was handled in the right way. I felt all the worries of this world leave me, and just observed the reporters dispassionately, who in their state of ignorance felt the urge to find as many faults as possible in the unfolding drama. I heard a whisper inside me saying that I was not a part of it anymore, and I would not allow it to become part of my being.

"I am not going to say anything more," I said. "We believe that the police will make a statement, so you will have to wait for that."

"But how could the victim fall over the railing and ..."

"I am not commenting anymore."

Still they would not give way. I then asked them, "Why are you asking all these questions?"

They had their answer ready, and most certainly they had said this a thousand times.

"It is in the public interest. People want to know what happened, and we are determined to tell them."

"Even if you know nothing?" I asked.

"But that's why we are asking you."

Then I had an idea as to how to finish the interrogation, and said, "Will you quote exactly what I say?"

"Of course."

"All right." Then I looked at them and said: "I know nothing. Write that."

They looked bemused and bewildered, and I knew I had confounded them completely. I was growing beyond the concerns of the world. My eyes were being opened; I could stand and not be taken over by the tragic event and dealing with the consequences. The words of Isaiah came back to me: the vision of all this, of the matters of this world, has become to you like the words of a sealed scroll. I was beginning to open it and read the words.

I turned around and went into the house. Mona was back inside and was shaking her head, clearly nearly ready to give up. I went over to her, made her sit down, then I put my arm around her and she leaned her head on my shoulder. She had been in the firing line the entire afternoon.

The newspaper people did not leave directly; they lingered for an hour or so.

I asked about JC. Mona said he had left last night with Maria, but she did not know where they had gone. The prophet was at home, but he did not go out to meet the reporters.

After a while, Rainer and Jens came into the house, but Hans left in his car.

Chapter Twenty-One:

THE TAX AUTHORITIES

Autumn 1988

I

Later that day, I went up to see the prophet. I told him everything I knew about the incident on the boat, and he listened attentively. "What do you make of it all?" I asked. "Richard appeared to be different in many ways, and Hans puzzles me. What has been going on between him and Richard?"

Carl shook his head and seemed bothered talking about Hans and any problems arising because of him. He said:

"I can tell you what I know. I once visited George, John's father, who arranged a party for the parents and students from the school where he was teaching. It was during the summer and we all enjoyed ourselves, including Maria and Hans, who loved meeting the students from the school. One of the parents was a widow with a young daughter, Claire, who attended George's school. Hans took Claire for a long walk during the party, and afterwards her mother was very cross with me and made terrible accusations against Hans. I talked to him and asked him if anything had happened; he swore to God that nothing had happened and so the whole incident was forgotten; and although Claire's mother kept returning to what Hans had done to her daughter, no further action was taken. Claire left the country to study in the States, so nobody ever talked about the incident after that.

"But when you brought me the letter from George, after his death, I started to wonder if Hans had told me the truth. However, it is now such a long time ago and nobody really knows what took place. I told JC about the letter and he just said that he knew and that we should go no further with the matter. But I was surprised when Richard became a student, and also to see his mother around so much. You see, Richard was Claire's younger brother and their mother seems to have been rather protective of her son. He was, as you say, different; as if he was living in another world and not really aware of what was going on around him. But from what you told me earlier – about the incident at midsummer – a question arises in me: What was Richard supposed to know, and why did that seem to bother Hans?"

Carl paused for a long time, apologized for talking about Richard and, as he had often done when we met in his shop in days gone by, he suddenly looked down, his mind filled with memories, most of which seemed sad. Then he lifted his head and came back to the conversation.

"I've already told you that Hans became a student earlier, but I have many regrets about my decision to introduce him, although JC accepted him, and to this day still seems to do so. Now here we are confronted with problems of all kinds, and I am not sure what to do. Do you think that Hans ..."

I interrupted him.

"I think we should do nothing. What has been set in motion will definitely bring more reaction, but we cannot stop it. It would be like trying to block the flow of a river. Sooner or later, the water would rise high enough to break through and with such tremendous force that much greater damage would be caused than if we had done nothing."

Carl looked at me with surprise.

"Now you are teaching me," he said. "That is good.

But there is something else," he continued.

"A few days ago we received a letter, addressed to the board of the organization, from the tax authorities. They have called a meeting with the board and all four of us – JC, Maria, Hans and I – have to be present. The problem is that they do not accept the accounts that Hans has presented, though they were sent in before the first of May as requested, and they have a lot of questions. Hans has claimed that he has paid wages to a number of students and that he has paid income tax on their behalf, but not payroll tax. Furthermore, they are questioning a number of transactions, some of them connected to accounts belonging to Hans. The meeting is called for the 25th of July here at the Farm, so we will see what happens."

I was surprised by this. I told Carl that while we were in Norway, Hans had been away, presumably in Oslo, but no-one knew what he had been doing.

Carl thought a little and then said:

"My theory is that Hans has lost a large sum of money by investing in areas with too high a risk and then, in order to hide the losses, he came up with the crazy idea of pretending to have used the money for wages. No one has been paid for the work they have done here, that's a fact. Then he has, no doubt, been working furiously to raise the amount lost before anyone could find out what he had been doing, but unfortunately for him, the tax people have come asking their questions a little too soon. I do not understand the transfers to his own accounts, because if he had access to reserve capital somewhere, why didn't he just transfer the losses from those accounts? But maybe he needed the money for further investments, hoping for a gain in order to repair the income-tax form unnoticed. That is my theory.

"Now we have to wait and see what comes out of the meeting with the tax officers and, as you suggest, let us see what JC will do when he gets back."

But events did not wait for JC's return. During the next few days, some of the farmers who leased land to us came wanting to cancel their leases. Soon half of the land we rented was gone, and there was no doubt that this was due to the incident on the boat, and not to the financial situation.

When I went down to the shop on the main road, I met Hans. He said that people in the little town were turning their backs on us, and there had only been a few customers.

John came in from the room behind. He confirmed what Hans had said, but there was not much we could do about it.

When Hans left a little later in his car, I told John about the incident on the boat, and that I had become surer that I saw someone disappearing to the starboard side of the ship at the moment when I came on deck. I suspected it was Hans. John became upset and suggested that we go to the police and tell them. I explained to him why we should not do that, and that furthermore, I thought it would be wrong not to wait for JC's decision on the matter. John was always a person who burned for justice; this had not changed since High School. That is why he could not forgive our teachers there, and even though I had agreed with him then, I had now changed my attitude to justice. I reminded him of the lovely blindfolded goddess of justice with the scales in her hand. What kind of justice could one expect from such a goddess?

I also told him about the tax form. He shook his head. "Why didn't you say anything about that while Hans was here? You could have asked him what it was all about."

I said I had deliberately decided not to take up the matter, hoping that Hans would find a way out of the mess and put things right.

I drove to the joinery and talked with the students there. I didn't mention anything about the problems, but they did not seem to have escaped their fair share. The Russian, Ivan, came to me: he was seriously worried. He said the police had been there and had asked to see his stay permit: as he didn't have it, they asked him to show it as soon as it arrived, at the police station in the city. I said that of course the permit had been applied for, but since he was not officially employed by us, he was just a friend living with us. The permit would turn up. It was a matter of time and we could tell the police to check with the immigration office instead of acting on their own. I promised him that I would settle the matter.

I then spoke to two Africans from Ethiopia, Salim and Ali. They confirmed that the police had been there, but they both had their stay permits and were simply a bit confused by all the newspaper articles and the gossip doing the rounds locally. I calmed them down as best I could.

On the way back to the Farm, I had to stop while a farmer let his cows cross the road.

When all the animals had passed, the farmer, who was walking behind the herd with his stick, stopped and addressed me. I opened the window of the car.

"I take it that you are one of those hippies from the sect over there. What is going on with you people? Killing innocent young boys."

"I am not a hippie," I stated calmly. "And it is not a sect over there, it is a school. And the people there are learning things that are very important."

"Come off it, you bastard. I read the papers, and don't think I don't hear what people are saying. You have a number of illegal immigrants and are hiding them from the police, and what about all the unpaid work you ask people to do? Surely the lot of you are brainwashed."

There was no point in starting an argument or even trying to explain things to this good man, so I just said, "Your cows are running away from you."

He looked up and saw that some of the cows had wandered away from the others and were on their way down the road. He started running after them, shouting and cursing, and when I had passed them, I looked back and could see that he had all the cows in the correct field. He was standing there closing the gate, and lifted his stick in a threatening manner. I won't try to guess or repeat what he said.

II

On my way back to the Farm, I felt good. Previously, with so much appalling information and news I would have been worried sick, searching for solutions and becoming angry, but it seemed that I had no fuel inside me for anger. I felt free, with a lightness that gave me a sense of flying home, and I really felt I was at peace and unburdened.

When I entered the main house, Mona stood in front of me. She was not flying, but seemed weighed down by iron chains.

"Richard's mother was here. She has just left. She wanted to talk to JC, but as you know, he is not here at the moment. She said she would go to the police. She was throwing out one accusation after the other about the death of her son, about the Foundation, illegal workers, and lack of policies regarding Health and Safety, and so on and so on. She said that we were not going to get away with this."

"We are in deep trouble," Mona finally stammered.

I was still flying, so all I could say was:

"Take it easy and don't let it get you down. There is nothing more we can do than to answer the questions as best we can and then see what happens. By the way, it will be a long time, possibly next spring, before all these investigations are over and then we shall see if they press charges against us."

"I wish JC was here," she said.

"So do I, but he isn't. Have you talked to Carl about it?"

She had not.

"Do, and then let us wait."

"But what about the death of Richard?"

"It is very sad; it was such a shock for all of us, but as things now stand, I think we must go on. There is nothing we can do. There is very little evidence. They cannot accuse anyone of murder, and if the forensic department want to go through the ship for evidence, they will find themselves in a very difficult situation. Perhaps I did not mention it, and possibly the others in their confusion did not either, but the ship is lying at the bottom of the harbour in Halden."

That calmed her a little. I went to my room and sat down. I started thinking about Richard, and worry started in my stomach and insisted on moving up to my chest and then to my head. Then I remembered to let it go, by keeping focused on what I knew: the worry is not part of my true self, but it still tries to lure me into misery. I am not to worry, I am free. I am the son of God, as everyone is. Let the worry and fear come and do not resist it; just let it run its course and transform itself.

This created a kind of friction inside me, but as I kept my intention on letting it be, it gave rise to a strong heat that spread all over my body. My house was built on rock and after some time, it gave way to a liberating feeling of joy. This was the whole secret of the teaching. I knew that now, and in a way it was unbelievable that there had to be an accident with accusations and mistrust all around before I could come into this state and to this understanding.

I remembered St Francis of Assisi. In one of the many stories that others told about him, Francis is sitting with one of the monks, Leone, and he asks him: "Wherein consists the greatest happiness?" Leone suggests various options: the whole Muslim world converts to Christianity; or all the kings in Italy serve the holy church and donate their wealth to it; or the emperors in Germany and France repent all wrongdoing and promote the faith in their subjects. To all these suggestions St Francis says: "No, that is not the greatest happiness, but I will tell you of what it consists; I am on my way home from my neighbouring parish in Italy, Perugia and it is winter. I am not dressed for the cold and when the rain changes to frost, the water on my cloak freezes and the icicles hurt me when I walk. My legs start bleeding, so when I come into a village I knock on the first door and ask if I can stay there overnight. The answer is no. So I go on to other houses and ask the same question and receive the same response, which is: 'We do not want you here. Go to the leper's place and leave us alone.' I am tired and hungry at this point, but if I am able to keep my composure and not blame, or complain or feel angry, but rest inside myself in humility, then inside me, in my heart, I will feel the presence of the kingdom of God. That is the greatest happiness."

III

Early on the morning of 25 July, I drove to the joinery. I told the students there to take the day off. I suggested a swim in the river; after all, it was summer. They liked the suggestion.

The other workshops also closed for the day, and John closed the shop. He went back with me and we sat in my room, at the window facing JC's house.

At 11 o'clock, two officials arrived. They were impeccably dressed and carried large briefcases. Carl, JC and Maria were there. Hans arrived some minutes later.

For a long time, John and I just looked at the bungalow, as if we were watching a movie. Then he said, "The foundation is facing a dire situation. Maybe the whole foundation will implode and we'll be back to square one."

"I don't think it will go that far," I replied. "I think we will get out of this with a capacity that we could never have imagined. We will be teachers for the rest of the world."

He liked that idea, but merely as a metaphor. When he was about to leave, he asked, "Do you want to come with me?"

"No, I'll wait here until the meeting is over, because I want to talk to Carl," I said.

I sat there for some time, waiting for the meeting to end, which was not until 3 o'clock, when the officials came out carrying their briefcases. They walked straight to the car and drove off.

I went outside and started walking towards JC's house. Hans came out and walked straight past me without so much as a glance, looking stressed and worried. Carl came out of the house, as if he was expecting me.

"Come on in," he said, and we went to his room.

I was somewhat impatient to know about the outcome of the negotiations with the tax inspectors, and Carl did not keep me waiting long. He told me briefly everything there was to know. Hans had tried to explain the accounts and answer questions from the officers, but he had not been very successful.

The accounts of the foundation were not being accepted, and Hans had been told to submit a completely new set of accounts within two months. This relatively long time was due to the number of receipts and bank statements he would have to go through.

"What did JC say to everything?" I asked.

"He said nothing during the meeting, but as soon as the officials left, he severely reminded Hans that he had misused his trust and that he had better come up with some explanation. Hans left at this point and, as we all know, he now finds himself between the devil and the deep blue sea. Unfortunately, he can cause many more problems if he abrogates his responsibilities by blaming someone else, or by simply refusing to do the work, because it may not be possible to produce a sound set of accounts. As I see it, he might have to stand trial, if he is charged with fraud."

We had just finished our little talk when JC came out of his apartment. He was not the least troubled, but looked as if he had just come back from a holiday.

He turned to me and said, "The time has come. We are now going into the wilderness. We will leave in a month's time. Try to prepare yourself."

I noticed Carl smiling. He knew about this.

"Do not take many things with you, we will only be staying for three months or so and we will live a very simple life. I mean do not bring books or lots of clothes, only bring a toothbrush and other really useful things in your case."

He made no mention of where we were going, and I was not completely sure of the purpose of this journey. Three months, I repeated in my head. And he had said: "only three months". He had once told me something about a certain time that would come, when one would have to go away from normal life, in order to clean out all the rubbish from one's mind, as he put it. He had used the metaphor of cracking the nutshell when the nut was ripe; destroying personality, in other words, to disclose the essence – the kernel. Maybe that was what he meant, and in that case I found it exciting. After my latest experiences, I was ready to take a decisive step forward.

"All right," I said. "I'll be ready."

"Good. Maria here will help Mona to take care of whatever matters come up to do with the foundation."

Maria said, "We will take care of everything."

Chapter Twenty-Two:

THE WILDERNESS

October–December 1988

I

It puzzled me that JC had arranged our trip a whole month in advance. Usually he informed us about changes or travels just a day or two before, but it seems that even this had a meaning.

In the beginning, I was looking forward to the journey; I was excited and I imagined how it would be. Then I realized that I had also started to worry about the journey, as I did not know what was expected from me and I didn't even know where we were going. JC had told me to prepare myself; I could not understand why I should prepare anything, if I only had to pack a toothbrush and a few other necessities, which really did not require much preparation.

After a while, it became clear that JC's intention was to teach me to take one day at a time. Apparently, the task for the journey implied a readiness for each moment and not trying to figure out what my next step would be. I had to go on the journey with complete trust, and leave my desire for control behind.

We left on 22 August 1988. It was a Monday. I remember the date because it was my brother Jim's 40th birthday. We had not met often over the past twelve years, and I certainly would have no opportunity of congratulating him on his birthday, but I sent him a prayer in my mind. As expected, Carl was coming with us.

We packed the car and left at 8 o'clock in the morning. We drove down to the A6 main road heading north and passing the bridge at Svinesund, we crossed into Norway and continued up over the mountains. It was a barren landscape, with only a few small bushes and crippled trees, just a few feet tall. We then descended through beautiful countryside until we arrived at the end of a small road, where we parked the car. James and Phillip had been waiting for us, and were ready to help us carry the luggage and provisions up the mountain. There were several bags and sacks of supplies – enough for the time we were to spend in the wilderness. I had not realized how much had been arranged in advance, but certainly James and Philip had been instructed to buy food for us.

Now we walked along a narrow trail for an hour or more. The last part of the trail ran along the side of a brook; the water tumbled down the side of the mountain with considerable force and as I listened to it, I noticed it had many voices like an orchestra, with many different notes and sounds of the different instruments.

At one point we crossed a ford on stepping stones; a little later we came out onto an open plain where the brook was resting, so to speak, on its way down the mountain. Here it had formed a lake, and beside it there was a log cabin.

James and Phillip, after drinking some water, set off for the walk back down to the car. There was very little conversation; I understood that JC had organized every detail of this trip. They said goodbye and wished me luck, and from the way they looked at me, I supposed they knew more than I did about the expedition.

We went into the cabin and put our luggage on the floor. There were four bedrooms (one of which was already occupied, because there was a bag on the bed), plus the kitchen and a small living room. The toilet was outside with a shower, which mainly used cold water.

To my great joy, I was given the room facing the lake. When we had settled into our rooms, JC asked me if I would like to go for a walk and look around a bit, while he and Carl preferred to lie down and rest a little before dinner.

I followed his advice and walked out into a land of dreams and fairy tales. The surroundings were simply breathtaking; the air was fresh and clean and I breathed it in with great pleasure. I walked around the lake and climbed up between rocks and stones. I reached the top of a peak and sat down to take in the wonderful view of the valley with the brook far below. This was real wilderness – no houses or people, just an amazing and profound silence, which reminded me of heavenly music.

I found a cave nearby. It was as large as a living room and there were rocks around the floor that could be used as chairs and tables. I decided, then and there, to make this a place of retreat for myself. Over the next few days I took up blankets, matches and candles to furnish it.

When the daylight started to fade, I turned back to the cabin and as I was coming in through the door, I smelt food. I realized I was hungry; the smell drew me into the kitchen, where someone was preparing the evening meal. When this someone turned around, I had the greatest surprise I have ever had. It was Krishna, from Bilga in India. He came straight over to me, put his arms around me and whispered:

"Welcome." He smelled of almond oil, curry and incense. "I am so pleased to see you. Dinner will be ready very soon."

Then he turned round and continued to prepare dinner. I must say, I was speechless.

After dinner, we gathered in the living room. JC spoke to me:

"I need to tell you about the purpose of our stay here because, as I said to you earlier, the time has come. You have prepared yourself so well over the past 6 months that now it is time to break through into awareness. For the first month, you are not allowed to speak – total silence is necessary. And when we are around you, we will not speak either, but when you are not around, we can speak to each other. The reason we are here is for your sake, not for ours. We are your helpers, your midwives if you like, and you do not have to do anything. We will prepare the food and do everything in the house, and if you want something to do, you can chop wood outside. That would be useful, as nights can be cold up here at the end of August.

"The aim of the silence is to learn to stop the continuous talking to yourself; this is necessary because you have to get rid of all the rubbish and nonsense you have in your mind.

Secondly: It is absolutely vital that you follow all my instructions to the letter. Do not question anything. Just follow them.

"Thirdly: There will be difficulties, but you must keep your focus all the time and not give way to imagination or negativity. I am going to be harsh with you at times; that is part of the whole training, but do try to stay focused at all times. Later, when you have accomplished this first state, there will be more and further instructions.

"I know that you have been looking forward to this moment all your life, without really knowing how it would come about, but your childhood angel, your seed and your longing and search for the truth is all now coming to its fulfilment. You are now going to be born again and your seed will become a grown-up plant, as long as you can agree to my instructions and my rules."

I took a deep breath. Of course I knew from books and from the talks we had had that this was a possibility at some stage. When I thought about the way I had handled the extreme difficulties we had met since the boat trip, I was simply thankful that I had been given this opportunity.

Krishna served some tea and we drank it in silence. Then everyone went to bed. I lay awake for some time. It struck me that just three months ago I would have asked a lot of questions, such as: How was it that Krishna was here? How are things in India? Did JC arrange for him to come? How did James and Phillip know about this place? Who does the cabin belong to?

But now I was silent, filled with music from the brook, clear as the air, full of trust in JC, confident that he knew exactly what he was doing. And then I fell asleep.

II

The next morning breakfast was prepared at seven o'clock. The daily routines were tough and I knew now, from all the time I spent in the school, that punctuality was one of the ways that JC organized activities: lunch at noon and dinner at 6 p.m. Then there would be tea or coffee around 10 in the evening.

In the beginning, it was very useful to follow the non-speaking exercise and not being able to make comments definitely had the desired effect, impeding the constant flow of inner talk. My mind became clearer and calmer and I enjoyed this, but after a few days, a restlessness set in. I had nothing to do all day long. I was not able to just sit around, meditate or engage in endless walks in the beautiful scenery, so during the second week, my mind was flooded with thoughts or, more precisely, with chat: words and more words, nonsensical repetition of words. It was as if there was a reservoir of words deep down in my being, coming from the core of the brain. I had the feeling that all these words came through a memory bank situated somewhere in the past. It was as if there was a volcano hidden deep under the surface from where the thoughts rose up like bubbles in a fizzy drink. There didn't seem to be any end to the multitude of things that insisted on being expressed.

Painfully, I realized that I was like a machine, an uncontrolled device that would go on for ever or for as long as there was fuel. It was a type of insanity.

JC noticed what was going on inside me. One evening he asked me to come and sit down.

"Listen," he said. "You are not supposed to stop the flow of thought. I thought you had already understood that."

I surely did. I had experienced it long ago under my training with JC, but for some unknown reason, it had almost become an obsession to get rid of the nonsense. But I was going further now: I was going to become a new man. This was my reasoning.

JC shook his head and raised his eyebrows, as if I was a completely hopeless case.

"Leave the thoughts. Let go of them. As soon as you identify with them, they become matter and then the thoughts take on the shape of reality and you are stuck with them. The good news still is that they are not real; they are nothing, only what you make of them. Let the many thoughts pass through you and let them go wherever they want to go, to some black hole in the galaxy, or to those who still want to have them. They do not belong to you or to anyone, except to those who cherish them and make them part of their own history. And if you need help, come to me. Something you can do right away is to work with your body, just in order to help divert the rubbish."

I followed his advice, and a lot of firewood was chopped and split over the next weeks, just as it had been at Krishna's place in Bilga. The wood store grew rapidly, and would last for several cold winters. It was strange that whenever I needed to silence my mind, I had to chop wood, which now seemed to be part of my fate.

Now I entered a blessed state of mind, with a pleasant feeling of having a well-used body as well, and I slept well at nights.

III

One morning I was, as had become my habit, chopping firewood. A bird or two were singing sporadically. JC came out of the house and walked slowly towards me and then, like a thunderstorm from a clear summer sky, he said:

"Who do you think you are?"

I was puzzled by this unexpected question, and before I could answer, he said, "I will tell you. You are nothing. You are absolutely nothing."

His voice was now calm and pleasant, as if he was telling me what a nice person I was, and how much he liked me. Then he raised his voice again and became much more direct.

"All that you think about yourself is imagination; it is something people have fed you with, praise or blame or whatever, and it is all stored in your imagination, where you have built up a person called Peter. This person does not exist. He is the reflection of all your perceptions and judgements about the world. It does not exist, except in your thoughts, so what remains is still the overwhelming concept of the useless little boy Peter, who wanted to be something in the eyes of others and pretended to know and to be what he neither understood nor was."

Then he posed a rhetorical question. "Do you know what the problem with you is?"

He did not wait for my answer.

"You are intoxicated with yourself, you want to have a good time, you want to be praised for all your inherited skills, and when someone, no matter who, questions you one little bit, you feel the need to defend yourself, you want to prove you are right. On top of all that, you become negative; you judge and withdraw into your imaginary safe cave of self-indulgence and do not want to be with anyone. Do you hear me? Then after a little while, you come back for the precious energy of the appraisal of others and so it continues, back and forth."

At this point he raised his voice, shouting at me, he was so angry. The energy of his words was like shock waves coming towards me.

"You are not what you think; and what you think you are is nothing. You are absolutely and irrevocably NOTHING. Deep inside you, there is something governing you: it is the fear of failure. Failure to be recognized and flattered, failure that someone will one day look through you and see that the game you are playing is pretence; it's false, it's all nothing."

Then he left me alone with my thoughts.

I was standing there with the axe in my hand. I dropped it and it fell to the ground with a thud. At first, I was totally speechless and amazed. I was in shock. Then anger started to roll through my mind like thunderbolt, but I also had, at that moment, the strength to remember. This was part of the plan. I had been told about this moment, but as with all theories you hear about, they turn out differently in reality. I felt split open, totally naked, but also aware of the meaning of this "attack", which is how it would have appeared to an onlooker.

I sat down in the grass. A new and unknown feeling started inside me. I had nothing to explain, nothing to prove, nothing to defend and no-one to blame. I was thrown back to point zero, to the beginning of my earthly existence; perhaps I was like a child of five or maybe six. There was a seed and a longing in me, but I had no idea how to deal with the world. Sensations from my surroundings came rushing towards me; they were no longer explained or interpreted by my mind; the world was completely new, not seen through the filter of knowledge or through the veil of personality.

Everything was new. It was like having landed in a foreign country without passport, money or travel instructions. It was as if there was no past, no friends, family, or events in my life; all were washed away and it even felt as if they had never occurred. There was nothing to cling to, nothing. Reality seeped into me, as if I was aware of it for the very first time in my life.

I felt an urge to walk out into the wilderness, to be alone. Tears were running down my cheeks as if a well inside had been opened. I finally realized that, for a large part of my life up to this point, my life had been an illusion, in which I had put my trust for so many years. Still, I had no regrets. It was very liberating. My state of mind oscillated between emptiness and a pure deep awareness of existence. I had very few thoughts in my mind, just perhaps a reminiscence of my personality, but now I needed to be constantly focused. I recalled JC's words about not letting anything undesirable enter my mind. I had to make up my mind about what I really wanted to be, which voice to listen to, and leave behind all the distractions.

I walked up into the mountains. I think I walked for a long time. It was around noon, as the sun was shining down from the clear blue sky above. I looked at everything around me in a new and wondrous light. I sat down near a little waterfall with the water splashing me, making me feel as if I was being caressed by a lover. There was a flower in front of me; on the leaf there was a drop of water and I looked at the drop as it slowly slid to the ground. It seemed to be a whole universe, reflecting the greenness of nature and the light of the sun, but inside it there was space – much more than one would expect from its tiny volume. It disappeared and was followed by another.

I went close to the stream, filled my hands with water and bathed my face several times. Then I lay down and looked up to the sky for what seemed an eternity.

When darkness fell, I found myself in my cave. I made a fire and sat there looking into the flames, remembering the eternal flame that thousands of people had shared with me before, as we were all one in this experience. I covered myself with the blankets I had left previously, and fell asleep. My dreams were devoid of the usual nonsense, with no strange or inexplicable scenes or actors. I was a plant that had been uprooted from a bad and unwanted place, full of thorns and thistles, and had been gently planted in good fertile soil. I had been born anew.

The next morning I was hungry. I had nothing to eat but did not want to go down to the house. The newness of life made me forget my hunger. The whole world was new, so I could no longer meet people that I had known from my past. Of course, JC, Carl and Krishna would not have a problem with my absence; they would realize that I wanted to be alone. My soul was, in one sense, barren, but not dead; there was so much that was germinating, so much that was a secret between God and me.

I stayed in the cave for some hours. Thoughts from the past tried to force their way into my consciousness, but I left them behind. I walked out of the cave. It was raining, a steady drizzle, and I had a sudden urge to take all my clothes off. I walked out into the soothing rain naked. It was exhilarating. I felt the water running slowly down my body and enjoyed every minute of it, though it was cold. At that moment, I remembered an incident from my early childhood. I was at my aunt's house and it was summer, perhaps the summer my brother was born, which means that I was only a year and a half. I remember that I had been running naked around the garden, which was a natural thing for a small boy to do, looking at the flowers and weeds.

I realized that memories were returning from my past and I became a little concerned. Was the past now going to intrude on my new being? Apparently everything I had previously experienced was still stored in the memory. Wherever that memory was to be found, the fact was, I had access to it.

Then I remembered JC's words. Be focused. The past will try to come back, but remember; you can decide now what you want to be.

Later that day, things became very difficult. It was as if the monsters of false personality occupied the landscape of my soul. First I tried to leave them alone and not give them energy, but little by little they became stronger; I was bewildered. My hunger made itself felt; I needed something to eat, but there was nothing. I sat down, meditated and tried to remember myself, but my difficulties continued. I knew that this was the ultimate phase, the last temptation.

It had stopped raining, so I stayed just outside the cave and concentrated on being in the present with no deviation into speculation or cravings of any kind, but by the time it was dark, I was in a state of depression. The darkness enveloped me and I could not see any light at the end of the tunnel. In this state of mind, I could not sleep, so I sat there the whole night confronting the demons that seem to materialize from all corners of the cave. I was not sure if I had created these surrealistic animals from the books I had read or what I had heard, but they appeared very real to me. They threatened me, invited me and tried to persuade me to follow them by promising fantastic benefits; power to rule over people, who would worship me and sacrifice themselves for me.

A creature in the shape of a serpent, or a bit like a dragon, rose up in front of me. Flames spat out of his mouth. He was furious, saying he would destroy me if I did not accept his offer.

I kept reminding myself that I should not give way to these threats and inducements; I delved into the depths of my mind to find a safe place, but utter darkness took over. I could not see any light, only emptiness. I started to pray and to call on Christ my Saviour. I had not done that often in my life, but it came to me instinctively. I think I travelled deep, deep down inside myself, hearing sounds of roaring beasts, insane laughter and ungodly phrases. I was to take part in something that every sane person would consider sacrilege. There were murders, rapes and indecent happenings and all the time, I was being invited to take part in the entertainments. I suffered and felt an exceedingly strong pain all over my body; I felt I was dying, but a picture of JC came into mind and I tried to be with him.

This went on all night long. Only in the early morning as daylight appeared did the temptations start to fade. I saw the daylight increasing, but inside I felt empty.

I walked outside the cave and looked at the life out there. It did not feel like life: it was as if death had taken over the whole world.

This state of mind persisted for some days. It was extremely painful, but I became more and more aware that some higher power was accompanying me and, in the end, it was the grace of God that kept me alive, nurtured me and increased my strength any time I was on the brink of giving up. One morning, when I woke up, I felt that I had conquered the demons. I was immersed in a blissful state; it was as if the good Lord himself was carrying me through stones and rocks, through death and hell, through human hatred and violence into the Garden of Eden, where I finally felt the deliverance from evil. Now I was safe.

I stayed in my cave for another couple of days. I walked around full of joy. I found some berries to eat and drank the water from the brook; now, I also knew what my task was to be and my destiny.

When I returned to the house, JC came to meet me. He embraced me and kept me in his arms for a long time. Then he looked at me and I think there were tears in his eyes.

"I suppose you must be hungry," he said finally. "Krishna has some food for you."

This time I did not wonder how Krishna knew that I would arrive at that moment; neither did I bother asking. I was tired, happy and extremely hungry.

I slept for several hours during that day and woke up after sunset. JC was sitting by my bed. We stayed silent and I realized that he was communicating with me without words. I heard his voice in my mind, but he did not move his lips. From now on, we were connected, inseparable for the rest of our lives, possibly even beyond death.

He told me that over the following days we would be doing exercises, such as yoga. It turned out that these exercises were extremely boring and repetitive, but he said that they were necessary, to help me maintain my new state of mind. We worked at them for many days.

The new man I had become still had memories of the past. I knew where I grew up, who my parents were. Everything that had happened in my life had become crystal clear, but now it was not personal; it was like a movie or a book from a library, something that in a strange way was outside me, but still a part of my life. I saw my life as a whole, like a hieroglyph on a wall, which existed only for a second but in some mysterious way contained everything.

I was still a good joiner; I was the academic who had been to university; I knew what my thesis was about; I was familiar with the scientific discussions around my subject and was able to discern the core of problems, without being affected. I still had some insignificant habits from the old days, but they represented no more than a slight itch on the chin. The most important transformation was the loss of negativity: I had no delusions about or false images of myself. I knew myself as I was, and from now on, the growth of my plant would go on indefinitely, directed by the new knowledge that I had gained and supported by JC, whether he was present or not.

I thanked God for the grace he had bestowed on me and was totally aware of the fact that, from now on, I would follow the voice deep inside – whether it be called the Holy Spirit, my teacher or my higher self, it would guide me whenever I needed guidance. There would be no more self-will or selfishness to lead me astray.

The exercises ended during the early days of December. JC came to me one day while I was sitting outside, looking at the lake. There had been frost during the night and the surface had a thin layer of ice, which melted during the morning.

"Tomorrow we are going back to the Farm," he said.

That evening, we lit the fire in the woodstove; I had carried some firewood in and couldn't help smiling at the enormous pile inside the shed.

After dinner, we sat around the fire. I started thinking about how the journey had been organized. I asked JC why he had brought Krishna and Carl too. He made a sign to both of them, and they went to their rooms to fetch something.

"You see," said JC, "each time a new one is born, there are always three kings to celebrate with him."

Carl, my prophet, came in. "I want to give you something in gold, the royal metal; and since I am a watchmaker, I will give you a gold watch."

It looked like my grandfather's watch, the one that had originally led me to Maria and my first time with a woman, but this one was brand new.

Krishna came with the incense bowl he had had in his temple in Bilga. "I want to give you the pleasant essence of life and in the fragrance of it you will be connected with me through all time."

Then JC looked at me and made a gesture as if he had nothing to give. He took a little bag out of his pocket. In it was a herb – myrrh.

"This herb is useful and will keep you healthy," he said. "It has a benevolent effect on the heart, liver and kidneys, all the important organs of the body. Myrrh is derived from a tree. When you cut the bark with a knife, the tree starts to bleed, so its healing effect stems from its pain and as you know, it sometimes has a bitter taste. So I not only give you health, but also something to help you in the struggle with yourself and your life. This struggle will continue, but now you know you have the power to overcome."

I thanked all three of them and sat with the presents in my lap, almost like a child on Christmas Eve. Funnily enough, I was still able to be a child. My heart was beating with excitement and overwhelmed with joy.

The next morning, we left the log cabin. This time, we had no helpers but carried the remainder of our luggage ourselves, as most of our supplies had been used up and I only had my toothbrush and a few clothes. Arriving at the parking place, we loaded the things into the car and set off. Carl and I sat in the back. On the way down to the main road, he turned to me and said, "You see, I was right about you. I am a prophet."

We left Krishna at the airport in Oslo to begin his long journey home. We bade each other a warm and happy farewell and I asked him to give my regards and love to the family in Bilga.

And so we continued with our journey towards the Farm.

I said to Peter that I now understood.

"I was thoroughly mistaken about you when we first met. I see now that you are not an ordinary person. You are a saint."

"No, don't say that."

"Yes, but you have gone through what most people do not even dream of and ..."

"No," he said. "We all have a part in the big drama. And the one who brings a cup of wine to the main actor on stage is as important as the main character, because someone has to bring it to him."

Still I had to confess that what he had told me was far beyond my comprehension. I had read many books about these things, even the story of the mystics, but the way Peter told me about it, it was as if I had joined him on his spiritual journey.

It was now crystal clear to me that Peter knew much more than he showed. I understood why so many times I had had the feeling that he knew what was going on inside me. He could read me like an open book.

Chapter Twenty-Three:

COMPLETION

December 1988

I

A thin layer of snow covered the landscape around the Farm. Each year, after the first snow fell, it was so beautiful to see the land covered in a pristine layer of white, with no trace of human activity. When we arrived back at the Farm, JC asked us to come up to his house. When Maria and Mona joined us, JC asked for a report covering the time of our absence.

Maria started by saying that many students had left, probably due to the pressures from the neighbouring community. The people in the nearby town had signed a petition urging the police and Council to take legal action against the "sect", as they called it. The view of the local community and local media was that there were many illegal students staying at the Farm. This was not strictly true, but there were some who had come and were still waiting for their permits to stay. Perhaps this talk of illegal foreigners was a sign of hostility to immigrants, especially those from Muslim countries. There was no doubt that the reaction to the Farm had been started by the accident in Norway. The newspapers had been silent about it for some time, as the reports from police and tax authorities had not yet been produced and, as Carl had said, they were not likely to be published until sometime in early spring.

JC asked how the farming was going. Mona said that it had been a hard struggle. She and Maria had decided not to sow the winter wheat or rye. The remaining land could then be used for the animals when they were let out of the stables in May, and there would be enough hay for the winter. JC thought this was a sound decision. Maria added that Hans had not been around much and, according to John, had only been to his office a few times to fetch some papers. John had said that Hans was closed and distant, living inside his troubled mind and unable to make contact with the outside world.

II

JC called a meeting that took place on 13 December. He had carefully chosen which students he wanted to attend. They were the most devoted, understood the teaching and put it into practice: Maria, Mona, Anna, James, Phillip, John, Gerhard, Rainer, Jens, Matthew, Michael and me. Of course Carl was also present.

When we were all seated, JC made an announcement: "I have decided to close the school and the whole organization."

Nobody said a word. The students looked at each other, speechless with shock. JC continued: "I will not be around much longer; I am coming to the inevitable end, as it will be for each of us when our time is up."

Someone asked, "Are you going to die?" He did not answer.

"Our properties in different places have to be sold. In Copenhagen the contract for the apartments has to be cancelled. Everything must be accomplished by 1 June. I will send three of you to Germany, two to Denmark and two to Norway. Each of you will take students from here to help you. Try to keep the centres in good order; continue the teaching and the meetings until everything is sold. John will stay here and work at selling the Swedish houses around the valley, the shop on the main road and the houses in the south of Sweden. Maria and Mona will travel around to the centres and support you as best as they can. There will be opposition and trouble in many places, but I know you can deal with it. Peter and Carl will stay here with me, two students will help Michael with the animals and another two will take care of the main house.

"The Farm will not be sold: that is, the main house, bungalow, stables and barns. However, I want you, Michael, to sell the animals and the machinery as soon as you can.

Once the properties have been sold, I want each of you to take what you need, from the money raised, for your living expenses. The rest will go into the foundation's account. I have found a lawyer and an accountant to see that any debts are paid; the rest will be donated to the church."

Needless to say this came as a huge shock to us all. It was clear, concise and straightforward and, from the way he gave the orders, there would be no discussion. However, at that moment in time, we all seemed paralysed.

JC looked around the circle waiting for some reaction, but there was none. Then he said:

"We often do not know what is best for us. What is going to happen will become clear to all of you, little by little. I am doing this because in the long run, it will be for the best. I have never let any of you down, so trust me now. I am not giving these orders to hurt anyone or because I cannot handle the situation. What is happening now is meant to be." Then he paused for a while.

"I was once told that Shakespeare said that the play is written, the actors are on stage and now all that matters is how well we play our parts. Think about that. Play your part well and then in the spring, during May or the beginning of June, you will all come back here, bringing with you those who want to follow you. Then we will be together again and can see how things will continue."

He was very aware that we all looked like sheep without a shepherd, as was written in the Gospels.

He finished by saying: "Do not forget that I am with you all the time, even to the end."

During the next few days, the students left in small groups. There was some talk, some disagreement, disappointment and lots of questions. What would happen to all of us now? What about the teaching? What about the teacher? Was he really going to die? I reminded the students that JC had expressed the importance of being in the present; to take one day at a time and not get lost in fantasies about the future. This proved to be a very good exercise, as I knew from my own experience; I also knew that to live this way was very difficult. It is like walking a tightrope, balancing and not looking down in case you fall. At the same time, we could not avoid the practical decisions we constantly had to make, but we did not worry about the future. Today's trouble is enough for today.

The twelve students at the meeting continued JC's teaching in the respective centres to which they had been sent. They were loyal, and straight away started to engage estate agents to sell the properties. Unfortunately, many students became angry and left. It was sad to hear how they spread lies about JC, gossiping to the media in their anger, wanting to vindicate their actions.

Christmas that year was very silent; we literally celebrated a "Silent Night". From now on, JC started to spend much more time alone. He had his food brought to him daily; on some occasions I brought it to him. He was usually sitting, as if he was praying or meditating, but a strong light shone around him. Mostly he was very serious. I guessed he was preparing himself for something, and I assumed he knew what was going to happen.

We celebrated my birthday two days before New Year's Eve. I was now 42.

III

John had a lot of work to do, as well as Michael and his helpers. I did not have much work at the joinery now that everybody had left and the houses were for sale.

Carl and I sat together for days on end, talking and enjoying each other's company. He could tell me so much. Now and then, he turned back to the problem of Hans. He could not understand how he had not been able to give his "son" more and help him to lead a good life. I told him that as far as I was concerned, he had been a very good father and mentor.

"I have never told you before, but you were always like a father to me: the father I didn't have. You always dealt with me with understanding and help, even when I was a boy. You really should not blame yourself. There was no way of knowing or preventing the way Hans has developed."

"I think you are right," he said.

We sometimes visited JC. He was always glad to see us, but when we touched on the current state of affairs, he became silent.

He would say, "My time is running out and I have to complete my aims for the school."

We knew he was talking about his death, but he would never elaborate.

One evening when we were playing chess, Carl suddenly felt tired and wanted to lie down. I helped him to his bedroom and sat next to him on a chair. He closed his eyes many times and smiled vaguely, looking at me.

"You were the best son I have ever had. I loved your curiosity and youthful ways. You gave me much joy in my life. Over the last few years, I have been happy, not least at seeing you going so far in the development of your seed."

He asked for some water and I fetched it. When I came back he looked very weak, but drank the water and then fell asleep. I stayed with him and saw his breathing became slower and slower, until it stopped. He had died.

I took his hand and blessed him. Then I prayed:

"God, our heavenly Father. Be with my friend Carl and guide him through the journey he is now undertaking. Help him in all his choices along the road and lead him safely to a good place where he will find peace, and if it is your will that he has to come back to this life, grant him to live it in understanding and love. This I pray in the name of the Father, of the Son and of the Holy Spirit. Amen."

I opened my eyes. It was the first time I had ever seen a person die, but I felt clearly that the body was like an empty shell. Carl, my dear prophet, had left, but I still felt his presence all around the room.

I got up and wanted to go to JC. He was asleep and his rooms were dark. Maria and Mona were away, so I walked to the main house to see Michael or some of the others, but everybody there was also asleep. I went back to Carl and sat at his bedside. I fell asleep in the chair, and woke up when JC put his hand on my shoulder. It was morning. He said:

"Will you take care of the funeral? I will contact Maria."

Maria and Mona came home from Germany late that evening. Maria wanted to spend some time at her father's bedside and I sat there next to her, holding her hand.

Over the next few days, Maria told me how her father wished everything to be arranged after he had died. We followed his wishes.

We were only about twenty in the little village church. I noticed that Hans was not there. One of the German students had been given permission to play the organ. Maria was in black, as were most of us. I had to borrow the appropriate liturgical clothes from the local priest. He knew about our difficulties, but was very pleasant and full of understanding and gave us all the help we needed.

The service was that in the Swedish prayer book. We sang the well-known hymn *Härlig är jorden* (The earth is wonderful). My address was short but personal. I said that Carl, who was a true prophet, had always had been like a father to me. I told how he had lived a fascinating life, excavating in Israel where he had met his wife, the beautiful Miriam, with whom he had his daughter Maria. Then I spoke about his difficult times during the war, about the loss of his beloved wife and his great joy at getting his little girl back. I said that he had loved Hans, whom he had adopted. He took the little boy away from a miserable life in an orphanage and gave him a home. I spoke about his calm and understanding way of talking to people. I recounted the first time I had met him and how after that, I visited him often. I explained how he had helped me on my way, as I knew he had helped others. I had tears in my eyes and it was difficult to speak, but I managed to continue.

"I know he has had a great influence on the school. He was JC's right hand and helper from the very start. With his visionary powers, he was always a great supporter of JC."

At the end we sang *Abide with me* and when the music from the organ died away, we carried his coffin out into the graveyard, where we had prepared a place for him. I threw in three handfuls of soil. Then everyone present came to the grave and took their farewell. Maria stood there for a long time. I walked up to her and put my arm around her. She was crying.

In March, we placed a headstone on his grave. There was a picture at the top of a clock: it showed 20 minutes past one. Underneath the inscription ran: In memory of my beloved father, the prophet Carl. 1901–1989.

Later, JC asked me to move into Carl's flat. That made it possible for me to be very close to JC, as he spent many hours in isolation, but when Maria was at home we often had our meals together – just the three of us. JC usually ate in silence, but he maintained eye contact with us. I shall never forget those evening meals.

Chapter Twenty-Four:

THE ADVERSARY

February 1989

I

In February, the tax authorities would wait no longer. Hans had not handed in a new declaration and, one day, someone from the police and a tax official came to the Farm and demanded we hand over all our record books and the accounts that were available. They had a warrant from a judge, had already been to Hans's office in the town and their car was loaded with files and boxes of papers.

Michael had by then managed to sell the livestock. Only the two horses were left, but the stables had been cleared out. The hay would be sold later in spring when farmers ran short of their own supplies: April was often a difficult month since the grass had not yet started to grow.

Some days later, people from the council, the immigration office and the health and safety departments came to the Farm. We were notified of the visit and JC cordially welcomed them, saying they were free to look around and ask any questions they wanted. He asked me to accompany them. I had difficulty suppressing my laughter at their astonishment that JC was being so accommodating.

There were no sheep and no students to be seen, except Michael and his two helpers. So where were all the illegal immigrants? Were they hiding? Michael invited them to search, and it became obvious that nobody was hiding among the hay bales. The officials left empty-handed, and since there were no problems and therefore no news, the newspapers remained silent. We said to JC that this was a victory. I thought that it was a very clever move to send the students away, but JC simply commented: "Wait and see. There is much more to come."

Around this time, the police report on the drowning was completed. During the autumn the police had questioned several students, in particular those on board the boat. I heard that Fredrik had disappeared. He was no longer in Halden. The police had asked around for him several times, but no one knew where he had gone. Based on the accident report, the public prosecutor decided to charge Hans with manslaughter. This was surprising based on the available evidence, but someone must have mentioned that Hans might have had a motive for getting rid of Richard: probably his mother.

Hans's trial was set for August. We had no idea when the tax authorities would come to a decision.

Certainly, there was much more to come. When I looked back on what happened, it seemed to me that we were moving with increasing speed towards a final resolution of the problems: Richard's death, the accounting problems, the closing of the school, Carl's death and now Hans's trial. We were falling through time, faster and faster, like a stone accelerating until it hits the ground and stops.

I asked Peter why JC hadn't tried to change the course of events. He said that he himself had asked that, but JC had explained that he would not interfere with the way things were going.

"Some people think they can change the world; that's an illusion. Hardly anyone is able to change himself, and the world is an even bigger issue. It is important to understand that there are many different orders of change. Naturally, there are small things that can be dealt with. At the same time, whenever you change something, it has an effect on something else; often this effect was not included in your calculations, so in the end the question is whether the change was for the better or worse. It is like taking medicine. There is always a side-effect, and sometimes the side-effect is so strong that you might have been better off not taking the medicine in the first place. Still, everything changes by itself all the time, because every cause leads to an effect and that in its turn leads to a new cause, and so on."

Peter continued: "I am sure that JC could have accomplished certain changes, but for him, the most important thing was not to relinquish his aim: an aim which none of us at that point understood."

At the end of May students started to return from the centres, and by the first week of June we were all gathered at the Farm. When I say "all", I mean those that had decided to come with the twelve: altogether we were twenty-nine students including Michael, myself and our four helpers. JC had indeed managed to wind up the organization; what remained was the two buildings at the Farm and the adjoining stables. The shop was still for sale, but John was working on that.

Just before midsummer, JC dissolved the board of the foundation and left any remaining business to the lawyer and his accountant.

For all of us the vital question was: What next?

The answer to that came almost immediately. As soon as all the students were back, JC started to work with all of us, day and night. We met daily in a large group, but he also met students individually or in smaller groups. He was handing out instructions about the future work, and it became clear that we were all going to be sent out into world to continue the teaching.

"But don't believe in the way of the world," he said. And he often used some phrases from the gospel, for instance *be wise as serpents and innocent as doves.*

JC showed us many exercises that we had never heard of. I became convinced that he had saved them for these circumstances. It was an intense period and very joyful, not least because summer was in full bloom.

To our great surprise, JC wanted us to celebrate midsummer in the old way. He asked Mona to buy lots of food and drink and to prepare for the party. He bought coloured lamps which were hung up in the trees around the two houses. We took part in all the preparations whenever possible. There was a truly loving atmosphere, which allowed all of us to just be ourselves.

II

Two days before midsummer, John drove up to the Farm at great speed. With shrieking brakes, he stopped the car and then came straight to me.

"Something terrible has happened!" he said, very upset. Calming down a little, he repeated, "Something terrible has happened!"

He was standing on the doorstep and obviously had no intention of coming in.

"Tell me," I said, "tell me." Still standing outside, he started:

"I asked the two African boys, who came with Gerhard from Germany, to come down and help one afternoon with the inventory of the shop. There are so many items to be logged and I wanted to have them all registered and counted before the sale. So I asked Salim and Ali to help me, in part because I wanted to show them that they mattered, that they were useful to the school. I know they did not come to the meetings often, but I wanted to encourage them. After all, they had chosen to follow Gerhard.

"I saw them walking towards the shop. Then some young lads surrounded them and the situation became threatening. I don't know what they said, but suddenly they started beating the two Africans. Salim hit back and then a proper fight developed. They were so many against the two boys, I decided not to interfere physically, but rang the police and an ambulance.

"Then there was a shot. It echoed through the whole town, and one of the Swedish boys fell to the ground."

Before I could ask any more, he said, "I must tell JC straight away." He turned around and walked towards the bungalow.

"But wait a minute," I said. "What happened to them all?"

"Our guys are in hospital in the city, as is the one who was shot. All were taken to hospital by ambulance."

"Is the one ... the one who was shot ... is he ..."

"I don't know," he said as he walked, or rather ran, to JC's house.

I drove to the hospital a little later. Salim was unconscious. Ali was not as bad, but the doctors had decided to keep him in for observation. At reception, I asked about the guy who had been shot, but they could not tell me anything. They were not allowed to, they said. I got hold of one of the doctors who had attended him and was told that the wounded young man was in a coma, but that his condition was under control.

I asked Ali to tell me what had happened.

"They started provoking us, by saying we don't want apes like you here, and all that stuff; foul things such as we should go back to the jungle and eat bananas; then Salim lost his temper and the fight really started."

Ali was very sad. He said that maybe he had jeopardized the safety of the school.

"Where did you get that idea from?" I asked.

"Well, we all know that things are getting worse; Hans has disappeared, the police are searching for him and many other students have left. What if the young man dies?"

"None of it is your fault."

"I know, but we like being here. We have finally found a place where we are respected. We probably don't understand that much of the teaching, but I have met JC and he is a good man, you know."

"I know. Since you came with Gerhard, you must know that JC is closing the school. Both of you can go with Gerhard wherever he goes and help him in his work. The shooting has nothing to do with you; you know that."

I continued: "Have the police spoken to you?"

He confirmed that they had, but they also wanted to speak to Salim when he recovered consciousness.

III

When I left the hospital I walked towards my car, but then decided to go somewhere to sit down a little and perhaps have a drink or a cup of coffee. I found a coffee shop near the hospital and went in, where I almost bumped into Hans. I said, "Hello. How are you?"

Of course he recognized me, but he looked very depressed and low. He hardly lifted his head to greet me.

"Shall we sit down a little and talk?" I suggested,

He did not seem to be bothered either way, and just nodded. I had a good hard look at him and thought he was in a serious way.

"Let's go somewhere else, so we can have something stronger. Come on, let's go over there."

I had spotted a bar, and since it was late in the day, I hoped they would be open. He followed me, although he gave the impression of having nowhere to go.

We sat down and I ordered him a whiskey and a beer, with a beer for myself.

He was sitting in the chair like a tramp who had been invited into the warmth, with no idea of what would happen next.

"Now, tell me. How are you getting on? We haven't seen you for a while."

"I am all right," he said. "Doing OK."

"Tell me, how are you really getting on? You don't look too happy."

He sighed. It was as if he was trying to change his hopelessness simply by sighing and getting new air into his lungs, but it did not last long, because he immediately slumped back into his depressive posture.

"Hans, please tell me what is going on."

"I don't care," he said. "I don't care."

"But you must care. The allegations against you are serious, so you must care."

He lifted his head and said, "Well. Things have got out of hand. I don't trust anyone anymore, not even JC. He has betrayed me."

At this point, I clearly realized that he had given in. I worked out that he felt betrayed by JC because he had finally understood that things would never go his way. Maria was not interested in following him, and all his ambitions and plans had come to nothing.

But I had to ask him the question that I had asked myself hundreds of times.

"Hans," I said. "Tell me please. What happened on the boat? Did you push Richard?"

I think he was considering his answer, looking round to see if an answer was written on the walls or ceiling. Then he said:

"I believe that Carl told you about me, which is why you are asking. Yes, I was accused of raping Claire, Richard's sister, but I didn't. I cannot know what she told her mother, but I am sure that Richard, who at the time was just a little boy, spied on us when we left the house to go for a walk. I have tried many times to ask him about it and told him that if he had seen us, he would have known that nothing happened, except that I wanted to have sex, we struggled a little, but I let her go. Richard kept saying that he knew nothing."

Hans scratched his chin, raised his eyebrows and said:

"The problem has always been that nobody believes me. I feel that people are against me, but I really want to be believed and accepted as I am. That evening on the boat, I walked around on deck, looking at the sea. I realized that the sunny weather was over, because huge clouds were arriving from the west. Then I saw Richard standing at the railing on the port side of the boat and when I passed him, I told him that he was a coward for not standing up and telling his mother the truth about that day with Claire. As a matter of fact, I intended to continue, leaving him by himself. Although I had always wanted justice, now I no longer really cared, but he turned around, becoming angry, and shouted at me to stop pestering him with my stupid questions.

"I said to him again that he was a coward, but then he did something totally idiotic. He opened the gate in the railing and said that he would jump and that I would be blamed, as people would say it was due to my behaviour. He said to me, 'Then everyone will know what kind of person you are.' I pushed him lightly on his chest, saying, 'Come off it, you bastard, you don't know what you are doing.'

"Then he took a step backwards and fell into the water with a splash. He started screaming; I looked around for a life buoy but couldn't see one. Then I heard someone coming up from below, I panicked and ran as fast as I could to the other side of the ship. I was standing there listening to all the activity when, little by little, it dawned on me that Richard had drowned. I was in a terrible state, confused, angry, and fearful, together with the overwhelming feeling that I was in serious trouble. I decided to pull myself together and felt I had no choice other than to pretend I knew nothing, because, as usual, no one would believe me. It was at that point that I came back and asked what had happened."

He put his head in his hands and started crying, gently and almost silently.

"I believe you," I said.

"No, you don't."

"Yes, I do. It is still possible to straighten things out. The charge against you is not murder, but manslaughter. And no one knows what happened that day on the boat. The police will ask you and there will be questions in court as well, but even if you are found guilty, the sentence may not be severe. JC wants you free of the tax problems. Have you heard that the school is closing and that the students are leaving the Farm to go to other places? Whatever debts there might be will be paid."

I looked at him and for a moment, I thought I had lit a vague feeling of hope within him.

I said, "I want you to know that I am thankful to you. You 'handed over' the teaching to me. You brought me to the school. JC has asked me to go England: you could come with me. After all, it is your country."

I felt instantly that it had been a mistake to mention England, as he said straight away, "I don't want to go to England."

"All right then, you could go somewhere else. Earlier I saw how you were changing and that you seemed to understand what the teaching was about. That made me happy."

It was clear that he did not believe me. Strangely, when someone says "no one believes me", it is often the case that the person in question does not believe in others. He was now acting like a person with low self-esteem – whenever someone says something positive, their first reaction is: "You are just trying to flatter me. I know that I am worth nothing."

It suddenly occurred to me that Hans probably knew nothing about the death of his stepfather.

"Hans, do you know that your father, Carl, died recently?"

His look of surprise told me that he hadn't known.

"Why didn't anyone tell me?" he said angrily.

"We had no idea where you were," I said. "You have been away for so long. John said he saw you a few times; but that was before ..."

I stopped. Hans was crying. He was sitting with his face buried in his hands. I waited a while.

"He died peacefully. I was with him and I also conducted the funeral service. His grave is in the local graveyard near the Farm. You should go there."

He looked up and said, "I might do that."

"I think it would be a good thing to do."

After a few minutes' silence, I felt I could be of help to him.

"There is something I would like to say. You have told me about your upbringing and the wounds you carry inside. I know it is difficult, and maybe you don't want to talk about it now. But I think it is time you started to forgive them and free yourself from the hatred and the blame."

"I shall never forgive them."

I shook my head. I knew that if he wished to, he could have gone through the present difficulties and come out on the other side with his self-respect intact.

"When you say you'll never forgive them, I have to ask, do you think the people who hurt you know that? Do you think you can harm them or have your revenge on them by not forgiving them? I am not trying to defend them; what they did was terribly wrong, but the only one you are hurting now is yourself. You are still carrying all the bad things in your mind and poisoning yourself with your hatred."

He seemed to follow my reasoning, but said nothing. Then I had an idea.

"Hans, would you like to do an exercise with me? Something that might be helpful to you?"

He looked surprised at the question, shrugging his shoulders as he said, "Anything you want, it does not matter."

"Try to imagine the person in this world you hate the most – a person you simply cannot forgive. Can you do that?"

He nodded. "There are many," he said.

"Close your eyes and try to keep a picture of the person you hate the most and then say to him or her: 'I accept you as you are and I want to free myself from all that took place. I will let you go and heal my mind and not carry the burden of your deeds any longer. I forgive you and I love you.'"

He did as I requested and sat for at least two minutes with his eyes closed, head raised, seemingly relaxed. When he opened his eyes, I asked him, "How did it feel?"

"It's strange, but I managed to see this person without attaching any concepts to him; it was as if he was a neutral person that I no longer hated."

"Right, there you are. Do this again and again with everybody you feel contempt for, or have a grudge, judgement or hatred against."

"It won't work. There are too many and I still remember what they did."

"But who was the person you thought about?"

"JC, and I still hate him."

I had to ask him a last question. "Were you down at the shop yesterday?"

"That's none of your business," he retorted.

When we parted I stretched out my hand and he took it, in the same way that he had long ago in his office.

"It's strange," he said. "Even though you are a naive idiot, I still like you."

He walked across the street and disappeared.

IV

The next day, you can imagine what was on the front page of the newspapers: *Young Africans attack Swedish youths. Young man, aged 18, wounded by shotgun.* This was partly correct, if Ali's story was the true version. Salim seemed to have started the fight, but still the way it was written left no one in any doubt about who was to blame in their eyes – the two black boys. I was at a loss trying to work out from whom the journalists had received their information. Apart from the incident with the two Africans, there was an article in one of the tabloid papers about the Farm's financial problems. Who had told them about this? I knew there were reporters attached to police headquarters, to the department of justice and even the local administration office, but surely they were not allowed to give out information on matters that had not yet been decided upon?

Anyway, it had happened. The papers were also implying that there was something fishy going on within the "sect". Why had so many properties been sold? Was this an attempt to withhold money from the tax authorities? Of course Hans had already been charged. As far as they were concerned, he had already been found guilty. What else could you expect with illegal immigrants among the students, drug dealers, plus all the other scum under the sun? In the light of all these accusations, it was not that surprising that so many students had left. After all, who wanted to belong to such a group of people?

I know that John also visited our friends in hospital. He had no further news to report.

The next day, he wanted to finish the inventory without help. He mentioned to me that he would be able to return early in the afternoon to help with the midsummer preparations.

But things did not turn out as he had planned. He returned at 3 o'clock in the afternoon without having finished, looking tired and sad. I asked him to tell me what had happened but to begin with, he didn't say anything. He sat on the chair, looking down, probably not seeing the floor, but rather the empty space inside himself. Then slowly, he started telling me what had happened, interrupted by long pauses.

"When I arrived at about 10 o'clock, I parked my car outside the entrance to the shop. The work was going well and by lunchtime, I had finished the inventory of the jewellery. I walked down to the hamburger joint and had some lunch, returning to the shop shortly after 1 p.m. To my great surprise, there were two police cars lined up on the road in front of the shop. I asked the policeman why they were there; they told me that it was because of the demonstration that was due to start at 1.30 p.m.; they were there to guarantee the safety of everyone involved, to protect private property and disperse the gathering in good order at the end of the demonstration. Apparently, this was normal police policy and just routine."

John looked at me; rubbed his forehead with his hand and continued:

"I went inside and tried to concentrate on my work, but the news about the demonstration was spinning around inside my head. Surely it must be a demonstration against the Farm and the whole organization? Otherwise, there would be no reason for the police to get involved by taking up a position right in front of the shop? The phrase: 'protect private property' sounded like a forewarning of something likely to happen.

"People started gathering around twenty past one. A little later, the protest march which had started in the town square arrived. I think there were more than fifty, possibly up to a hundred. They were carrying banners with slogans saying things like: The sect has to leave! We want the murderer convicted! We don't want illegal refugees here! No more stealing in our shops! Pay your taxes like everyone else! Stop your indoctrination and exploitation of young people! We want to live peacefully as before! No more trouble! Get out!, with many more placards in the same vein. I stood watching everything from behind the curtain in Hans's office. They marched up and down for a while and then the group stopped and gathered around a speaker – probably one of the people who had initiated the petition to the council. I heard most of his speech. It was one lie after another, but people were cheering and shouting.

"I realized that the motive behind it all was fear. No one had been stealing in the shops and no one who was with the 'sect' had been forced or tricked using false pretences. The people were simply afraid of anything that was different, anything that didn't seem to fit into the old, well-known way of life. Similar ideas and fears have been aroused in other places where refugees had been housed, following their arrival into the country. Suspicion against newcomers has always been strong. Why are they here and why should we pay for them? All the various accusations, which ranged from stealing from the shops to raping the young girls, were born out of fear."

John stopped and shook his head.

"Oh Peter, the world is rotten. Why can we humans not live together without being afraid of each other and blaming all our shortcomings on others? I tell you, it made me very sad to see some farmers in the crowd, the good people that leased their land to us who, in the beginning, were interested in taking part in our way of living, of our little community. They gave us advice on farming matters. I know Michael often met them to discuss things. They were our friends. It's unbelievable that their attitude towards us has changed into one of suspicion and enmity. It's just not fair – we haven't done them any wrong. We were always welcoming and open to them, and did not try to convert them to our teaching. They were free to believe what they wanted, and some of them went to the service in the local church each Sunday.

"And suddenly everything is upside down. Something has been set in motion, probably by the accident on the boat, about which no one actually knows anything apart from the version which the newspapers have given. In some inexplicable way, the mistrust and antagonism has steadily increased. There is no way of turning the tide now. I see that so clearly."

I understood that he was badly shaken by the incident, but I also knew that he had heard JC talking about "the way of human life", as he called it. I reminded John about that:

"Do you remember what JC used to say to us? There is no justice in this world; everything goes on mechanically and you cannot blame a machine for working the way it does. Then he used to laugh. There is something in what he says. You always want justice, and justice implies that some are right and others wrong. The wrongdoer never admits his guilt, and if found guilty in court will be punished according to the laws prevailing at the time. The next time the wrongdoer may be deemed to be right and the good ones punished. This is what JC meant about 'the way of life'.

"And so it works in society, but not among us, because we are freeing ourselves from the laws of the world. We want to lift ourselves above the talk of right and wrong and substitute it with truth. JC used the parable of gravity: we are tied down to the earth by gravity and no one can lift himself by his fingernails, but with the help of right thinking, or rather by changing the way we look at things, we will be able to defy gravity and actually fly high above slander, fear and the judgement of others."

John knew I was right, although his feeling of injustice at that moment was stronger than his willingness to let it go. He continued to tell me about what had happened:

"Well, the demonstration was coming to an end. The speaker ended his speech and people were supposed to go home. The police tried breaking up the crowd, but the shouting increased and threatening voices filled the air. Someone started throwing pebbles at the windows. The police made a cordon around the crowd and, using megaphones, tried to persuade people to leave, but instead the situation worsened. Now stones were flying through the air, windows shattered and I decided to get away unseen as quickly as possible. I got into my car and reversed out onto the road, where a policeman saw me. He understood that as I was coming from the shop, I needed protection. He walked towards me and tried to keep people away. When I reached the road, I set off as fast as I could. The rear window was smashed by a stone, with glass splinters scattering throughout the car, but I carried on and succeeded in getting away. Finally, I arrived back here. I wanted to tell you about everything before I told anyone else."

"Just one more thing," he added. "I think I got a glimpse of Hans. He had a cap on his head but still, I am pretty sure it was him. That made me sad."

"John. Do you know how to conquer gravity?" I said. "It is a matter of forgiveness, but in a way that we do not usually think of. You cannot forgive the farmers or Hans, but you can forgive yourself for letting them take up such a large space in your mind and your heart. You can pray: God forgive me for letting them become an attack on myself and in that way, separating myself from your peace. Amen."

John had tears in his eyes. I said, "You should go and tell JC. I'll tell Maria."

Then I said, "I think we will all be leaving soon. I see now what a wise move it has been to close the school and dissolve the organization. There will be nothing left for the wolves; they are now fighting amongst themselves."

Chapter Twenty-Five:

PETER THE ROCK

Midsummer 1989

I

That last midsummer's evening was a totally different event from all the previous ones. The atmosphere was overshadowed by the demonstration two days before. The whole organization was crumbling away, exactly as JC had arranged it.

The party started in the usual fashion, with good traditional food and preparing for the dances.

JC was a master at doing the unexpected. He must have taken all the recent events into account, but still he encouraged us to celebrate. He said, "This is our last midsummer."

He had presents for all of us, and he enjoyed watching us unwrap them. By this time, Ali had left hospital and told us that Salim had regained consciousness and, furthermore, the Swedish youth was recovering. This was indeed good news.

The dances never started. JC suddenly stopped the music and asked us to sit around the bonfire with him.

We sat in a circle, exactly as we had the first time I was with the group in Copenhagen. JC looked around. He was calm and full of love, but serious.

"Now everything is prepared," he said. "Tomorrow it will all be over. You will all have to leave in the morning. Take all the cars available. I want Peter and Maria to stay with me the longest. I need you two here around me," he said, addressing us.

And then he added – which sounded strange – "to the end." I think we all were waiting for the final explanation, but it did not come.

"You are all aware of the situation we are now in," he went on. "The opposition is strong, but not stronger than me. I will fulfil my aim with the school. Many have left us along the way; they followed as far as they could and there is no blame attached to them for leaving. You who are here came because you trusted in me. Those who have left can still be useful. Therefore, I want you all to gather as many as you can around you and continue teaching them.

"You will found new centres, new places where growth is possible. But you shall not build an organization, any church, creeds or rituals. You are all of you the living examples of the truth. The system that I taught you is now abandoned, but its truth is still true. Therefore you will reconstruct the system, all you have learned, and present it in a new form to those who are willing to listen.

"The teaching will spread all over the world. It will have different forms, but the core of the message is the same. Nourish the seed in others whenever you meet it; how far you go depends on your willingness and the grace of God. The new movement will, at times, not even be visible, but it will grow under the surface of life. It will permeate and transform everybody who comes into contact with it, and one day, it will be so strong that the purpose of our all-loving Father will be fulfilled."

He put a piece of wood on the fire. The sparks rose up into the summer sky.

"As you know, I dissolved the board of the foundation and on Monday, the lawyer and his accountant will take care of what is left. We will keep the house in Gilleleje. That is where everything started, and I want that house to be a meeting place for you and a place for you to come and rest from your travels, at least in the beginning. You all have your instructions as to how to proceed from now on. The intensive days we have had together are the basis of the new start.

"This month, together at the Farm, we have shared love. Love is more important than words or systems. We only need words to help beginners to understand, then soon they will live the teaching, so the teaching does not have to be written in holy books. It will be alive and will be passed from one person to another, in the name of Christ and our loving Father. No further explanations are needed. Do not be troubled in your hearts when you leave me. I have said it before and I say it again:

My love I give to you and I will always be with you, no matter where you go. Trust in that."

He then closed his eyes and sat motionless for a long time. We all sat there together in silence. What he had said now was, in a way, the conclusion of our time together. It was also the final closing of the organization. Everything had now been fulfilled. To my surprise, he ended with The Lord's Prayer.

Then he thanked us and retired alone to his flat. We all felt like motherless children, but then I said, "Friends, let us dance and celebrate. I believe JC would want us to do that."

The next morning the students left and Maria and I stayed with JC.

II

In the Christian tradition, Midsummer Day is the day of John the Baptist. When John met Jesus at the River Jordan, he is supposed to have said that "from now on I will decrease, but you will increase". In the Northern Hemisphere this is mirrored in the seasons. At midsummer, the sun is at its highest but then the day starts to decrease in length until Christmas, when Jesus is born again and the days start to lengthen. I remember that this puzzled me as a child. I asked my father why people in Australia have the longest day around Christmas!

He just said that the Australians would have to find another explanation. I started thinking about this on Saturday morning, after everyone had left. JC was sitting quietly in his room with his eyes closed, as if he was praying; the door was open. Would he now increase in power while the power of the adversary would decrease? I did not realize that the final assault was still to come. But, when I looked back on the days immediately after, I felt sure that JC's work would grow, like a shrub that has been cut back to allow new growth from the base.

It was a very long day for us. We were waiting for something, but did not know what. JC did not want any dinner, so Maria and I ate alone. When darkness fell, we lay down on my bed, fully dressed, holding each other tight. I felt her body next to mine, and our minds were joined in sublime silent communication.

Perhaps we slept a little, and we woke to hear loud, angry voices coming from outside. I went to the window and saw a crowd of people; I estimated thirty or more, carrying thick sticks, gathered at the front of the house by the road. And there was Hans, in the middle of the crowd. He seemed to have a leading role because he came to the front of the crowd, raised his fists and shouted:

"This is the end. Come out and show yourself like a man, if you dare to. We don't want you anymore. We are tired of your lies and deception. Come on out now, if you dare, and talk sense to us. We want to hear your explanation for everything that's been going on."

I turned away from the window and walked into the room. JC was sitting immovable in his chair.

"I think we have to go," I said. "The mob out there is crazy. They might do anything when they get worked up. Let's go."

JC sat silently and did not move.

"No," he said. "I will stay."

"But you can't – they are crazy, all of them. They do not know what they are doing."

Then he said slowly, but with definite authority, "You must leave now, both of you. This is my command. Go."

Maria collected a few things. She walked to JC, put her arms around him and kissed him. Then she said, "Thank you for everything, I will always love you." She walked through the back door and disappeared.

I walked to the window, where I saw the people becoming angrier. "Perhaps it is time to leave. We can still walk out through the back door and up into the mountains," I said. But JC stayed where he was.

"Peter," he said, "I am an old man and I have known this was coming for a long time. For me, this is the end, but I know that this end will generate an energy so tremendous that the world will not be the same again. It is also a new beginning."

I could not believe what I was hearing. "What energy are you talking about?" I asked.

This was the first time I had actually challenged him, as if I was now his teacher, correcting his decisions.

"You don't understand, but remember what I said to all of you a few days ago. You are going to places that have been predetermined for you and you will continue my work. You will inspire hundreds of people and through you, the teaching will grow. One day, there will be so many of you that it will make a difference on this planet. You are to teach the art of self-remembering and in that way change the world, to speed up the development of humanity, and then the plan of our creator will be fulfilled. I have told you that already. Didn't you listen?"

He sounded angry now, but I still thought that maybe he would come away with me. These people were about to destroy the place, kill him and walk away, satisfied that they had avenged their perceived wrongs. What purpose would that serve? But JC did not move. He said to me in a very firm and commanding voice: "You have to leave now. You are of more use if you leave than if you stay. GO!"

I understood: there was nothing more to be said. I heard the voices outside growing louder and more threatening. I looked around, took my wallet and some money I had in my cupboard and went to the back door. I opened it and the strong fragrance of the summer evening came wafting towards me. I turned around one more time and JC just nodded with a gentle, loving smile on his face.

"Maybe we'll meet again," he said as I left the house.

I walked up the mountain, hastily at first and then more slowly. I could not help thinking about JC, sitting there alone, with a hostile crowd outside his door. But I knew now that this was part of the plan – this was what he had hinted at many times in the recent past.

When I had almost reached the peak of the mountain, I heard a shot. It echoed through the valley below and was carried up the mountain. I stopped for a moment and then I walked on. When I reached the top, I looked back one last time. Flames were coming out of the roof of the house, sending a last message to me: It was over. I started my descent down the far side of the mountain.

III

On my way down, I thought about JC. I recalled the many miraculous moments he had blessed me with. I could not believe that it had all ended like this, but there was no doubt about it anymore. It was over.

I came down to the point where the hills levelled out; there was a pasture and many sheep were lying in a group in the middle of the field. The moon was shining, with its reflected light. There would be full moon in a couple of days.

There was a shed in the field, which the sheep could go into when the weather was bad. I went in there, sat on the hay and leaned against the wall. Everything was silent now. I saw smoke rising behind the mountain top. I was tired. I wondered in which direction Maria had gone, also where all the others were. I knew that I was the teacher now; I was taking JC's place in the drama. I hoped that I would meet my friends again and help them all to go on with the teaching. But maybe that was unnecessary. JC had no doubt already arranged everything.

I must have slept for a time, because when I woke up, dawn was breaking on another summer morning. It can't have been more than four or four-thirty; there was a mist hanging over the field and down into the valley, which meant that it was going to be a warm day. I got up and started walking down, when a voice inside me told me to go back, which I did.

I walked to the top of the mountain and descended towards what had once been our beautiful Farm. The main building was still on fire, but JC's house had burned right down to its stone foundations. Some wooden beams were still smoking, metal objects and kitchen utensils were recognizable from where I stood, but of course the furniture and the decor had gone. I did not want to search the grounds, because I did not want to find the remains of my teacher. It was almost certain that he had been shot and left in the burning house. Surely at some stage, the forensic teams would go through the houses, and it was up to them to come to a conclusion.

I noticed that the barn was intact. I walked over to it and opened the huge doors. Then I saw Hans's body hanging from a beam. He had taken his life. The ladder that he had used to get up there had fallen down.

My first thought was to take him down. I raised the ladder and climbed up, but, realizing that I needed a knife to cut him loose, came down, found one in a hay bale, and climbed up again. His body was getting cold, but was not yet stiff. I struggled for a long time to free him, and carried him down over my shoulder.

When I reached the ground, I laid him gently on his back. The look on his face as he lay there showed no distress or desperation, but was almost one of relief. I said a blessing over him, then I took his hand and talked to him.

"Jude. Why? Why? I know you had a bad start in life. You were thrown into the vortex of life and never found love. You wanted to find it with Maria, but you really did not know how to handle love. You craved it. Love cannot be demanded, you know. You looked for love in the wrong places and never found it.

"I know in the end you had no choice. You thought JC had taken your love away and you were disappointed that your beliefs and his did not coincide. You did not understand what he was doing, and your mistakes in handling the accounts made you an outlaw. You didn't know what to do. You probably did not know what you were doing all along; always searching, wanting and wishing things to go as you wanted. And you failed. You felt that no one believed you. You wanted to clear yourself of any suspicion. You pressed Richard to go forward and tell them all that you had done nothing to Claire. It was all just a misunderstanding. And things went so wrong.

"You have been fighting to save yourself all the time, hoping that one day you would receive recognition for what you were, hoping for a new life, a new society; but in the end, it all came to nothing."

I was quiet inside now. It came to my mind that it was Jude who brought me to JC.

"Dear Jude, you 'handed over' the teaching to me. You actually saved my life and were the agent that enabled me to give it meaning. I am grateful for that."

After a little while I continued:

"We all do the best we can, and I know that in the end everything will be put right, and all that happened was a part in the play. Hans, I forgive you, by not letting my mind carry any judgement against you. I want to set you free, and whatever you have done is now in the hands of God. I cannot correct other people's mistakes, but I can pray that Christ the mediator will take your case to the only judge there is. And he is merciful and understands everything. I will now leave you in the hands of God. He is the one that will set you free, by forgiving you. And although you are not in your body any longer, I know that life cannot die. Therefore one day you will be ready to receive love as I did. Peace be with you."

I blessed him once again and stayed some time with him. Then I searched his pockets and found his wallet. I opened it and saw his driver's licence: Jude Hansen, born 11 June 1931. There was a little money and some addresses, but I did not care about that. I knew when the police found him, he would be identified.

I walked down the road towards town. The morning was becoming brighter. On the way down, an ambulance and the fire brigade were coming up the hill, together with the police cars. They did not bother about me. I was invisible to them as I walked down to the shop and the office.

I knew they had nothing to do up there in a way, except to take care of Hans's body. They had come much too late. No one had informed them; no one in the crowd had said anything, which was not surprising. They could hardly hand themselves in and face up to what they had done. And down in the town, no one would have seen the smoke from the fire. But I wondered why none of the farmers in the valley had contacted the police or the fire brigade. They must have seen the flames and the smoke. They must have heard the shot. Did they not react because they had all taken part in the assault?

I found no answers to my questions, but obviously someone had called the police, perhaps anonymously. Anyway, there they were.

I said to Peter, "I find it very strange that Jude could hold such extreme beliefs about JC. How could he think that JC would start a socialist revolution? It is an absurd idea from what you have told me." Peter said:

"The fact is that most people misjudged JC. Some thought he was a saint, although as I have told you, he never tried to give the impression of being holy, if you know what I mean. Some people thought he was an imposter; some that he was a fraud, that he was using people for his own ends. There was also talk among people in the village and among the farmers that he was an alcoholic, that he was a glutton and wine drinker, a lover of women, whose services he made use of.

"All along, JC never tried to correct people's opinion of him. He lived gladly with that and concentrated on his mission and the work with all of us. He did not own anything. He only had his clothes and a car for his private use, which was the least he could claim, considering what he had brought to the foundation.

"Sometimes I had the impression that he welcomed the adversity and opposition. He once said, 'This is what is giving me the strength to continue and transform myself and others.' I think Jude misjudged him totally; he projected his own aims onto him, loathing the students who were creepers, as he called them, and believing that he was one of the few who really understood. At the same time, I understand that Jude had connections with the extreme right. I realize now that he was a very confused man.

"I do think that Jude was a mystery and so was JC."

When I reached the shop and the office, I found the doors wide open. The sign outside was still there: "For sale", it read. The windows had been smashed and, no doubt, things had been stolen. Many items were definitely missing. The shop was almost empty.

I went into Jude's office. The shelves were empty. The tax people and the police had done their job, but even here there was destruction, with stuff spread all over the floor. I opened the drawers of the writing desk. Most of them were empty, but in one of the drawers I found the letters from John's father, George – the letters we had been looking for many years previously.

I knew why Jude had taken them and why he had been hiding things from us all along. I left the letters, not even bothering to open the bundle with the rubber band around it. I just left them.

IV

I managed to get a lift on a lorry down to the ferry at Helsingborg. I had my wallet and my money, which were the only things I had managed to grab the previous evening. There was enough money to cross to Denmark, and from there I took the train to Gilleleje.

Maria was there. I told her about my experiences at the Farm. She was silent; we ate our supper without saying a word, both feeling bereaved, but we also knew that this end was the beginning of something new.

After supper, I felt a strong urge to go for a walk.

The evening was bright to begin with; after all, it was the end of June. I started walking towards the area where we used to go swimming when we were children; it took me about twenty minutes. The sun was setting, there was a wonderful red sky to my left, but the warm day had created an onshore breeze that was rather chilly; as the sun slid below the horizon, it became increasingly difficult to make out the contours of the land. I walked up the hill at Strandbakkerne and when I stood on the top, I saw the sea in front of me with the different coloured lights reflected from the coast of Sweden becoming dimmer and dimmer. At that moment, I was in a neutral state of mind and emotion; it was as if I was waiting for something.

I noticed a man walking down along the seafront. He stopped and looked up in my direction and then he waved, as if he wanted me to come down. I had a strong impulse to run down the hill, almost stumbling over my own feet.

When I came nearer I saw the person more clearly; I saw his face and indeed it was him: it was JC.

I was perplexed and said, "I knew it. I knew you could not die."

I ran towards him, then stopped because he lifted his hand as a sign not to come closer. I was out of breath after the running, but I stammered out, "Is it you?"

He smiled and said, "Yes, it is I."

I fell down on my knees, with my forehead buried deep in the sand – which I managed to get in my mouth, but that didn't worry me. There were tears running down my face, not of sorrow but of sheer happiness.

"Get back on your feet," he said gently. "This is the last time we will meet in this world and from now on, I will be somewhere else."

"But where will you be?" I said, confused. I continued:

"I am so thankful for all you did. People and even some of the students questioned your actions; they became uncertain, suspicious and – God knows how it was possible – they even turned their backs on you; but please forgive them, they did not understand and I did not understand at times either. I also betrayed you with my own agenda, disregarded your loving and wise guidance ..."

"It is all right," he said. "Everything is completed now."

Once again, I asked him where he was going.

"I am going to a place you do not know, but one day, you will. It is a place where there is no turmoil and no tangible matter."

"But," I said, "can't I follow you there now? I have nothing else in my life to live for, nothing to do, no agenda: please let me go with you now."

"You cannot," he replied. "Have you forgotten the task I gave you? There is a plan for you, a part to play in the theatre of the world." He added, "There is something for you to live for."

At that moment, silently in my mind, I recalled all the many moments when he had guided and taught me, shown me the possibility of another world, another dimension. He had taught me that there is a world behind the veil, much more real than the ephemeral existence we live here. I had come to realize that and make it a part of my own being.

Now he smiled again. His presence radiated love, and the notion of wanting to have him here permanently became answered without even being expressed in words.

"It is not possible to keep anything in this world permanently," he said. "You know that, but we will meet again; we are connected and you have, through being my student all these many years, taught me a lot. You helped me. When I meet the angels, I will say to them that everything important I learned in this world was taught to me by a priest called Peter."

He smiled, and I wiped my eyes with the back of my hand. Then he said to me:

"Take good care of Maria, and take care of my brothers, wherever you go. I have chosen you to continue the work and I send you out into the world. You know that there will be wolves, snakes, doves, and sleeping people, but also the angels will walk with you. Lead my brothers and help them to accomplish their tasks and tell all people in the world, whoever you meet, about the good news: There is no death, but there is a seed; take care to tend it and make it grow and pray for guidance wherever you go. I will be with you to the end of time."

I was going to say something, and I took a step towards him. He turned and walked away. And as he walked, he gradually vanished into the mist.

I fell down onto the sand again. I thanked God for my life, for my good fortune, for all the people I had met, and I asked him to forgive all my trespasses against my brothers. I knew that this had already happened through my experiences in the wilderness. I was a new man. Then I prayed: "God help me and lead me in my task to bring the news to my brothers and sisters and to help them in their tasks."

I walked back to the house. Maria met me at the door. She was wearing a red dressing gown.

I told her that I had met JC.

"So have I," she whispered. "He came after you left and said to me that he would go and meet you as well. Isn't that wonderful?"

"Yes it is," I agreed. "It really is fantastic." Then I added:

"Now I understand what JC has done for us. He closed the school, sent us away and stayed in the house to wait for them. He saved all of us. Can you imagine what would have happened if the school had still been open? And if there had been all the students from different countries staying at the Farm for the annual celebration? It could have been a massacre.

"The authorities would have investigated the organization and the damage would have been enormous. Perhaps not only Jude would have had to face trial, but possibly JC, you and some others. And we would all have been scattered without having any instructions or ideas as to how to carry on. He saved the teaching by his wise arrangements. He came into the world to bring us the good news of liberation. And he saved all of us by sending us out to continue his work. It is amazing that he could foresee everything and arrange it all, down to the smallest detail."

Maria agreed; she had had the same realization. Then she came close to me and said, "I have something for you." She took out a gold watch from her pocket. It was the one Carl had given me after the time in the wilderness.

"I brought it with me when I left," she said with a smile.

I embraced her long and tenderly. Then she said, "This time you do not need to damage your watch to have an excuse to visit me."

We both laughed and, hand in hand, we walked upstairs.

Here Peter ended his story.

The next morning he woke me up by knocking on my door. When I opened it, he stood there ready to leave. His rucksack was on his back, and he seemed to be shining like the sun.

"I wanted to say goodbye to you and to thank you for listening to me for the last couple of weeks."

I asked him to come in, but he just put his arms around me and hugged me. A sensation of warmth spread through me, changing itself into a deep love for him. I feel sure that if anyone had been there as an onlooker, they would have seen the whole room filled with light.

Then he left.

I stood on the same spot for some time. It occurred to me that I did not even know his last name. Didn't know where he could be found. I had no telephone number and no address. I jumped out into the corridor, but there was no one there. Then I ran to the window in my room and I saw Peter crossing the road towards the main station. When he was about to enter it, he turned around and waved. I saw him, but I am sure he could not see me. There again, I could be wrong. But he was gone. And to this day, I have not seen him again.

December 1999

After Peter left, I collected my things, paid the bill at the reception desk and walked towards the main station. I thought about calling my wife and asking her to fetch me, but I chose to take the train. We lived north of Copenhagen in a fancy area called Hellerup. The train ride took only a few minutes, but I needed those precious minutes alone.

I realized that Peter and Maria had spent the past month preparing for their journey, perhaps trying to raise some money. Maria had already left for London when I met Peter. It was preordained that he would meet me, in order for his story to be told and published; he had indicated several times that we were meant to meet. But no matter how strange or unlikely it sounded, it was a fact that we had met and I had promised to write his story. Now my promise has been fulfilled. I am only sorry it has taken so long. Today it is New Year's Eve 1999. The day before yesterday was Peter's birthday, and tomorrow a new millennium begins.

Over the months after my encounter with Peter I looked in the newspapers for information about the murder and fire at the Farm, to find out what had happened. Finally in November the police report was published. The police had found the remains of a human body, but there was so little remaining that the forensic team could not make a definite identification. It remained a mystery. Witnesses on the other side of the river reported hearing a shot. The bullet was found, but not the weapon. The police found it incomprehensible that no one had reacted to the fire or the shooting straight away. This made them question the neighbours of the Farm, some of whom were charged with instigating the riot and arson. Hans was dead, so all charges against him were dropped.

There are many things that I have not told you, and though I recorded our conversations, there were times when we talked off record, so to speak. We spent many evenings together.

I remember Peter telling me that JC had never had been sick. He never went to a doctor, or a dentist. Perhaps he was not even registered with the authorities. He was a mystery.

A few months after his death, people claimed to have met JC. The newspapers reported the stories, but only because they were sensational, not because they believed them. I only know what Peter told me, and I believe that he was telling the truth.

Now, more than ten years have passed since I first met Peter. Sometimes I think about him, and sometimes he comes to me in my dreams. Sometimes I think we are still together. I have no excuses for not writing his story earlier, but many things changed in my life since our meeting, and it all took time. I ended my career at university and applied to train for ordination. My wife was surprised, but adapted very quickly to my plans.

I was ordained on 11 June 1995, on the devil's birthday like Peter, and on the birthday of Jude. In the astrological calendar, where each day of the year has a special meaning, it says that 11 June is an exceptional day. People born on this day will have a strange mixture of love and hatred. They will be strongly dedicated to an aim, usually spiritual. The outcome of the aim will depend how they tend their innate possibilities, their seed. The possibilities will be there no matter how much they go astray, for some higher power will always lead them back.

But days and dates are also just what we make of them.

Two years ago, I had a letter from Peter. On the back of the envelope was written "P". He had found my address through the directory of the church in Sweden. He wrote:

Thank you my friend. I just wanted to tell you that I have met my son. He is a lovely person. He is with me in my group here. How is it going with "our" book? I suppose you are working on it.

God bless you and once more: Thank you.

Love
Peter

I was so glad to receive his letter, and also, I am so grateful to him for sharing those days with me in Copenhagen.

I am a priest now. In the beginning I really did not know if I would handle this task; but there was a hope inside me, which I still cling to: that there will always be people around who are longing for the truth, and I hope that I shall be able to give it to them, to the best of my abilities.

I sometimes believe that in the church, there is something one could call the holy church. Peter taught me that it is a seed, a collective seed that belongs to humanity. At times it is trampled down and crushed, but it always grows anew, struggling to give fruit, and even when it has been betrayed, harassed and despised, someone will water it from time to time. Someone must tend it and protect it, and it will never die because it belongs to all of us; for although we are many, we all are part of the same body, the one and only seed.

I remember how Peter's described JC quoting Shakespeare: "The world is a stage. The play is written and the players are on stage. What matters is how well we play our role."

My life changed radically from the meeting with Peter. I cannot help thinking that all this happened because my flight to Birmingham was delayed. One question often comes to my mind:

Who arranged the delay?